Katie, Kelly and Heck

Katie, Kelly and Heck

JACK M. BICKHAM

DOUBLEDAY & COMPANY, INC.

GARDEN CITY, NEW YORK

1973

All the characters in this book
are fictitious, and any resemblance
to actual persons, living or dead,
is purely coincidental.

First Edition

ISBN: 0-385-07501-4
Library of Congress Catalog Card Number 72–84890
Copyright © 1973 by Jack M. Bickham
All Rights Reserved
Printed in the United States of America

Katie, Kelly and Heck

ONE

The stagecoach lurched over a heavy obstacle in the mountain roadway, then plunged steeply downward into a pit. Dust gushed up over the coach like a brown wave, spilling through the windows as if poured from buckets. The brakes were applied. The coach rocked forward violently, then grumbled and jangled to a stop, shaking from end to end.

"We've crashed!" the freckled, twelve-year-old boy yelped delightedly. "We've wrecked and we're lost and the Apaches are gonna come!"

"Nonsense," said the only other occupant of the passenger compartment, a red-headed young woman with pretty green eyes. "You just behave yourself, Heck Blanscombe."

"I bet the Apaches'll be here any sec!" Heck argued, half pleased and half frightened by his own prediction.

Katherine Blanscombe patted at her stubborn chin with a handkerchief hopelessly too small to do any good against all the settling dust. "There won't," she said firmly, "be any Apaches."

"Boy! I bet if they did come around, *you'd* show 'em a thing or two, huh, Katie!"

"Don't be silly," she responded, hiding her smile.

"Hey, I wonder why we stopped."

She had been wondering the same thing. "I don't know. This country is simply impossible. Look at our clothes!" She brushed at her skirt.

Heck ran the shade up on the window on his side. "There's just a big ole hill on this side. Are we still up in the mountains?"

Katie peered out. The stage had paused on a narrow spot in the dust road overlooking a declivity that made her stomach quake. Less than six feet from the high rear wheel of the coach, the

1

roadway simply vanished into a void. The cliff face tumbled down more than a thousand feet into a wooded canyon, and then, far across, the earth vaulted itself upward again in hills and rugged mountains that shaded from brown to green to azure to lavender as they receded toward the far horizon. For an instant Katie had the feeling that she and her little brother were the last two people on earth, a feeling she knew was silly for a twenty-two-year-old woman, but one she had felt another time or two since leaving Cleveland.

As usual, Katie reacted to the slight sense of fear by doing something.

Leaning out the window, she craned her slender body around to try to see the driver and shotgun man on the bench seat above and forward.

"You up there!" she called imperiously.

The coach shook a little as weight was redistributed, and then the round, bushy-bearded face of the shotgun man peered over the side at her. "Yessum?"

"Why have we stopped here?"

"Got to rest the hosses a minute. Hard climb gettin' up here."

"Where are we?" Katie demanded.

Bushy-beard grinned and spat brown juice. "Almost there, ma'am. Matter of fack, you git out an' look up ahead, you'll see the town of Salvation in the valley below, big as life an' twice as."

"Oh boy!" Heck yelped gleefully. "I want to see!"

"You stay where you are, young man!" Katie told him sharply. But as she spoke, she leaned farther out the window, trying to see ahead. Her view was blocked by the side of the coach.

"I want to *see!*" Heck repeated.

"You sit still, I said! It's too dangerous!"

Heck glared at her, hesitated a moment, and then stuck his tongue out at her. The coach, unlike many they had ridden in during the long journey west, had doors on both sides. And before Katie could even react to Heck's tongue being pointed at her, Heck had opened the door on his side and jumped out.

"Heck!" Katie screamed.

"Wow!" Heck yelled outside, running forward. "I can see it, Katie! It's far down there, boy! —Hey! Wow! Ouch!"

"Watch it there, boy!" one of the men up front thundered.

2

There was a sound of gravel and dirt sliding, and Heck's voice yelping in pain.

Katie leaped out of the coach on her side, hardly seeing the sickening void right at her toes. She ran around the front of the coach and team, making the horses leap and stamp wildly with alarm. Vaguely aware that the driver was having his hands full in holding the horses, she cut in front of them anyway and saw the drop-off and stopped, her heart in her mouth.

Heck had gone over the drop.

But it wasn't the drop into the canyon. It was on the inside curve of the road, and Katie saw that the brushy, rocky terrain sloped upward only a few hundred feet away. The drop from the roadway, she realized, running to the brink, had to be shallow.

She peered down.

Twenty feet below her, on the shale-strewn bottom of the roadway fill, Heck was brushing at himself and shaking his head groggily.

"Heck Blanscombe," Katie called down, "you get up here this minute!"

Heck looked up at her. He had a gash on his cheek. "I don't know if I can," he called, and began to bawl.

Katie took a deep breath and went down the shale slope on her feet, sliding and running sideways and sending little avalanches in all directions. She reached Heck's side and grabbed him by the ear. "Come *on!*" she breathed, and started back up, hauling him.

At the top the shotgun man was peering down anxiously. "You need a hand, lady?"

"No," Katie called, scrambling. "Of course not. I always climb mountains in a long dress."

The shotgun man took off his hat and scratched his head, watching. That made Katie really mad, and she managed to scramble on up to the roadway, dragging her little brother with her.

"By gum," the shotgun man grinned at her, "I thought we'd lost the tad for a minute, there."

"What would you have done if I hadn't been here?" Katie fumed, brushing tons of dirt off her dress. "Just gone on without even looking down to see if he was alive or dead?"

Heck groaned, "It wasn't his fault, sis!"

Katie whirled toward the boy, ready to tongue-lash him. But he

3

was bleeding and he looked white as snow under the coating of dirt, and his eyes were the size of pie plates.

Katie grabbed him in her arms and began to cry.

"Aw," Heck choked, his voice muffled against her breast. "I'm okay!"

Katie brushed her tears away. "If you ever do anything like that again—"

"I won't!" Heck promised. "I won't *never*."

"Well," Katie said, brushing herself, embarrassed at her outburst.

"You aw right now?" the shotgun man asked solicitously.

"Yes," she told him. "And I'm sorry I was rude."

"Shucks," he grinned. "You was skeert. Natural to cry when you git skeert. I've seen men do it."

Katie took a deep breath. Her legs were shaking. "We'll get back in the coach now."

"Might's well take a look-see at your new home, sinct you're already up here where's you can see it."

Katie remembered, turned, and looked out northwest, over the curving brink of the road.

Far below, in a sweeping break in the mountains where the desert washed in from the south like a massive brown ocean, was a little gray clutter. By squinting, Katie could see that the clutter was composed of dozens of small shacks and buildings, denser at the center, as if the hand of an idle giant had spilled play blocks at random. Farther up the valley she could see a large building surrounded by what appeared to be a fence.

"There she be," the shotgun man mused. "Salvation. And you can see the old fort up yonder. Not much of a fort no more. But they still got a troop there."

Katie felt a wave of disappointment and regret rise inside her. She had known it would be bad—desolate, small, barren. She had *known* that, and all the way out here she had been preparing herself for it. Still, without realizing it until now, she had had hopes. It might be a little valley with fruit trees, she had told herself. It might have a church and flowers and nice people. There were parts of Arizona that were really very nice, people had told her, and the Apaches weren't much of a problem any more. After all, this was 1882.

But looking down at the little town, Katie felt her insides continue

4

to sink. It wasn't pretty. It didn't have trees. She saw no church steeple. It was little and dirty and desolate and horrid.

But it was the place where she was going to build the new life she and Heck had to find.

She took a deep breath and tried to get interested in facts. She had to learn about her new home, she reminded herself.

"How many people live in Salvation now?" she asked.

"Aw, I dunno. Seven hunert, a thousand, maybe."

"And isn't that Fort Jefferson?"

"Ust to be. Army closed it. Got no real name now. Only since there's been a troop stationed in it again, local folks an' the sojers call it Fort Forgot."

"Forgot?" Katie echoed.

The shotgun man grinned and spat. "Story is, the general sent them fellers up here an' forgot 'em."

"That couldn't be," Katie replied seriously. "They must—"

"Aw, I know. It's just a joke. The boys git paid regular, an' new sojers come in now an' then, an' they git supplied an' such. It's more of an army joke than a town joke. The sojers don't think Salvation is much count, for a town."

"It looks all right to me," Katie said hopefully.

"Well, it ain't bad. Got a lot of nice folks. An' you don't have centipedes or tarantulas near as bad up in this country as you do down around the Tonto Basin."

"Do they bite you?" Heck asked, rubbing his nose on his coat sleeve.

"Naw!" the shotgun man grinned. "No problem atall!"

"Is there a church?" Katie asked hopefully.

"Well, they used to be a Holy Roller place, but it burnt. Folks meet in the schoolhouse on a Sunday, I think."

Katie set her jaw. Her vision was watery and she was afraid she was going to cry again. "It looks very nice," she said.

The shotgun man eyed her worriedly. "Another real nice thing about this country," he said, trying to be helpful. "You don't hardly ever get much smallpox. It's the altitude."

Within a few minutes the horses were rested enough to allow them to continue. Katie and Heck climbed back into the coach and the shotgun man got back on top with the driver. Wooden brakes

5

groaning, they started down the crumbling roadway toward the valley far below.

In the back, Katie wet a handkerchief from her water bottle and wiped Heck's face as clean as possible. Still shaken by his fall, Heck watched her solemnly and didn't say a word, even when she rubbed ferociously at the cut on his cheek. Then she put her arm around him and he leaned back against her side. They rumbled along, being jostled from side to side. Sifting clouds of dust made it impossible to see anything outside. The coach was as hot as a furnace. Heck dropped off to sleep, his hand holding Katie's.

She looked down at Heck's hand, still pudgy like a child's, but beginning to elongate, like a man's. In sleep, her little brother's face was that of a child. Sometimes when he was awake she saw fleeting traces of manhood there.

She sighed. For what seemed the millionth time she wondered if she was really doing the right thing.

Well, it was awfully late to be worried about it. She and Heck had both lived with their grandparents the last four years, since mom and dad had been killed in the train wreck. Katie had worked in a bank. It had seemed that this was to be their life forever—or until life separated them for good—except that the letter from the attorney in Philadelphia had changed everything.

Joe Blanscombe, Katie and Heck's father, had had a brother who was seldom spoken of since, as Katie's father had always put it, "He went out of his mind after the war and headed west someplace." But the Philadelphia lawyer had written to say that Henry Blanscombe, the seldom-mentioned uncle, had evidently felt better about relatives.

Henry, it seemed, had gone into business in a place called Salvation, Arizona, and had built up certain properties, to wit: Blanscombe's Rest, a hotel; the Roadhouse, a cafe adjacent to the hotel, and Kelly's Emporium, an amusements establishment located in the rear of the hotel on a perpetual lease basis. Uncle Henry owned fifty percent of each of these businesses, sharing ownership with one Michael Kelly. And when Uncle Henry had died recently, he had left a will assigning his fifty percent to the children of his brother Joe, to share equally, to operate and derive profit from, or to sell.

Katie had taken a day to get used to the idea, and then had

6

announced she was taking her younger brother west. Her grand-mother had a conniption fit and grandfather almost had a coronary, but Katie had been firm, and explained her reasons with fine logic.

Now, crushed by fatigue and wondering if she would ever get all the dirt washed out of her hair, Katie was trying hard to remember all those fine reasons she had given grandmaw and grandpaw. It was difficult because she was disheartened and scared.

But there they all were, she told herself, working to get her nerve up again. They were *good* reasons, too. *One:* she couldn't get the best profit from Uncle Henry's businesses, even if she elected to sell, unless she had been on the scene a while and understood the local market and competition. *Two:* there was nothing for her or Heck in Cleveland—nothing for her but a marriage, perhaps, and nothing for Heck but a job working steel or coal. *Three:* she had to give Heck the best; it was her duty; somehow she felt Heck would love the West, grow up fine and straight in manhood there. *Four:* with their parents dead, it might be better to go somewhere else . . . build a new life . . . forget the pain and prove themselves. *Five:* but Katie had never told anyone about *five.*

Yet there it was, old number five.

Well, maybe she was silly. But was it really so impossible to believe that it was all fate, and the man she awaited was really out here in Arizona, unknowingly awaiting *her?* Was it so stupid to *see* him, tall and dark and handsome, brave, strong, generous, loving —on a horse—taking her in his arms and telling her she never again had to worry about money or food or shelter, and taking care of Heck, too, making him the foreman of their thousand-acre ranch?

Katie sighed again.

She was awfully old for such daydreams, she told herself. Given another year or two, she would be a spinster. Most of her friends had married long ago. She had to keep such nonsense in the back of her mind. She was here to take over the businesses. She intended to stay, at least for a year, and learn. She could make a profit. She was smart and she knew bookwork. Out here in the West a woman would have a chance to prove herself. It was all going to be fine. *Fine.*

But oh, God, it was *so far* out here. She had had no idea. And every mile had made her feel smaller and more alone, although she

7

would never let anyone know this, especially Heck. She had her bluff in on Heck. There wasn't a male of any age that she couldn't bluff; her grandmother had said that.

Only here there might be . . .

She pulled herself up short again. Business, she reminded herself. She had to be tough.

Especially if there was as much dust, as many tarantulas, as much fear of Apache raiding parties, as few courtesies, as she feared.

But she wasn't going to be scared, she told herself. Even the *thought* of being scared was enough, usually, to bring out the Irish temper from her mother's side of the family, and as long as she could stay angry, and fight, she would be all right. She really would. And God help anyone who tried to give either her or Heck a bad time, because she wasn't here to turn around and go back. No. She was here to stay, no matter how awful it was.

TWO

Mike Kelly was going to bust. He knew it. The armpits of the black suit were too tight, the sleeves too short, the waistband of the black trousers was cutting into his gut, the fancy button shoes were killing his feet and bending his toes all sideways, and the celluloid collar was cutting his neck off. Any second, he thought, feeling sweat drip down his sides and soak into the galling waistband, he was going to plumb explode.

Nevertheless, Mike Kelly stood in front of the stage station in Salvation, back against the 'dobe wall as far as he could get to grab the scant afternoon shade. Sweat coursed down his face. His feet sent up pain signals. His belly grumbled and his blood pressure felt like it was going to blow the top of his head—and the derby resting on his matted, curly blond hair—clean to the moon.

Up and down Main Street, nobody else was paying much atten-

8

tion. An army wagon was loading at the grain store, two carriages were parked along the street near the post office corner, a flatbed wagon stood unhorsed near the blacksmith shop in the next block, a few men strolled here and there, a lazy hound dog snoozed under the front porch of Primrose Cafe, and the old boys on the whittlers' bench in front of the stone bank building were whittling and chewing and spitting, as usual. No one else was waiting for the stage.

It was the fourth day in a row Mike Kelly had met the stage, and he had long since run out of patience and fresh underwear. She probably wouldn't be on this one, either, he thought bitterly.

He had to meet her if at all possible, however, even if he met the daily stage every day until his socks rotted. Her wire had been cryptic: ARRIVE THIS WEEK BY STAGE. K. BLANSCOMBE.

What a hell of a way for a woman to sign a telegram! Mike Kelly groaned mentally as he thought about it. Her name was Katherine; he knew that much. And she was Hank's niece, so she had to be a lot younger than old Hank. But the tone of her earlier letter, and now the wire, had made Mike Kelly begin to think of her as tall, bony, beak-nosed, with a wart on her chin and a black umbrella. What kind of a *woman* would sign her name by initial only?

He had to be nice, however, Mike Kelly reminded himself. *Very* nice. K. Blanscombe, even if she was covered with warts and had the personality of a black widow spider, now owned fifty percent of all his worldly goods. He had to get along with her, at least until he could figure out a nice way to send her packing East again.

But meeting the stage every day all week, just because she had been too stupid or independent to put the day of arrival in her wire, was already a little above and beyond—especially since it meant putting on this monkey suit every afternoon just as the temperature topped one hundred.

Mike Kelly sighed, bit off a chunk of plug tobacco, and began chewing.

The door of the stage building beside him flapped open. Homer Farley, the stage agent, waddled out with his suspenders flopping. He was barefoot, and except for the tops of his sweat-stained long johns, all he wore was a pair of brown trousers.

"Stage's coming," he told Mike Kelly.

"I know," Mike sighed. "It almost always does."

"You figger she'll be on it today?"

9

"I don't know if I do or not."

"You *hopin'* she'll be on it today?"

"I don't know if I do or not."

Homer Farley pointed down the twisted street toward the far corner, where the town bent. "Here she comes."

Down at the curve, the stage appeared in view. It raised some dust as it cornered, obscuring the view of the saloons and sheds behind it. As it passed the burned-out ruin of the old church, and approached Primrose Cafe, the hound dog loped out and took a half-hearted snap at the horses. The horses were too tired to care, so the hound went back under the porch.

Mike Kelly tried to adjust the celluloid collar so it wouldn't cut quite so deep into his flesh, but the collar was so slippery with sweat, and so stuck to his neck at the edges, he couldn't budge it. He shrugged his shoulders in the tight coat and waited uncomfortably as the stage jangled up to the porch and reined up in a calamity of sifting dust and groaning harness.

"Howdy, Mike!" the driver called cheerfully, climbing down.

"Is she?" Mike asked.

The driver strode stiffly to the coach door. "Yep."

Mike grunted in surprise and tried to fix the collar again.

The driver opened the door. A little kid, sandy-haired, on the skinny side, with a dust-smeared face and wearing sissy eastern clothes, hopped out and looked around. "Boy, oh boy!" he cried. "Hey, sis, wait till you see!"

From inside the coach came a muffled feminine answer. "What do you see?"

"Everything looks like a ghost town!"

Mike Kelly spoke despite himself. "Watch your mouth there, boy."

The kid turned to Mike's voice and looked up . . . up to Mike's height of six feet, three inches. "Huh?"

"Bad luck to call a place a ghost town," Mike told him. "Especially when it ain't."

Before the boy could reply, the coach shook a trifle and a young woman, her dark red dress coated with fine dust, climbed down. Mike Kelly took one look, sucked in his breath, and figured it was a mistake.

That was because she was pretty. She was more than pretty. She was cute. Hell, she was *beautiful*. She was little, by Mike's standards, much shorter than his shoulder, and tiny-waisted, pale, with red hair piled high atop her head under the bonnet, and a pert mouth and fine, even features. She was also young, much too young to be a K. Blanscombe.

The girl brushed herself off, dabbed at her face with a little hankie, and looked up and down the street. Her expression was crestfallen. But then she squared her shoulders as if bracing herself for something, and turned to stare smack into Mike Kelly's face.

"Oh!" she murmured. That was because Mike was close.

She had astounding green eyes, and her surprise made them even wider.

"Howdy," Mike Kelly grunted, snatching off his derby.

The girl recovered her composure and gave him a look that would have made a blue norther feel like a hand-warmer. She turned her back on him and watched the driver and shotgun man handing down luggage.

Mike didn't know what to do or say for an instant. He glanced at the coach door. Nobody else aboard. But *this* couldn't be K. Blanscombe. She didn't even have a blemish, much less warts.

Mike cleared his throat. "Ma'am?"

The girl stiffened and kept her back turned.

The boy said with a frown, "You better leave my sister alone, mister, if you don't want a black eye."

This made Mike Kelly's Irish temper flare a little and he reached out to touch the girl deferentially on the shoulder. She jumped a foot.

"Sir," she said icily, "if you touch me again——!"

"I'm looking for a lady name of Blanscombe," Mike Kelly told her.

Her marvelous eyes widened a little again as she stared at him. "I'm Katherine Blanscombe."

Mike grinned with relief and stuck out his hand. "I'm Mike Kelly."

"Hey, Katie," the boy said, "he's the guy that owns half our business!"

The girl was frowning at Mike's outstretched hand, making no move to accept it with her own.

Mike grinned wider. "Katie, is it? Well by golly, that's great. I always like——"

11

"Miss Blanscombe to you," Katie said frostily. "Do you have some identification?"

"What?" Mike grunted.

"Identification," Katie snapped.

"Oh," Mike said, trying to figure out what was going on. "Yeah. Let's see." He rummaged in his pockets, but the suit was so tight that he couldn't get his hands in very far, and then he remembered that he hadn't put anything much in the pockets anyway, for the same reason. All he could find on him now were a few matches, a poker chip, a sack of tobacco, some papers and a pocketknife.

While he was still fumbling around like an idiot, sweat pouring all over him, the driver came over and gave Katie a little salute. "All your gear's piled up right there, ma'am."

"Thank you," Katie said loftily. "Oh, could you vouch for this man?"

The driver blinked. "Him?"

"He says he's Mike Kelly. I expected someone older."

The driver grinned. "That's him, all right."

"Thanks," Mike said disgustedly, and spat.

Katie glanced at the gob of tobacco juice on the roadway and shuddered. Manfully she extended her hand to Mike anyway. "How do you do, Mister Kelly. It was good of you to meet us."

Mike relaxed a little and grinned at her again. It was going to be all right, he thought. "My pleasure, ma'am." Her hand was adorably soft.

"This is my brother, Heck," Katie said, introducing the boy.

"Good looking boy," Mike said, shaking hands with the kid. "You have a nice trip?"

"Ghastly," Katie snapped.

"Yeah," Mike said. "Well—"

"Which way is the hotel?"

"You mean my hotel, or the one you'd wanna stay at?"

"I mean *our* hotel," Katie corrected him. "And why should I stay at any other?"

"Oh," Mike said. "I see. Uh—it's down yonder." He pointed down past the bank corner. BLANSCOMBE'S REST, the white-on-red sign said, sticking out over the gingerbread second-story roof. It was the only two-story building in that block, and even stood taller

12

than the feed store or domino parlor, with their two-story false fronts. Mike pointed it out with a certain sense of pride.

"Why," Katie asked, frowning, "is it painted red?"

"Stands out that way," Mike explained.

"That will be changed," Katie snapped, picking up one small suitcase. "Will you bring the other things, Mister Kelly? I should like to check in and rest before further discussion."

Stunned, Mike Kelly watched her take her brother's hand and waltz up the street as if she owned it, looking neither right nor left at the handful of men gawking from porches.

The stage driver and shotgun man were standing by, grinning at Mike.

"Who the hell does she think she is?" Mike fumed. "I can't carry all this crap!"

"I think," the driver replied, "she thinks she's the Queen of England. She's some dinger, I'll give her that."

"Well," Mike spluttered, "I'm not carrying this stuff!"

"You better," the driver told him. "Ain't no way to start out with your new business partner, fussing at her."

Mike looked up the street. The girl and her little brother had swept right up onto the front porch of the hotel and were going in. "Aw, gawd," Mike groaned. "She hadn't ought to go in there like that! The girls'll get all upset. And that kid—"

Up the street, Katie and Heck went into the hotel.

Groaning, Mike Kelly made his decision. He swooped down upon the pile of luggage, got a suitcase under each arm, hung a couple of strapped bags around his neck, hefted the steamer trunk, which felt like it was loaded with rocks, and staggered down the street as fast as he could stagger, his derby hat clenched between his teeth.

In the little, gilt-painted, red-carpeted lobby of Blanscombe's Rest, Katie stood rooted by shock.

The lobby was only a twenty-foot-square area with a desk in the back and a doorway leading to a hallway and stairs. A front window beamed gritty sunlight over a long crimson couch and several over-stuffed velvet chairs in blue and gold and purple.

On the couch sat two women. In two of the chairs sat two other

13

women. They wore spangled silky dresses cut to reveal plump, bare shoulders and arms. They had long hair piled up and heavy red makeup and beauty marks pasted on their faces and a lot of other identifying tags, but Katie had already gotten the general message.

One of the women, a large bleached blonde wearing seventeen strands of imitation pearls, got heavily to her feet. "Afternoon, dearie. What do you need?"

Katie's voice came out in a croak. "Who are *you?*"

The blonde wiggled and looked Katie up and down, then glanced at Heck. "Is he with you, dearie?" She reached out to pet Heck's face.

Katie slapped her hand aside. "How *dare* you!"

"Hey!" the blonde growled. "What's the idea? Nobody gets ugly with Ruby Smith, dearie. What do you want here, anyway?"

At this moment, Mike Kelly lumbered in with his mountain of luggage. He looked hot and upset and silly in his suit, but Katie felt a little pang at the way he moved and how handsome he was. Her shock and anger prevented her from realizing any of this very clearly.

"I see you met," Mike smiled, putting down the suitcases on top of the steamer trunk. "Ruby, this's—"

"I don't care who she is," Ruby bawled. "I want her out of here!"

"Well, now," Mike murmured nervously, "wait a minute, Ruby."

Katie attacked. "Mister Kelly, what are these—these women doing in my hotel?"

"*Your* hotel!" Ruby bellowed. "This is—"

"Well," Mike Kelly stammered, "the fact of the matter is—"

"Hey, sis!" Heck piped up. "You know what this place *is?* This is a dadgum—"

Katie put her hand firmly over his mouth and bolted for the door.

14

THREE

Tears of rage blurred Katie's vision as she hauled Heck onto the front porch. She almost forgot where she was for an instant, and got a shock as she looked up and down the street for something familiar. There was nothing familiar. Instead of the paved, curving streets, stone or brick buildings, sidewalks, trees, horse-drawn trollies and nicely dressed pedestrians of her home experience, she saw a dusty, twisted roadway lined by falling-down sheds, false-front clapboard buildings and adobe huts, sun-warped board sidewalks with holes here and there, a few battered wagons and some flea-bitten horses under saddle, and, nearby, a bare wood bench lined with old men in overalls, the spittoons in front of them half buried in wood shavings. A rotund Indian woman in blankets had been strolling by as Katie and Heck burst out of the "hotel," and she stopped and stared at Katie with round, lackluster eyes.

It wasn't home. It was the end of the world.

Mike Kelly barreled out of the building after her. He had lost his hat, and his celluloid collar had sprung open so that one end flapped in the air. "Wait a minute! Wait a minute!"

Katie whirled on him. "Were you that eager to ruin a legitimate business enterprise, Mister Kelly?"

Mike Kelly's mouth fell open. "Huh?"

"My poor uncle Henry wasn't cold in the grave yet, and you turned his hotel into a—a place of sin!"

"What?" Mike Kelly muttered. Then light dawned in his attractive eyes. "Oh, *I* get it!" A grin spread across his face. "You think I *changed* things—you figure old Hank was—"

"You'll regret it!" Katie told him. "There must be law, even in a place such as this! I'll have you in court!" Heck was tugging at her hand, trying to get free.

15

"Listen, lady," Mike Kelly told her. "I didn't change a thing. Whatever you find here, that's how old Hank had it set up."

"Liar!" Katie snapped. She released Heck's hand.

Mike Kelly's eyes went narrow. "Don't call me a liar."

"My uncle would never countenance such an enterprise. He was a gentleman!"

"Your uncle, lady," Mike Kelly told her, "was a good old boy. Everybody liked him. But your uncle smoked black stogies and chewed tobacco and got drunk every night and hated kids and kitty cats. He was one of the orneriest, no-count bums—"

"Heck!" Katie screamed.

It wasn't an expletive. She had just caught sight of Heck, trying to edge his way back inside the hotel.

Heck stopped when she yelled at him. "I just wanted to check something," he mumbled.

Katie grabbed his hand again. "I know what you wanted to *check,* young man, and if I ever hear of you going *near* this place again, I'll have you strapped until you can't sit down for a week! Do you hear me?"

"Aw," Heck growled, sullen defiance in his eyes.

Katie shook him. *"Do you hear me?"*

Heck hung his head. "Yessum."

Mike Kelly told her, "You don't need to worry about him in there. He's just a tad. Ruby wouldn't let any of the girls—"

"I'm bigger'n you think," Heck shot back angrily.

Mike grinned at the boy and reached out to tousle his hair. "You bet you are, sonny. Only—"

"Keep your hands off him," Katie said icily.

Mike Kelly paused, hand in midair, and frowned at her. "You sure do want to fight, don't you."

Katie heaved a deep sigh and got rigid control of herself. It was no good to allow emotions to run wild, she reminded herself. She had always prided herself on being controlled. Especially with men. She needed all her control now.

"Mister Kelly," she said coldly, "you have slandered our uncle's name. What else you may have done remains to be seen. I suggest that you show me my other business holdings immediately, so that I shall have the proper information in hand when I consult an attorney."

16

Mike's face twisted in obvious pain. "You don't want to sue anybody. Dammit—"

Katie looked at the doorway next to the hotel. A beer mug was painted on the front glass. "This, I assume, is the Roadhouse?"

"Yeah," Mike Kelly said. "Only—"

Katie marched to the door and went inside.

It was a single large room with a low, raftered ceiling from which lanterns hung. Along the side wall was a long, dark wood bar, and behind the bar were enormous gilt-framed mirrors. The other walls were hung with red draperies, and here and there hung a painting of a voluptuous nude. There were also some deer or elk horns. Small tables studded the room. Most were unoccupied. Three men had a desultory poker game going in one corner, and at another two cowboys were drinking beer. At the bar, several soldiers, in cavalry uniforms, stood with spurred boots hiked up on the rail as they drank redeye whiskey.

Heck and Mike Kelly came in behind Katie.

"Heck," Katie ordered, "wait outside."

"Yessum," Heck said, too eagerly.

Katie grabbed his hand. "Never mind. I'm holding onto you."

"Aw!"

Katie turned to Mike Kelly. "This is nothing but a common saloon."

"It ain't common," Mike said with a growl. "It's the best saloon in this whole part of the country. You can ask anybody."

Katie glared at him and started for the bar. She tripped over something. She looked down and saw a pair of booted legs extending out from under one of the tables. She gasped and bent over to peer underneath. The soldier was young, and he was snoring peacefully, a bottle of liquor clutched to his chest.

"You, there!" Katie snapped at the soldiers at the bar. "What's the meaning of this?"

One of the soldiers grinned at her. "That's Larry. Don't worry about him."

"He's inebriated!"

"Ain't it the truth!"

"Call the sheriff. Call your—your provost!"

"Leave him alone," one of the other soldiers pleaded. "It's okay. He's on a pass."

17

Incredulous, Katie stared at the speaker, a freckle-faced youth who couldn't have been over eighteen. "Do you always come in here and simply get—inebriated like this?"

"No, ma'am," the boy soldier told her seriously. "Only when we get paid."

Katie turned to Mike Kelly. "Please direct us to a decent hotel. If any."

Mike scratched his head. "The Shady Nook is just down the street. That's where I was going to take you before you—"

"I just *imagine* you wanted to hide this corruption!" Katie flared.

Mike Kelly's eyes widened the way they did when he lost his temper. "No, ma'am," he growled. "I didn't mean to hide anything. But I just wanted to get you settled before showing you around. A lot of folks come out here and don't know our ways. I didn't know if you'd be one of them or not."

"But I obviously am?" Katie challenged.

Mike Kelly was trembling. "You are," he said in a tone like distant, threatening summer thunder.

Katie squared her shoulders. "You will find, Mister Kelly, that I am not the—the tenderfoot, I believe is your quaint expression —that you assume me to be. I know the law. I know my rights. I own and control fifty percent of these businesses, and you may be assured that things will change around here as soon as I have consulted the proper attorney."

"Yeah?" Mike Kelly bellowed. "Well, you just consult all you want to, lady! You just consult your rear end off! I been trying to be nice to you, but you sure wear my patience out fast. I come down to meet your dadblamed stage in this monkey suit, just for your benefit—"

"You didn't need to wear that outlandish costume for my benefit," Katie broke in. "I'm not enamored of people who look like monkeys!"

Mike Kelly stared at her and his eyes bulged. Then he tore his celluloid collar off and hurled it across the room. "That's it! That does it! I tried! But you want war, lady. It'll be war!"

Katie quaked inside at his towering anger. He was the first man she had ever met whom she couldn't overwhelm, and it was frightening. There was such a—a *physical* quality to this man.

18

But she didn't show anything. With glacial calm, she pulled Heck toward the door.

"See ya, Mister Kelly!" Heck called back.

Mike Kelly didn't reply. He stood there, glowering, fists on his hips.

Katie let the door slam behind her.

"Who," one of the soldiers asked in awe, "was *that?*"

Mike Kelly drew a deep breath to help him control his shaking. "Her name is trouble," he said, going to the bar. "K. Trouble. Bernie, pour me a double."

"A double for trouble," the freckle-faced soldier said. He giggled.

Mike looked him over. "You going to take care of him?" he asked the corporal.

"I suppose," the corporal said.

"Well, he's going to fall down any minute."

The corporal nodded. "That girl live here, does she?"

"She does now," Mike said. "Temporarily."

Bernie, the bartender, swabbed the counter with a wet towel and poured him a drink. "She's the new owner."

"Wow," the corporal breathed.

"Half owner," Mike corrected bitterly. "*Half* owner. With half, she can't do a damned thing."

"Yeah," Bernie grunted. "But neither can you."

Mike downed the double shot. It hit like a bomb. He had to watch it, he thought. She could drive a man to drink real easy.

"Another?" Bernie said, the bottle poised.

"No," Mike said, and shoved away from the bar.

"I'd sure hate it, man, if that girl messed things up," the corporal said.

"She isn't going to mess anything up," Mike replied.

"Yeah, but the old Roadhouse and the girls next door are all that make Salvation livable, Mike. You run nice places. Your games are on the level, the girls are nice and you don't water your liquor. If that girl messes you up, all we'd have left is some place like Ray Root's place."

"You don't have to go to Ray Root's stinking hole," Mike growled.

"Well, I know there's bad blood between you and old Ray, and I sure wouldn't want to take my business there. But if that girl messes everything up—"

19

"She's not messing anything up," Mike said flatly. "Count on that."

The freckle-faced soldier chuckled. "A double for trouble," he said, and passed out, sort of sliding to the floor.

The corporal sighed.

"You said," Mike reminded him, "that you'd take care of him."

"I will," the corporal said. "You just take care of that girl."

Mike grunted and went outside. He stood on the porch, eyes slit against a wind that was rising out of the desert to the southwest. Already Rudder Mountain, to the west, was partially obscured by blowing dust, and the wind whistled down Main Street, turning tiny dust devils and driving bits of scrap and trash and tumbleweed under raised porches. It was hot. His monkey suit clung to him like wet mud.

It was going to be bad, Mike thought. Katie Blanscombe was as much like old Hank as a kitten was like a rattler. Mike had loved old Hank. It had been Hank who gave him a chance, took him practically off the garbage heap and made him a partner. Together they had built something—something good. They had never cheated in their games, they'd run off any girl who tried to steal money from her clients and operated the cock fighting pit on the up and up, and had been like brothers the whole time.

Mike shrugged, readjusting his body inside the clammy suit. Salvation, he thought, wasn't the greatest place in the world. But he had made it home. After the years of drifting along the trails, he had *made* it home. People respected him, mostly. As long as the army kept a troop in the old fort, there was business enough. Even Ray Root hadn't been able to cheat or steal enough business to hurt profits too badly. Mike had imagined he had it made, that, at age thirty, he had a fine future with the bad trouble and the drifting all behind him.

But that was before old Hank died and the wire came from K. Blanscombe.

She was going, Mike thought, to give him hell. She was the coldest, nastiest, most stubborn, hateful woman he had ever run into. What made it worse was that she didn't have warts. She was too young for warts, and she probably wouldn't have any when she was sixty.

20

Even at sixty, Mike thought, she would probably be the most beautiful, bewitching woman any man had ever laid eyes on.

Which only made it infinitely worse. Even the thought of how pretty she was made him madder. It didn't seem *right* for her to have those eyes and that mouth and that hair and that way she moved things around when she walked. What the hell right did she have to have all that equipment and then be so cold and hateful with it? It was unfair.

Mike sighed again.

The door of the hotel banged closed. Mike partly turned. Ruby walked out to stand facing him. There was fire lurking in her eyes.

"Well?" she said.

"Well what?" Mike grunted.

"Did you get rid of her?"

"She's gone down to the Shady Nook."

"All her crap is still in our lobby."

"I'll have it sent down there, Ruby."

Ruby shifted her ample weight, making the dusty sunlight glitter on her spangles. "I didn't like the way she acted. I didn't like it at all, Mike."

"I didn't either, much."

"Is she going to give us trouble?"

"Well, I imagine she's going to try."

"The girls won't like her meddling around, either. And when Dolores gets a good look at her, you're in a lot of trouble."

"Dolores doesn't have to get a good look at her," Mike said.

"She will, though. Dolores is a very jealous girl. You know that. I never had a girl working for me that took a shine to a man the way Dolores took a shine to you. And I think you like her too."

"I've never—" Mike began to protest.

"I know that," Ruby muttered. "Wouldn't I know that? But you like Dolores. You've been nice to her. You're nice to all the girls. But you've been nice to Dolores, too, and she's young and fiery and maybe she doesn't understand that you're just a nice, soft-hearted guy with too much generosity for your own good. She's in love with you, and when she gets one look at this woman you've brought in here, you're in bad trouble."

21

"Look," Mike expostulated. "I didn't bring that woman in here!"

"She's here, though. She's your new fifty percent partner. And when Dolores gets a good look at her, and sees how cute she is, Dolores will probably try to stick a knife in her."

"Well you just keep Dolores from seeing her, then," Mike snapped.

"It's going to be bad trouble," Ruby said darkly.

"You said that."

"I'll say it again."

"Don't."

Ruby softened and gave Mike a motherly smile. "You sure you can handle that one, Mike? She's mean. I know her type. She can hurt you."

"I can handle her. I can handle anyone."

"I don't want to see all this ruined."

"Do you think I do?"

Ruby smiled. "All right, all right. I *hope* you can handle it."

"I can," Mike said grimly. "If she wants a fight, she's got it. But I'll tell you right now how it's going to end. I'm going to run her rear end out of this town and end up owning the whole shebang."

"I don't know," Ruby began, "if you're . . ." She let her voice trail off.

"You don't know if I'm what?" Mike prodded.

"Nothing," Ruby said.

"No. Say it."

Ruby met his eyes. Hers were weather-beaten and soft and sort of sad. "I don't know if you're mean enough."

"I'm mean enough," Mike said. "I'll *get* mean enough."

The hotel room in the Shady Nook was on the side, with a window overlooking some trash cans. The wallpaper was yellow, with purple flowers, and the furniture consisted of an oversized bed with a rope mattress and flowered covers, a pine dresser with a pitcher and water basin, two straight chairs and a small round table. Heck was on the bed, bouncing up and down and making it creak. Katie was at the window. She had the shakes.

"What'll we do now, Katie?" Heck asked, bouncing.

"We send for our things," Katie said.

"Then what?" More bouncing.

"Then we clean up, rest, have something to eat, I suppose."

"Then what?" More bouncing.

"Will you please stop bouncing?"

"It *feels* good. What happens then, Katie? Huh?"

"Well," Katie sighed, "tomorrow we get you in school."

The bouncing stopped.

"Then," Katie added, "I see an attorney."

"I don't think I ought to go to school," Heck said.

"You'll attend school, young man, and that's that."

"I seen some boys my age out there on the street, and they wasn't in school."

"You *saw* some boys, and they *weren't* in school."

"Right."

"Well, they're ne'er-do-wells. You'll attend school."

Heck started bouncing again. "You sure lit into Mike Kelly."

"He hasn't seen the half of it," Katie sniffed.

"He's sure a big man, huh?"

"I didn't notice," Katie said frostily.

"Yeah, I bet you didn't!"

Ordinarily Katie would have reacted sharply. This time she didn't. For some reason, Heck's remark made her eyes start flowing like spigots, and she stood with her back to him, looking out at the trash cans. The tears kept coming. She was angry and embarrassed and frightened.

Everything, she thought. That was how much had gone wrong. Just everything. The town was horrid and the hotel wasn't a hotel and the saloon was horrid and Mike Kelly was a hideous man with no grace or style or consideration. Her tears flowed harder and faster, in silence.

Mike Kelly, she thought, probably didn't understand that this was a new start for her and Heck—a new life, and one she couldn't give up. She remembered how much money remained in her purse. There was no way they could go back. She hadn't enough money left. And even if she had been rich, she wouldn't go back—not to her friends' smiles and the I-told-you-so's of the grandparents. She had made a choice. She had to stick with it.

It was going to be a struggle, she thought. But everything now depended on her winning. Her pride, her future, Heck's life—

23

everything. She had the feeling that she would never be able to hold her head high again if she lost this battle.

So she simply could not lose it. It was desperately important.

"Sis?" Heck said quietly, as if worried.

She kept her back to him. "Yes?"

"Are you *cryin'?*"

"Of course not!" she snapped, dabbing her eyes. "It's just all this dreadful dust—"

"You *are* cryin'!" Heck said, jumping off the bed to confront her.

Katie did what came naturally: she counterattacked. "Get out of those filthy clothes," she ordered sharply, stifling the tears. "March yourself down that hall and find the bathroom. By the time you're clean, I'll have fresh things for you to put on."

"What's the *hurry?*" Heck protested. "These clothes feel good! They're just *breakin' in* proper!"

"We're going to find an attorney," Katie told him, bracing herself.

"You just said we'd do that tomorrow."

"Well, I've changed my mind. —Never put off until tomorrow, Heck, the things you can do today."

Heck eyed her belligerently. "Are you gonna *really* give ole Mike Kelly a bad time?"

"I wouldn't," Katie said, "be at all surprised."

"Aw!"

"March!" she ordered sternly.

Heck marched, showing his bitterness in the set of his shoulders. Katie watched him go into the hall, and then she took a deep breath and got the last of the tears wiped away. There was no use, she told herself, delaying. At least some action would keep her from thinking about Cleveland.

FOUR

Hugh Corkern, attorney-at-law, was so startled to see a customer that he almost dropped his bottle. He managed to catch it between his knees behind the desk, cracking his elbow on the edge in the process. The blow was right on the crazy bone and he tried to grin at the lovely young woman standing so imperious in his doorway, but he knew the expression was more of a grimace.

"Come in, come in!" he choked, screwing the cap on the bottle and shoving it into the bottom drawer.

"Mister Corkern?" the girl asked coolly.

She had red hair and marvelous green eyes. "That's my name," Corken babbled, "and law's my game. Ha ha. Do come in, young lady—and young gentleman."

He had just spotted the skinny kid lurking behind the voluminous folds of the girl's long dress, and gave him a fiercely conspiratorial wink. The boy didn't appear impressed; he stayed near the door as the girl swept into the office, knocking the stuffed owl off the end of the bookcase, and sat down in the chair facing the corner of Corkern's rolltop.

"My name," she announced, "is Katherine Blanscombe. This is my brother and ward, Heck."

"Pleased to—"

"You *are* an attorney-at-law, Mister Corkern?"

"Ah, yes," Corkern murmured. "I—"

"I need advice," the remarkable young woman said briskly, dusting a flawless small hand over the folds of her dark blue skirt.

"Advice can be invaluable," Corkern said, "especially in matters of—"

"I don't know whether it's a civil action in which I have to sue," she cut in again, "or whether I have grounds for a criminal

25

complaint. Let me ask you this question at once: you don't represent a man named Mike Kelly, do you?"

Corkern had been sitting in his office for five hours today with two houseflies and one small lizard his only company. He had had a few *small* drinks, to pass the time. Now he felt he was being propelled along in total confusion by some mighty force, and the fact that all the force was coming from this one little girl added to his confusion. He struggled to catch up. "Mike Kelly? Do I represent Mike Kelly?"

"He operates an establishment here as Blanscombe's Rest, another known as the Roadhouse—"

"Oh!" Corkern broke in. "Mike *Kelly!*"

"Do you know him?" Katherine Blanscombe's eyes looked dangerous.

"We've, ah, met," Corkern said.

"Do you represent him?"

Corkern almost laughed. Mike Kelly had almost as much use for lawyers as he had for old whores and smallpox. "No," he said. "I don't."

"All right," Katherine Blanscombe said. "My uncle, Mister Corkern, was half-owner of these business establishments. He left his half to me in his will, which is in probate here. I have come to Salvation to exercise my proper rights of half-ownership. I find that Mister Kelly, who owns the other half of these businesses, has turned them into disreputable houses. I want him stopped."

"You want *who* stopped?" Corkern asked, baffled.

"Mike Kelly!"

"Stopped from *what?*"

"From operating these places in a disreputable and immoral manner!"

"Uh—"

"I feel I might sign complaints against him in criminal court for operating a disorderly house and for encouraging public drunkenness," the amazing girl went on briskly. "That's one possibility. I could also sue him personally, of course, for all the damage I'm sure he has already done to the good name of the businesses since my uncle's death. But that might cost more money than I have right now. It seems to me that the best course of action might be injunctive. But then I don't know the law here. What do you advise?"

Hugh Corkern leaned back in his chair and held his head. He was quickly getting a violent headache. "You can't sue Mike Kelly!" he blurted.

"And why not?" she demanded.

"He's a popular man in this town!"

Katherine Blanscombe knotted her hands in her lap. "Very well, then," she said, taut-lipped. "I can see I've come to the wrong office. I fully intend to secure my rights in this matter, force Mister Kelly out of active participation in this business, and assume control myself. Without delay. But obviously you feel such a lawsuit wouldn't succeed—"

She got to her feet. "Come, Heck," she told the boy.

"Wait a minute!" Hugh Corkern bleated. "Wait a minute!"

She turned regally. "Yes?"

Oh, God. It was ridiculous. But she was the first customer today. Hell, she was the first customer *this month!* Was he going to sit here and let her walk out and go down the street to Busher & Cline, who already had all the clients in town anyway?

It was a matter of self-preservation, Hugh Corkern thought in this instant as he faced her. A fee was a *fee*. It had been almost three years since he finished the law course by correspondence, and he hadn't had a decent case yet.

"I certainly didn't mean," he said, sweating, "that maybe you don't have a *case*—I mean—maybe you *do*. I mean I'm fairly certain you do. Have a case, that is. I'd like to represent you. It sounds very interesting. Yes. Please, ah, sit down again, Miss —uh—"

"Blanscombe," she murmured, taking the chair again.

"Yes," Corkern muttered. He fumbled with a tablet and quill. "Uh, you want to sue, ah, Mike Kelly." Get the fee, get the *fee*, he thought.

"What I really want," she said, "is to file a complaint saying he's operating a disorderly house. Then I want to seek an injunction that would bar him from operating any of those businesses."

"Close him down?" Corkern said, a coppery taste in his mouth.

"Close him down," she snapped. "Once closed down and enjoined from operating his businesses, he would be forced to sell his interest to me, or at least to become a silent partner. I could then reopen the cafe and the hotel as decent, law-abiding places."

"And Mike—I mean, ah, Kelly—would be—?"

Her eyes were frosty. "I'm not concerned with what would happen to him, Mister Corkern."

Corkern nodded, jotted a meaningless note, and felt the chill going up his back. She was young, she was beautiful, and she had the attitude of an Apache snake woman, he thought. He wondered if Mike Kelly had any idea how much trouble he was facing.

But the girl was waiting for an answer.

Corkern gathered himself up. "We could, ah, file a complaint," he began, "and—"

"Good. I want to do that, then."

"And," Corkern went on, "we could file the request for an injunction."

"Good. I want to do that too, then."

"But," Corkern kept going doggedly, "there is one serious problem."

She looked at him steadily. Her eyes really were stunning. He wondered how he could phrase this so she wouldn't walk out.

"Well?" she said finally.

"I don't know how far we'll get with the judge," Corkern said cautiously.

"Isn't that your department?" she asked frostily. "You must word the petition, or whatever you call it, so the judge sees the truth and justice of our position."

"Well," Corkern muttered, *"yes.* But the *problem* is—you see—the judge—well, a lot of men in Salvation, ah, *like* the kind of business Mike Kelly operates. You see," he went on quickly, "not that they necessarily frequent such places themselves, but they see a range of entertainments as a lure to people traveling through the West, and they believe such places, uh, by providing outlets, as it were . . . uh—"

"The judge," Katherine Blanscombe cut in, "would rule in favor of Mike Kelly because he likes Mike Kelly."

Corkern took a breath of relief. "Yes."

"Is the judge a married man, Mister Corkern?"

The question startled him. "Yes. He and his wife live over on Clover Street, the end house, as a matter of fact, and—"

28

She cut him off again. "I want to retain you. I want the complaint filed and I want the injunction requested. Now about a retainer fee."

"Yes," Corkern murmured, feeling sweat bead his forehead as he watched her dig into her purse. "The fee. Of course." Should he ask for twenty dollars? That was pushing it; maybe fifteen? He was calculating furiously.

She took some gold pieces out of the purse. "Will thirty dollars be sufficient?" she asked.

"Yes!" Corkern gasped. "I mean—yes, as a starting retainer fee, that is, I, ah, believe it should, ah, possibly—under the circumstances—meet minimum—"

The gold coins sounded heavily on the top of the desk. "There you are, Mister Corkern," she said, her eyes slightly regretful and worried as she looked at the money. "Heavens knows we have little enough left. But this is a matter that must be resolved, or we simply have no future here at all."

Corkern's hand shot out and he dumped the coins into the top drawer. "You know the judge will be a problem."

"You take care of the filing, Mister Corkern. I'll take care of the judge."

Corkern stared at her. He wanted to know what she meant. But he was afraid to ask.

"When," she asked, "do we file?"

"We file tomorrow," he said, startled again by her bluntness.

"Good," she said, and she smiled for the first time. It was a pretty smile, very young and girlish, and it softened her entire appearance. "Thank you, Mister Corkern. You've been most helpful."

Corkern shook hands with her, patted the boy on the head, and ushered them out. Closing the door behind them, he rushed to the desk for a drink. He needed it, and before this was over, he thought, he wouldn't be the only one.

With the first shock of meeting his new partner subsiding, Mike Kelly recognized that he might be in for some unpleasantness.

Not, of course, that a little girl like that could really hurt him in any way. But Mike did some hard thinking, while making sure

29

her bags were delivered to the Shady Nook, and decided it wouldn't hurt to make sure all his fences were in place.

Changing back to his usual Levi's and a red flannel shirt, Mike left the loft room over the saloon and headed down Main Street. It was a pleasantly warm mountain afternoon, a few white clouds settling in near Rudder Mountain and the country beyond, and there was a chance that later it might rain. Mike felt some of his usual good humor come back as he sniffed the keen air and strode along, arms swinging, watching the sodbusters load wagons, the miners lead burros, the few waddies lounge around on the lookout for a pretty girl. Salvation, he thought, might not be much of a town by some people's standards, but it was a mighty fine place by his. It was home, he knew half the people around, and getting out among 'em made him feel better.

"Hey, Mike!" Homer Farley, the stage agent, called as he went by. "How come you to git outta your clown suit?"

"Through clownin', Homer!" Mike called back, and grinned.

Hank Blanscombe's death, Mike reflected, had been a bad enough shock. People had figured Hank was mean enough and tough enough to just live forever. Mike hadn't really been ready to go on without the old sot, either in business or out of it.

For the truth was that he had loved old Hank. It had been a hard blow to sustain, losing him that way. But then Mike had begun to see that you simply had to go on, you couldn't sit around with snot in your nose all your own life, and part of going on, in his case, meant running the businesses the best way he could.

Which was what he had been doing, assuming he would send old Hank's share of the profits back east to Cleveland or wherever it was that Hank's kinfolks lived.

Thus the letters and then the wire from "K. Blanscombe" had shaken him up, and he had still been trying to adjust to that surprise when the girl had arrived. He just hadn't been ready for what she meant in terms of new surprises.

But now, he thought grimly, he didn't have time for the luxury of more idleness. He didn't know what the dratted girl might do, but first things first: let the top customer know what was in the wind.

Consequently Mike hiked out to the end of Main Street, past the old rock-crusher building, the burned-out feed lot, the municipal well that had gone bad, and a long line of stores, shops, sheds, saloons, offices and houses that got progressively smaller and smaller and seedier and seedier until finally they just stopped, and he was walking up across the broad grassy incline that led up to the gates of Fort Forgot.

It never had been much of a fort, really, and these days, despite the scare started by Nakaidoklini and his mystical religion last year, and Nantiatish's raids in the Tonto Basin just a few weeks ago, Fort Forgot was still—well—*forgot*. They might be beefing things up over at Fort Bowie and even at Fort Thomas, but nothing had been going on locally. The local Indians seemed in no mood to go on the warpath again, so the military situation was still normal too. The huge open fields sloping up to the fort were knee-high in lush mountain grass, with blue-stemmed wildflowers peeping up here and there; the flag whipped in the breeze over the main guard tower looming over the fort's walls, but the walls themselves were not exactly teeming with soldiers. As a matter of fact, as Mike Kelly walked up to a place near the huge wooden gates, he couldn't spot any soldiers on the wall at all.

He paused, hands on hips, and squinted up at the high walls, black against the bright blue sky. He listened and the only sounds were distant bird calls and the clatter of the flag halyards.

"Hey!" he yelled.

The fort was utterly still.

"HEY!" he yelled louder.

Up on the top of the wall, a blue-capped soldier rose slowly and peered over, rubbing his eyes. "Howdy your own self. Advance and be recognized."

Mike moved a little closer to the wall, his face upraised to the guard, whom he recognized as a private named Smith.

"Zat you, Mike?" Smith called.

"You need glasses," Mike called back.

The guard leaned out of sight. "Hey, Billy, open up. It's Mike Kelly."

Directly in front of Mike, there was a groaning of metal hinges inside the great peaked gates. One of the gates shuddered backward a few feet and a soldier, wearing his blue pants and the tops to long underwear, walked outside. "C'mon in," he said. He was stubble-bearded, paunchy, about forty.

"I want to see Lieutenant Bumpers," Mike said, stepping inside.

"I expect he's in headquarters, sir," the guard muttered, shouldering the gate closed.

Mike shrugged and walked across the compound. The rear of the walled area was a clutter of storage buildings and barracks and barns, but the front half was empty by comparison. On the left was a long, one-floor unit once used to house officers and now used to store food. The windows were boarded up. To the right was a matching long building which was now the only barracks used to house troops. Some of the shutters had fallen off windows and it needed paint. In the center, a two-story building, with a long porch all the way across the front, had always been and still was headquarters. Rain guttering hung in rusty shreds, gaps showed in the front porch flooring, and the screen was off the hinges. In front of the headquarters, two soldiers were walking around picking up bits of dead grass and putting them in canvas bags. The compound never seemed to get any maintenance, but the army trained its men well in picking up and keeping neat. Mike had always imagined that one day there would be nothing left up here but one very old private, picking up splinters after the last wall fell down.

He walked past the soldiers and onto the porch, carefully avoiding holes. The front door was ajar. He stepped into a central hallway which was spic and span and smelled of dead mice. A very old cannon stood there in the middle of the floor. Off to its right was a doorway which led into an office area. Mike went that way.

In the front office, Sergeant Vickers was sitting hunched at his desk, staring at a booklet of regulations or something. He was frowning with seeming concentration, his weight on his elbows, his head down.

"Sergeant," Mike said quietly, by way of greeting.

Sergeant Vickers didn't move a muscle. A fly buzzed around his head and lit on his nose and walked around dubiously.

Mike stomped his foot loudly.

Sergeant Vickers jumped like a man hit by lightning. "Huh? What?" His eyes focused. "Yes, sir!" he snapped, scowling Mike into focus.

"To see the commander," Mike said softly.

Sergeant Vickers frowned. "He's extremely busy today, sir. But I'll see if he can spare a minute."

Mike built himself a fresh pipe of smoke while the sergeant went into the next office, discreetly shutting the door behind him. It was very quiet in there.

In a minute or two Sergeant Vickers came back. "You can go in, sir."

Mike nodded and brushed by him to enter the commander's office.

It was impressive, large, airy, well-scrubbed, with books on one wall, guns on another, and a huge, tattered battle flag on the third. The other wall was mostly windows, and looked out onto the compound. And there, standing behind a broad, empty desk, stood Lieutenant Harley Bumpers.

"Come in, Mike!" he boomed authoritatively. "Brace up a chair. Smoking lamp is lit. State your business."

He talked like that a lot, so Mike was not concerned by it. Harley Bumpers was close to forty, on one side or the other, wore U. S. Grant porkchops on the sides of his face, and was usually amazingly staunch and cheerful for a man to whom fate had given the worst assignment in the entire United States Army. While Mike took the offered chair and fired up his pipe, Harley Bumpers bit off the end of a cheroot, spat the fragments into a corner, cracked a wood match on the seat of his pants, and made great clouds of stinging smoke. He glowered at Mike like a man about to hear the South had risen again.

Mike told him, "We've got a situation in town."

"Situation?" Harley Bumpers snapped. "Explain. Provide details. Take your time. Spit it out." *Whap-whap!* his elbows crashed onto the desk top as he leaned forward, glaring.

So Mike briefly explained about Katherine Blanscombe and what she had said.

"You think she'll cause trouble?" Harley Bumpers asked.

"She might try. She's stubborn."

"What can she do?"

"I've thought about that," Mike told him. "Number one, I figure she may come to see you."

Harley Bumpers looked startled. *"Me?"*

Mike nodded. "To tell you you ought to keep your troops out of my places. —Sin, et cetera."

"All right," Harley Bumpers scowled. "Proceed."

33

"She might also go to the church," Mike suggested.

"Check," Harley Bumpers snapped. "Continue."

"Also, she might try to go to court."

"Court? Why? Explain."

"To get me declared a public nuisance or something like that. Or to try to say I won't let her exercise her half-interest control."

Lieutenant Harley Bumpers frowned mightily. There were times when he considered himself a tactician, and on rare occasions he broke his habit of monosyllables and launched into "situational analyses," as he liked to call them. Watching him, Mike could tell he was about to launch.

"As I see it," Harley Bumpers said briskly, "from a standpoint of practical application, what we have here is a situation where a girl, she doesn't understand what really happens in a place such as this, it's far from Cleveland, Ohio, certainly, as anyone will tell you with experience in both. Now. You're locally competent, but a key factor is that antagonists not only have to be evenly matched, they have to recognize, at a minimum level, because otherwise, to put it more clearly, if she doesn't see her own level here, then of course your position is enhanced in reality but not in terms of her viewpoint because she can't see that you have greater insight into various applications, that is to say, the court might *rule,* but what chance is there, because when all is said and done, if you follow my line of reasoning, which I think is based on human factors as old as the hills, certainly, but sometimes the obvious is overlooked. Now. You have two choices, action or inaction. Often the best course is hard to see, namely, the difference between feeling action must be taken and some recognition of the effects, *but not tactically.* And as far as her visiting me is concerned, I make it standard policy to listen, I see that as part of my role, but I certainly don't often see that role as extending into the realm of positive action, at least insofar as change is concerned, or not altering the status quo, because as anyone can clearly see, while the role of a commander involves many things, it's not necessary to overextend beyond the limits of jurisdictional competency, and she's a newcomer and Indians are my main business. Therefore it seems to me that we may be dealing with a non-issue here, or at least the issues are not at all clear, and until such time as the tactical situation is clarified at least in some respects, then without new information, or a visit on her part. Contrariwise, nothing else may come into play, or if it does, not soon. Right?" Harley Bumpers blinked at Mike and seemed to be thinking about the things he had just said.

Mike proceeded cautiously. "In other words—"

"Right!" Harley Bumpers said. "That's the key application."

"But you won't put my places off limits?"

"Well, certainly not, or at worst probably, either later or at this time barring some change in circumstances."

Mike took a deep breath. "Thanks, Lieutenant. I wanted to make sure."

Harley Bumpers put his cigar down in a dog-skull ashtray on the corner of the desk. "It helps to clear the air."

"I'll keep in touch," Mike promised, going for the door.

"Any time," Harley Bumpers snapped. "Glad to be of service."

Mike opened the door. "So long, Harley."

"Have you heard anything about hostiles?" Harley Bumpers called after him.

"Hostile what?" Mike asked, turning back.

Harley Bumpers scowled. "Indians, of course."

"No."

"I sense," Harley Bumpers said, "there will be action soon."

"Don't look for any," Mike suggested, "or you might find some."

Outside, the rain clouds seemed closer. The afternoon was getting along. If it rained, it would be a big night for indoor sports.

Leaving the post, Mike felt a little better. He had headed the girl off on the army angle, anyway. And the church didn't worry him because few in town took church seriously enough to let it interfere with good business.

As to the possibility of a court case, Mike felt perfectly at ease. Judge John Edwards liked his cards much too dearly to issue any order that might close down the only honest game in town.

Katherine Blanscombe, he thought, might be a beautiful, spunky girl. But she wasn't going to win this battle.

FIVE

Approximately fourteen miles downriver from Salvation, there was an area of about forty square miles where salt deposits surfaced along the waterway, poisoning every decent creek and making even the ancient springs brackish and nasty. In addition some prehistoric catastrophe had practically leveled an entire small mountain, making the terrain resemble a bombed-out rock quarry. In a countryside of azure hills, clean-flowing streams, beautiful evergreens and fertile land, Dead Cow Valley was a horror, a desolate hole, a scenic chancre. Naturally, in the Treaty of Old Timbers, consummated in 1876, this was the area designated as the new, perpetual home of the Tikoliwani band of Apache Indians.

The Tikoliwanis now numbered only seventy souls, counting squaws. Most of them were old, and not particularly unhappy; Dead Cow Valley was monstrous, but living there beat being shot up by the United States Cavalry. On the other hand, a few of the younger braves yearned for happier days, and heard distant rumors of the Red Man rising once more to cleanse the land.

The arguments were endless, and one phase of it was going on at this moment, late on a rain-threatening afternoon, in a tattered brown teepee near the center of the ratty little Tikoliwani encampment.

"We must *find* a way!" Running Deer, one of the malcontents, said angrily, slamming his forearm into his palm. Running Deer was young and often angry.

"Our brother is right," agreed David Swooping Hawk, another young warrior. "We must find a way to rally our people and attack the fort itself, and drive the army out of our lands."

Several of the other braves, older heads, grunted approval.

At the head of the ceremonial circle, Alvin Singing Duck, the youthful chief of the tribe, rubbed his head in perplexity. "If we go on the warpath," he said carefully, "many will die."

"Our great brother, Geronimo, has left his reservation and is loose in the land," Running Deer intoned. "The Apache must strike on all sides with the ferocity of wounded lions."

David Swooping Hawk gestured savagely. "Yes! We must fight and pillage and burn and kill, drive the white-eyes from our lands!"

Running Deer's forehead wrinkled. "Well, I didn't say anything about burning or *killing*. What we need is a noble gesture, to prove our worthiness in battle."

"The army at Fort Forgot is weak," David Swooping Hawk argued.

"The army can be reinforced," one of the other braves pointed out.

"Are you cowards?" David Swooping Hawk asked bitterly. "Are you afraid to die?"

The braves looked at one another uneasily, and then to Alvin Singing Duck, for proper leadership.

Alvin Singing Duck sighed. "We do not fear dying," he said finally. "But some of us would prefer to do it at an older age."

"It is well for you to say this," David Swooping Hawk retorted angrily. "You journey weekly to the town of the white-eyes, where you lead hunters on expeditions into the mountains for good pay. You live half in the white man's world, yet you are our chief. A chief must be true to his own people, and lead them to great victories!"

It was good oratory, the kind that was popular around the campfire because it was brave and good and strong and true, and called for no specific action. Most of the braves, old and young, grunted and shuffled their feet and muttered approval.

Alvin Singing Duck himself was forced to nod and hold his elbows together in the fashion that indicated general approval of a point well made. But at the same time he recognized he was in growing trouble. David Swooping Hawk was putting pressure on him, and he had to respond wisely and well, or his entire leadership role was endangered. Chiefs had been known before to wake up with a sudden pain in the chest, and find not a gas bubble, but a deeply implanted knife.

Therefore Alvin Singing Duck, although only twenty-four years old, knew he had to come up with something pronto.

"Brothers," he intoned, spreading his hands, "the time may not yet be ripe for strong action. Let us follow the ways of our fathers, and their fathers before them. Let us seek the sage advice of Wakinokiman, wisest of the wise."

"Wakinokiman! Wakinokiman!" several of the braves grunted, approving.

Running Deer looked questioningly at Alvin Singing Duck. "Shall I seek him?"

"Seek him," Alvin Singing Duck ordered.

Running Deer uncoiled his bare legs and ducked out of the teepee. Silence fell over those who remained. David Swooping Hawk furiously rolled a cigarette, and some of the others pulled out chunks of peyote to chew. Alvin Singing Duck bowed his head as if in meditation, and thought fast.

The *last* thing Alvin Singing Duck wanted was a war. He didn't even want an argument. The soldiers at Fort Forgot, he knew, were among the sorriest in the world, but they were still soldiers. That meant good horses, repeating rifles, decent food and God only knew how many reinforcements if somebody put them into a tight crack. Going on the warpath meant taking a shortcut to the happy hunting ground. Dead Cow Valley might be a lousy place, but as long as peace reigned in the area, anybody could go to Salvation and steal a little liquor and pick up a little work, as long as he was willing to pretend to be as stupid as the white men. War would mess up everything.

On the other hand, Alvin Singing Duck was not at all sure he hoped Wakinokiman would counsel total inactivity. What the tribe needed was some excitement. The blood had to be stirred up and some grand plan had to be found that would get everybody's mind off self-pity. Further, Alvin Singing Duck was not completely free of tribal superstitions, even after the years of leg irons and catechism at the church school back east; he had seen superstition work too often, and he had also seen rational white men and some of the things they did in the name of *their* religion.

So Alvin Singing Duck waited for the arrival of the tribal wise man with mixed uncertainty and hope.

After a few minutes, Running Deer reentered the large teepee, bringing with him what first appeared to be a tent pole in a blanket. But the tent pole had an incredibly wizened, brown face, long white

38

hair, and bony hands and feet that stuck out of filthy rag clothing. Wakinokiman's eyes, deeply set, sparkled brightly as he entered.

"Great seer of our tribe," Alvin Singing Duck said formally, "we stand at the crossroads once more, and seek the advice of the ages. Speak to us of our problem, our future, and our course of action."

Wakinokiman nodded and sat down in a slow collapse of folded robes and brittle brown bones that stuck out at weird angles. He said nothing but went straight to his work, taking from inside his robes an old sock that immediately filled the teepee with a harsh aroma.

Running Deer murmured, "I have told him our problem."

Silence plunged over the group, and every eye strained to see the wise man in action. Wakinokiman, it was said, was 317 years old, and as he opened the sock with palsied hands, he looked it.

Out of the sock tumbled a small clutter of dried owl entrails.

Wakinokiman stirred them on the ground with his fingers, meanwhile uttering an eerie, crooning little song through his nose that sounded like *"Oh-ih-ah-nee-ah-ooh-awk-oh-oh-uh-noo-ee . . . oh-ih-ah-nee,"* etc.

Then, suddenly, he stopped crooning and stopped stirring with his fingers. He bent close over the entrails and studied them, one eye closed.

The silence was total. Alvin Singing Duck held his breath. A faint wind stirred the parched folds of the teepee walls.

Finally Wakinokiman looked up.

"In the heavens," he said in that fantastically old, reedy voice, "the wild beasts prey upon the children of the stars. The rivers run to the seas, the horsemen of the sun and moon chase one another about the night, and the tribes of our people wait in suffering."

He paused an instant. Heads nodded, but no one dared speak.

Wakinokiman continued, "A day will come when our peoples must fight once more. On that day they will fight well and die bravely. Here is how you will know the coming of that day: *a fair maiden will carry a chicken; blood will become as milk; in a still place there shall be thunder, and a child, as our prisoner, will bring us strength.*"

Wakinokiman paused, looked at them, and closed his eyes.

The silence was breathless as they waited.

The ancient man said no more.

"Is there more?" Alvin Singing Duck finally asked huskily.

"I have spoken," Wakinokiman murmured, "from the wisdom of the owl. When these things come to pass, the day will be at hand."

Unsteadily, Wakinokiman gathered up his used entrails, put them back in the sock, and teetered out of the teepee.

"What does it mean?" Running Deer asked hoarsely. " 'A fair maiden will carry a chicken—' "

"Is it gibberish?" one of the younger braves asked sharply. "Must we wait forever for a saying that has no meaning?"

Before Alvin Singing Duck could rebuke the youth for this remark, David Swooping Hawk surprised him by replying fiercely, "The old man has never predicted falsely! He holds the wisdom of our tribe! Do not be a fool by doubting him!"

"That's right," Alvin Singing Duck agreed, relieved. "We simply have to wait for the prophecy to be fulfilled." He felt a lot better. While they waited, they would have hope. The prophecy made no sense, but was manifestly impossible, a tangle of unreal jargon. The old seer had been wise after all: he had provided them with a reason for living while at the same time making a war impossible.

"We should have asked him," someone said, "if the wait will be long."

"The wait," David Swooping Hawk said darkly, "will not be long. I feel this in my bowels."

Alvin Singing Duck wondered improbably how a feeling of urgency in the bowels could be interpreted so literally. He denied the impulse to ask; sometimes he was smart enough to recognize a white man's thought when he had one.

Instead he said solemnly, "Whether the wait is little or long, we must endure it cheerfully. Meanwhile, I shall continue my journeys to the white men's town of Salvation; there I can observe for signs of the portents."

"Good," Running Deer pronounced. "It is wise."

"I, too," David Swooping Hawk put in calmly, "will help our people spy upon the omens. I too shall journey to the town of Salvation with my brother and chief."

Startled, Alvin Singing Duck asked, "What will you do there?"

"I shall be meek," David Swooping Hawk said, baring his teeth like the great teeth of a puma. "I shall find humble work—and observe for the signs."

40

Alvin Singing Duck thought about a demurrer, but decided to let it go. It had been a tough meeting, and Wakinokiman had carried the day. If David Swooping Hawk wanted to go to Salvation to await a woman carrying a chicken, blood becoming milk, thunder sounding in a still place and a child being captured, the hell with it; what harm could he do?

"Alvin Singing Duck," he declared formally and with great solemnity, "accepts David Swooping Hawk's offer of aid in Salvation."

David Swooping Hawk smiled fiercely and they clasped arms.

It had been, Alvin Singing Duck thought, a good day.

In Salvation, darkness had fallen and gentle rain had begun to fall. Judge John Edwards, having finished his second beer at Mike Kelly's place, walked home slowly, his boots slipping slightly in the forming mud. He was weary, but it had been an easy day and he felt ready to face Cora, his wife.

Not that Cora was terribly difficult to face, of course. John Edwards was six feet, four inches tall, and a large man. Cora was five feet, two, and had never weighed over one hundred pounds in her life. The judge was not afraid of her or anything like that. It was just that he had learned it was best to—well—*brace up* for her. She was really a very good woman and he was lucky to have her, as she often reminded him.

So the judge braced up as he approached his small home. The procedure consisted mainly in reminding himself that his home was not a court of law, and while he was a stern taskmaster in the court, he was a very lucky man to have Cora and had to be meek and humble, et cetera, at home.

Walking carefully from rock to walk across the wet front yard, he reached his front porch. A light glowed in the living room window. He leaned against the wall and hopped on one foot while tugging off a boot, then put down his sock foot while tugging at the other. Rain had swept onto the porch, so cold water penetrated his socked foot instantly, and he gritted his teeth to keep from muttering the kind of words Cora did not appreciate.

His boots off and in one hand, the judge wiped them with his free hand to make sure they wouldn't drip, then swatted his pants legs to remove any loose grass or other debris, removed his hat, and quietly opened the door.

Wood floors gleamed. Every stick of furniture was precisely in place. The oil lanterns were turned to the perfect height for maximum illumination and minimum smoke. A small, cozy fire crackled in the fireplace.

The judge softly closed the door and tiptoed down the hall toward the side porch, where he was supposed to leave wet or dirty items of clothing.

"John?" the familiar voice called from the kitchen.

"Yes, my dear," the judge murmured.

Cora hurried into the hall to greet him. She was not frowning. She was a little woman, beginning to gray, still pretty in a firm-jawed, straight-backed way that emphasized the level, keen quality of her eyes.

"Good evening, dear," she said quietly, and then shocked him by briefly hugging against him.

"Is anything wrong?" the judge asked quickly, almost dropping the boots.

"No," she smiled sweetly. "It's just nice to have you home on such a rainy evening. Here, John. I'll take those nasty boots. You just go right into the living room and relax in front of the fire."

Thunderstruck, the judge watched her carry the ucky big boots into the pantry area.

"I've fixed chicken pie for supper," she called to him. "And I thought we might have a little glass of wine before we sit down."

He almost stumbled as he moved into the living room. Why, he wondered, this kind of greeting? What had he done? Or forgotten? *My God,* he thought, *our anniversary!* —But it wasn't their anniversary.

What, then? Birthday? —No. Christmas? —No. Company? He couldn't think of anyone he had invited. *What,* then?

Feeling like a doomed man, he sat in his favorite chair, making sure he didn't wrinkle the doilies. In a moment, Cora came humming in from the kitchen and handed him a small glass of port wine. "There," she crooned, "that's nice, isn't it!"

"Are you, uh, going to join me?" the judge asked nervously.

"I have to attend to the food, dear! I'll sip mine in the kitchen. You just relax and keep your feet nice and toastie, and I'll call you soon." With that, Cora went back out, still humming.

Judge John Edwards closed his eyes. Was it *his* birthday? He tried to think back over the day. It had been routine in nearly every respect. *What was going on?*

When Cora called him for supper, there was still no sign of a plot. The kitchen was redolent with the delectable aromas of chicken pie, coffee, fresh-baked bread and cake. Cora served him nicely and chatted about her women's club during much of the meal. Judge John Edwards relaxed slightly and decided he didn't give her sufficient credit. She was simply a nice person, which he had, of course, always known. He was a lucky man to have her.

After supper, they retired to the living room. The fire crackled gently and the rain on the window was calm and steady.

"Did you have a nice day, dear?" Cora asked.

Had she asked that before? Or was he defensive? "Normal," he said, and smiled.

"Did the Masters will case end?"

"Yes. There was no problem."

"And were any new interesting cases filed?"

"Nothing that amounts to anything," the judge replied.

Cora's voice softened further. "Did anyone file an injunction case?"

"As a matter of fact," the judge grunted, "yes. Absurd case. I glanced over it. Hugh Corkern filed it. He finally got a client. Some woman evidently just came to town, and she—"

The judge stopped, a chill shuddering down his spine.

He looked sharply at Cora. "Why do you ask?"

She smiled sweetly. "I heard about it. Isn't it an unusual case?"

"I didn't," the judge said dubiously, "know people walked around town, talking about court cases."

"Well, actually, dear, the young lady involved, Katherine Blanscombe, called on me this afternoon."

"*Here?*" The judge was aghast.

"Where else would she find me?" Cora asked drily.

"Um. Yes. Well—"

"She seemed like a *very* nice young lady. She's very sweet and quite young, and has perfect upbringing."

"Why did she come here?" the judge asked suspiciously.

"Why, just to call, dear. She had my name as president of the women's club." Cora switched gears deftly. "You plan to rule on her case immediately, I assume?"

The judge was getting damned uncomfortable. He wasn't sure yet what was up, but he didn't like it; he didn't like it even a little bit.

He said cautiously, "There are two matters, one criminal and one civil. They relate. She says in her complaint that Mike Kelly is running a disorderly house. Ridiculous."

"Does she want him arrested?" Cora asked sweetly.

The judge grunted. "Fat chance. No, she wants the place padlocked. As a public nuisance."

"Well, I think it's nice of her not to want Mister Kelly put in jail."

"Oh, she's evidently a truly beautiful person," the judge retorted sarcastically. "All she wants is for us to put him out of business, and then—in her civil suit—she asks the court to allow *her* to operate the businesses under new management. Hers."

"Well, it sounds reasonable to me."

"Reasonable!" the judge exploded. "*Reasonable!* Jehoshaphat, woman! Is it reasonable for some runny-nosed girl to come into a strange town and try to put a law-abiding citizen out of business? Is it reasonable for a *woman* to be messing around in matters of law at all? Is it reasonable to allege that the only honestly run house—uh—house for gambling in the entire town should be shut down? Is it reasonable to expect a court of law to push one partner *out* so the other partner can get *in?*"

Cora smiled at the judge.

The judge read the smile, and finally understood.

"*No!*" he choked. "The law is the law—"

"But," Cora cooed, "it all comes down to the court's definition of what constitutes a nuisance, isn't that right, dear?"

The judge stared at his wife, and the horrible truth continued to dawn brownly. "No," he whispered. "No."

"It seems to me, dear, that a judge planning to run for reelection next year—you *are* planning to run for reelection, aren't you, John?"

"You know I am," the judge snarled.

"Yes. —Well, it would seem to me, dear, that a judge planning to run for reelection would want to make rulings likely to offend the

44

fewest persons, within the confines of the law, of course. *Many members of the women's club have been concerned for a long time about the terrible things that go on at Blanscombe's Rest. And if this nice young woman has a legitimate interest—*"

"You can't ask me to rule against Mike Kelly!" the judge cried. "You can't, Cora! You *can't!*"

Cora smiled benignly and patted his hand. "I just want you to consider it carefully, John, dear. She is a *very* nice girl."

"But you can't expect me to mess up Mike Kelly's business," the judge groaned. "You can't expect me to worry whether the women's club will support me next year. You can't *infer,* Cora, that *you—* want *me*—that is to say—Cora! —You *can't*—?"

Cora continued to smile at her husband with a fondness of the kind usually seen in the eyes of a wolf about to pounce on a rabbit.

With one more drink, the judge could have wept.

With supper out of the way and the enormous first day behind her, Katie had Heck back in their hotel room. Outside, the rain drummed softly and steadily, and the lights of the main street seemed faint, like distant tinsel.

"It's a very nice school," she told Heck, who sat cross-legged on the bed, scowling at her.

"You show me a nice school," Heck growled, "an' I'll show you a bunch of junk."

"It's very nice," Katie repeated. "I spoke with the teacher and some of the children. You'll like it, Heck."

"When do I got to start?"

"Tomorrow."

"*Tomorrow!* Aw, we just *got* here, Katie!"

"Precisely," Katie agreed. "Idleness is the devil's workshop."

"Haste," Heck countered bitterly, "makes waste."

"Never put off until tomorrow—"

"Yeah!" Heck cried. "And you dragged me all *over* this dumb ole town today, too, and I didn't see anybody my age, even!"

"You'll meet them at school," Katie said, smiling. "Now you'd better see to the suitcase you haven't unpacked yet. I imagine we shall be staying in this room for a few days yet, and we may as well unpack."

45

"Aw!" But Heck rolled off the bed and slouched over to the suitcases against the wall, pulled his over to a chair, and opened it. He began putting things in a dresser drawer.

Relaxing, Katie allowed herself to droop to the edge of the bed. The bed creaked. It would probably be lumpy, she thought. Tonight it would hardly matter. What time had they gotten *up* this morning? Four? And that had been how many hours—and miles—ago?

She was, if the truth were known, wearier than she had ever been in her entire life. She had been going constantly since their arrival . . . first the disastrous confrontation with Mike Kelly, then the hotel, then Hugh Corkern's office, then the newspaper office to study back issues, then the cafe for lunch, then back here so Heck could take a brief nap before he fell down, then to the school, then to the church, then to see the judge's wife at her home, then back here for Heck, then the dismaying walk around town, then the general store and the cafe again for supper, and back here once more. Her legs ached, her back hurt and there was a general throbbing behind her eyes.

She had done all the right things, she told herself grimly. There was no going back; she had to make a go of it here. That gave first priority to dealing with that horrid Mike Kelly once and for all. People might say she was soft, and just a woman, but she would show *them*. And just because Mike Kelly was big and handsome in a rough, uncouth sort of way, he wouldn't charm *her* into any kind of submission!

She was slipping into desultory thoughts of what she would have to do to get Blanscombe's Rest back into decent condition when a tapping on the door startled her.

Heck, still at the dresser, turned, wide-eyed. "Who's *that?*"

Katie swallowed her moment's fear. "Well, I don't know," she said archly. "But I really doubt that it's a wild Indian."

"Are you gonna answer it?"

"Of course." She got to her feet.

"I wish we had us a gun!"

"Nonsense!"

But her nerves jangled slightly as she unlocked the door. "Yes?"

"Clerk, ma'am."

She opened the door a few inches. The wizened old man from the registration desk blinked at her.

"Beggin' your pardon, ma'am, but you have a caller in the lobby."

"A caller?"

"Mister Ray Root, ma'am. He said to say, if you don't know who he is, he runs a cafe and casino that's in competition with Mike Kelly."

Katie hesitated. She had no idea what the man might want. But if he was in competition with Mike Kelly, she thought, he might not particularly *like* Mike Kelly, and that gave them something in common. Besides, she was curious.

"Tell Mister Root," she said, "that I'll be there directly."

"Yessum," the old man said, and scurried away.

Katie closed the door and went to the tiny oval mirror on the wall. She patted her hair and inspected her face. She looked wilted and pale, but neat.

"You goin' to see him?" Heck demanded.

"Yes," Katie said.

"I'm goin' too."

"No, you're not. You're going to stay right here with the door locked until you hear me knock and identify myself."

"Aw!"

"No back talk, young man!"

"That's just it! There's *never* any back talk with you!"

"Lock the door after me, mind?"

She went into the hall and listened until Heck shot the bolt inside. With a nod of satisfaction, she went down the corridor.

In the small front room that served as a lobby, only one person was in evidence: a tall, dark-coated man with rather long black hair that glistened under a heavy layer of oil. He wore a flowered vest and wide mustaches, thin-legged pants and slightly muddied black boots that shone, nevertheless, like patent leather. His flat-brimmed hat, beaded, was in his hands.

"Miss Blanscombe?" he said, showing a great number of small, even white teeth.

"Yes," Katie said, extending her hand.

"Enchanted," the man said, clicking his heels and bending from the waist to kiss her fingers. "Allow me to present myself. I am Ray Root."

The finger-kissing was shock enough; Katie had never expected continental manners in Salvation when she had only read about them in a civilized place like Cleveland. But Ray Root's entire manner and appearance quietly bowled her over. He was tall and slender, and given to a flinty kind of handsomeness that was modified slightly by wrinkles which, on close inspection, hinted either he was older than he first appeared, or more dissipated. He smelled of tobacco and clove and coffee, and although his smile was friendly, there was something behind his quick dark eyes that made Katie's pores shrink as if his eyes were undressing her. Katie made some tentative decisions about him: (a) he was attractive, (b) he was aware of it, and (c) he was a cad. In her mood, this did not necessarily make her dislike him.

"How do you do, Mister Root?" she asked formally.

"Three things," Root said, continuing to smile brightly. "First, allow me to add my small welcome to an attractive newcomer to our fair little city. You'll find, Miss Blanscombe, that first impressions indicate a raw, frontier hamlet; but Salvation has much beneath the surface, including a small but active cultural life."

"Indeed?" Katie said, surprised again.

"Indeed," Root said. "Second, may I say that I have heard about the lawsuit you have brought against certain, ah, establishments, and if I may offer my support, please don't hesitate to ask."

"In view of the fact that you said you compete with Mike Kelly," Katie said, "I can understand your interest."

Ray Root frowned and his mustaches twitched. "Yes, yes. But actually, Miss Blanscombe, my interest is not in eliminating competition. Far from it! I believe competition is at the heart of America's progress, the kernel of her way of life, if you will. But I must say that I share your concern for establishments which fall under suspicion of operating, ah, shall we say . . . less than in a manner that is aboveboard."

"I assume, Mister Root, you'll get to the point."

"Call me Ray," Root urged. "I hope to be your friend."

"The point, Mister Root."

"The point. Yes, of course. —The point is simplicity itself. I offer support. I have no ax to grind. If I can help, you have but to ask."

"And the third point?" Katie probed.

Ray Root blinked. "The third point?"

Katie was amused. She had the feeling he was harmless enough. "You mentioned three points you wanted to make."

48

"Oh yes. The third point, Miss Blanscombe—may I call you Katherine? The third point, Katherine, is that I wish to offer to make myself available to you tomorrow, at your convenience. I feel sure that a comprehensive tour of Salvation and its environs would interest you, and enhance your understanding of the general situation. I understand you have a young brother, and he, too, of course, is invited."

Katie hid her frown. He was going a little too fast for her. Her natural caution asserted itself. "I appreciate the kind offer, Mister Root. However—"

The front door slammed open and rain gushed in. Katie turned, startled, and saw Mike Kelly, hatless and muddy to the knees, charge into the lobby. He caught her with a fiercely angry glance, swung toward her and pointed a shaking finger at her.

"There you are!" he bellowed. "By God, the two of you in cahoots already!"

Ray Root blanched slightly. "See here, Mike—"

"Shut up, Ray!" Mike stormed, stalking toward them.

Katie stiffened as her own anger rose magically. *What,* may I ask, is the meaning of this? What are you doing here, Mister Kelly, and—"

Mike Kelly towered over her. His face was red and his eyes bulged as if they might explode. "I just heard about that silly blankety lawsuit, *that's* what it's all about! What the hell kind of a person are you, anyway? What are you trying to do? If you think you'll get to first base with some stupid maneuver like that, you've—"

"*Mister* Kelly," Katie cut in sharply. "I'll thank you, sir, to take your bad manners elsewhere, or my attorney will have another charge to file against you, that of battery."

"*Battery!*" Mike bellowed. "I'll battery you! I'll charge your—I'll—"

Katie turned icily to Ray Root. "You were saying—Ray?"

Root smiled uncertainly. "I was saying that a tour—"

"What are you pulling here?" Mike Kelly cut in just as loudly as before. "Listen, woman! You get to town at noon, and the same day you file some stupid idiot lawsuit against me and then start getting thick as hops with the worst gambler and drink-watering—"

Ray Root said huskily, "Don't go too far, Mike."

Mike Kelly ignored the threat in his voice. Mike was past worrying about threats. "I'm talking to her, Ray. You keep your face shut, see?"

"But I am not talking to *you*," Katie told Mike. "My attorney has said all I wish to say to you, sir."

"What do you want to *do* this to me for?" Mike cried. "I run a nice place and I never had a cross word with Hank in my entire life! I loved the guy! And then you come in here and start plotting with *this* no'count card sharper—"

"That," Katie clipped, "will be enough!"

Mike stared at her in disbelief. "I came here to talk."

"You came here to bluster and threaten. It won't work. I have nothing more to say to you."

"You won't even *listen* to me?" Mike Kelly asked, and he honestly looked like he could have wept with frustration.

"You've turned an honest business into a den of thieves," Katie told him.

"I—!"

She turned to Ray Root. "I don't know what my schedule will be tomorrow—Ray. But possibly a tour of the area with you would be not only informative, but very pleasant. Could you call about noon?"

Ray Root's grin was oily enough to fuel a tanker. "Be my pleasure, little lady."

"You're going out with *him?*" Mike Kelly gasped, stunned.

"Is it any of your business?" Katie shot back imperiously.

"You're crazy!" Mike groaned. "I come over here to try to talk *sense,* and you—"

"Good night, Ray," Katie said warmly to Ray Root. "And thank you."

Root grinned and shook her hand this time. He looked awfully pleased.

Mike Kelly, however, looked like someone who had just been run down by a freight train. His face was drained of color.

In a voice that was almost inaudible he whispered, "I came to *talk.*"

Katie turned her back on him and marched toward her room.

She was delighted. So he thought he was a ladies' man, did he, with his hotel full of nasty girls and his lovely wavy hair and beautiful blue eyes! Well, she had showed *him* a thing or two—and she wasn't finished yet by a long shot!

Her hand trembled as she rapped on her door.

"Who is it?" Heck called.

"Katie."

He let her in. She locked the door behind her.

"You're all pink," Heck said. "What happened?"

"That fine Mister Kelly came over while I was talking to Mister Root," Katie said with satisfaction. "I put him in his place. I bet he doesn't think he's so smart or irresistible now!" She went to the basin and wrung out a cool cloth to place on her burning face.

"Boy," Heck sighed. "You sure do want to hurt him, huh."

"I don't want to hurt him," Katie replied through the cloth. "He just has to be shown he's not so smart and not as cute as he thinks he is. He has to be put in his place, and see he can't use his smile to get his way with *me,* anyway."

Heck said nothing. Katie put the cloth down. Heck was looking at her in a very odd and thoughtful way.

"What does that look mean?" Katie demanded.

"*I* never heard Mike Kelly say he was smart or cute or any of that," Heck said.

"He doesn't have to *say* it," Katie retorted. "It stands out all over him!"

"Does it?" Heck asked.

"Of course it does!"

Heck grinned crookedly. "I bet you're stuck on him."

"*What?*" Katie gasped.

"The only other person you ever was this nasty to," Heck pointed out, still grinning, "was Homer Frankler, back in Cleveland. And I know you were stuck on him for a good long time."

"I was *not* stuck on Homer," Katie snapped. "I—"

"Aw, no," Heck said. "You jus' cried two months after he got married to that other lady. And now you're bein' mean to this poor guy here, and he ain't done nothing at all to you, but you walk around spoutin' about how he thinks he's cute, an' all, and I never heard *him* say any of that. I think you think he's cute, an' all. I think you're scairt half to death of him, an' that's why you're bein' so mean, to prove you ain't."

51

"That's—that's the most ridiculous thing I ever heard!" Katie snapped.

"Maybe," Heck said, shrugging.

Katie placed the cool cloth on her face again. There were times when Heck simply astounded her. Where had he gotten *this* wild notion? It was crazy. It was ridiculous. It was absurd. It was . . . *Was it true?*

Oh, no, of course not. She rejected the idea totally. It was silly and childish and fantastic. She *knew,* after all, why she had to put Mike Kelly in his place, right here and now and for good. She was *not* attracted to him. She did *not* like his smile. She did *not* feel all oozy and itchy to run her fingers through his wavy blond hair. She did *not* like him at all, not even a little bit. *No!*

She put the whole idea completely out of her mind with a mental grunt of irritated satisfaction, and then, two hours later, after Heck was already asleep, lay in the dark room staring at the ceiling and kept telling herself that she was not lonely, either, or scared, or homesick, and that she *detested* Mike Kelly, and that was all there was to it.

SIX

Mike Kelly left his loft room and descended stiffly into the saloon at about 8 A.M. The Roadhouse was at its sorriest at such an early hour, and its appearance fitted Mike's mood: chairs were on tables, dirt and cigarette butts were swept into little mounds here and there, the morning sunlight sifted through fly specks and faint cobwebs on the front windows to glint dully off mountains of beer mugs, plates, cups and whiskey glasses stacked in the big kettles behind the bar for washing; there was a sour smell of stale beer in the air, and along the walls everything looked a little mangy—the railroad headlight lanterns, the cuckoo clock, the elk's head, longhorns, antlers, stuffed bass, mounted owl, old cavalry spurs and rifles, the saddles, blankets, revolvers, pennants, bear skin, buffalo hide, picture of Abe Lincoln that lit up and gave him a halo when you put the lantern behind it, lion head, fishing pole collection—all of it looked sorry at this hour, in this light. It was no hour for a saloon. Even the twelve gilt-framed nudes behind the bar looked musty and artificial. Mike sighed and poured a cup of coffee from the pot behind the piano.

"Up mighty early, boss," a familiar voice grumbled.

Mike turned to see Shorty Shelbourne, his chief bartender and manager, pushing a broom out from behind the big gaming wheel. Shorty had been given his name because he was six feet, eight, and weighed somewhere over 350 pounds. The meat scale at the butcher shop only went to 350, and Shorty fiercely resisted the idea of being weighed on the big bull scales at the auction barn. Right now, stripped to the waist, glistening with sweat, and scowling morosely, Shorty looked formidable even to Mike.

"I couldn't sleep," Mike admitted.

Shorty grunted understanding and leaned on the broom, biceps rippling. "That girl's got you down, huh?"

"She doesn't have me down," Mike snapped. *"No* girl gets me down."

"Right, right," Shorty agreed carefully. "Must be the weather."

Mike squinted outside where the sunshine was porcelain-bright. "Rain's all gone, anyhow."

"Yeah," Shorty muttered. "But the mud's there. People start comin' in here after while, drag in twenty tons of mud, slop all over the place. Never will get it nice an' clean."

"Might hire an extra man," Mike suggested absently.

"Alvin brang a buddy back from the reservation with him. Name's Hawk. Ast if we had anything."

"Does he talk American?"

"Seems like. Alvin said he'd work good."

Mike shrugged. "Put him on at least long enough to help scrub the place down late tonight or first thing in the morning. Make sure he understands we don't have anything permanent."

Shorty nodded. "How about Fairbanks?"

"He's finished here," Mike said briefly.

"He's a good card dealer, Mike. He was real surprised when you come in last night an' give him his walkin' papers."

"I think he cheats," Mike said. "His table take has run a little too high for six weeks straight."

"You ain't caught him," Shorty pointed out.

Mike sipped the scalding coffee. "I know it."

"Nobody else's caught him. Nobody's even complained."

"I *know* it," Mike repeated.

"You won't give him another chance?"

"I think he's been low-carding people," Mike explained. "Not much—just enough to increase his cut. I can't prove it and maybe nobody ever could. But I suspect it. And I'm not going to have cardsharps in this joint fleecing my customers."

"So he's out, huh."

"He's out."

"On *suspicions*."

"That's enough," Mike rapped, beginning to lose his temper. "It's my God-damned saloon, Shorty!"

"I know, I know," Shorty said soothingly. "But it's hard on the man, Mike."

"Not as hard as it is on my customers if he's cheating a little, as I think he damned sure is."

Shorty sighed. "Okay."

"Okay," Mike repeated, still angry.

"When's the new whiskey shipment git here?" Shorty asked.

"I wish I knew."

"We're low."

"I *know* we're low."

"You don't want to, uh, stretch it a little?"

"What the hell *is* this?" Mike expostulated. "Hang-the-clown-suit-on-Mike-Kelly-Day? No, dammit, we're *not* watering the booze!"

"Okay, okay," Shorty sighed again. "How about the white lightnin' in the cooker out back?"

"It's got two days to cook yet."

"I don't suppose you'd, uh—"

"No!"

"Okay, *okay!*"

"What *else* do you want to plague me about today?" Mike growled.

"Roof leaked," Shorty told him cheerfully.

"Get it fixed."

"Rowady Baxter was by. Wanted to know if you'd be fightin' cocks tonight as usual."

"There'll be some guys back there, I imagine," Mike sighed.

"I got some orders for you to sign, and do you want to go over the IOUs?"

"Later."

"When you go to court?"

"I don't know yet."

Shorty seemed to realize he had gone as far as he dared. He started shoving the broom again. "Oh, an' Ruby wants to talk to you when you got time."

Mike looked up sharply. "Ruby's up at *this* hour?"

"Amazin' grace," Shorty said reverently.

Amazing was the right word, Mike thought, looking down into the black depths of his coffee mug. The days Ruby got up before noon could be counted on the fingers of Two-Finger Duggan's bad hand. If Ruby was up this early today, it had to mean some kind of difficulty for someone.

He hoped the difficulty was not for him. He had enough right now, thank you.

Not that the trouble getting the whiskey was new, or the leaking roof was much bother—or that he was even truly worried about that stupid lawsuit. It was just the combination that bothered him. He had always believed that if a man ran a clean business and did his best, everything would work out okay. Now he was getting all this mess, and it didn't seem *right* to him.

If Katherine Blanscombe just were an ordinary-type girl, he brooded, things could be so much different. He had worried about her arrival, and had even been a little irritated by it. But he had been *hopeful*. He had been willing to *try*. Now she was trying everything she could think of to hurt him, and there was no earthly reason for it, and the sense of injustice rankled him. Worse, she had to be beautiful. He could have accepted meanness from an ugly girl—that sort of seemed in proportion, somehow. But beautiful women were supposed to be *nice*. Why did she insist on messing everything up this way?

Mike sighed and finished the scalding coffee. Thinking about that

55

girl wasn't getting him in to see Ruby. It was time to face the music next door, where big Ruby was probably waiting.

Feeling a little creaky in the joints from the bad night's sleep, he went through the beaded curtains that led to Blanscombe's Rest next door. The little lobby was quiet, but not deserted. Ruby, wearing a black wrapper and red furry house slippers, sat morosely on the flowered couch. Her blond hair was piled up messily atop her head, and without makeup she looked like a faded tintype.

"So there you are," she grunted.

Mike grinned and sat down in the chair facing her. "Here I am."

She pointed to her coffee cup. "Want some?"

"No, thanks. Shorty said you wanted to talk."

"What's this about a lawsuit?" Ruby demanded bluntly.

"Oh, it doesn't amount to anything," Mike said soothingly.

"People are *talking,*" Ruby countered, her faded eyes worried.

"People always talk, Ruby."

"You should have told me. Why didn't you tell me?"

"There's no need for you to worry about it," Mike told her. "I—"

"No need to worry!" Ruby exploded. "Here I am, taking care of the gents, and I start hearing them talking about how they heard this girl that came in here yesterday and raised a big fuss—how she's filing a case against us, and if she wins, we'll be closed down! And you tell me I'm not supposed to *worry?* And you don't even *tell* me about it? That's not like you, Mike!"

"I didn't think word would get around," Mike admitted disgustedly. "And I *didn't* want you to worry. Hell, Ruby! What chance does she have? That judge isn't going to take this place from me! It's mine, fair and square. We run a clean operation. Nobody gets cheated, nobody gets robbed, the girls act right and don't talk about their clients—"

Ruby interrupted him with a long sigh. "Mike Kelly," she muttered, "I've always thought you were one of the world's biggest fools. People like Ray Root take twice the house cut you do. They bring in girls from any old place, and if the girls rob the sucker, nothing is even thought about it. You run this place like a goldarned *convent* in comparison—all these rules, checking the girls, running off Sadie just because you *suspicioned* she might have tricked that drummer out of his roll—and half the dadblamed place is full of old girls

56

down on their luck that you just practically take care of, like a charity ward—"

"Well, all right," Mike said, losing patience. "So I'm a bad businessman. So what?"

Ruby looked at him with those sad, tired eyes that had seen it all, and there was real maternal feeling there. "So you're a silly babe in the woods, Mike Kelly. That nasty little girl is going to take you to the cleaner's and you ain't even going to know it until she's shrank your britches so bad you're running around with a bare fanny."

"Nuts," Mike grinned. "She's wasting her time. There's no *way* she can win in court. I bet there's a good chance the judge will never even call the case for the docket. People *know* me, Ruby! Nobody's going to wreck things for me here! I've got too many friends, and the judge is one of them!"

"Ah, Mike," Ruby sighed again regretfully.

"You just leave it to me," Mike said, standing. "There's absolutely no problem. Just a little irritation, but that's all. Take my word for it: the case will never even be called."

Ruby shook her head. "Ah, Mike," she sighed. "Ah, Mike, poor Mike."

"Baloney," Mike snapped, and headed down the corridor behind the registration desk, intent on getting to the back stairs so he could go down and check the outside entrance to the whiskey still on the alley.

The whole thing, he thought, was ridiculous. Poor Ruby. The nerve of that little girl with her pretty eyes and nice hair and everything, getting people like Ruby all shaken up—

"Mikey?" a little voice purred as he passed a room door.

Mike stopped, getting a little chill. Bad tactics. He had forgotten that he was *never* safe using this corridor.

He turned with a smile on his face and a sense of resignation down deeper. "Morning, Dolores," he said gently.

Dolores was standing in the doorway to her room. A slender, blonde girl with stunning blue eyes, she wore a little bluish wrapper draped about halfway around. She was like a pale little porcelain doll, fragile, tiny, woman-like, really breathtakingly lovely and very, very young. Her eyes were filled with nothing less than adoration.

"How are you, Mikey?" she asked in that helpless little-girl voice.

57

"Fine, fine," Mike grunted, feeling a size too big for the hallway. "I was just hurrying out back—"

"Would you like to come in a while, Mikey honey?" Dolores asked hopefully.

"Well, I, uh, got this stuff to do, Dolores."

"I want you to come see me, honey," she said babyishly. "You know I do, Mikey. Come in just for a minute, okay?" She reached for him.

Mike got out of the way. "Maybe, uh, some other time, Dolores. You just, uh—well, it's bad business, the boss and the girls, I've told you all that—"

"I know," Dolores moued sorrowingly. "But oh honey, could you come by later this morning? This afternoon? How about tonight, Mikey? I'm sure you could come by tonight, and I'll lock the door and nobody will bother us or even have to know, and I *do* so want—"

Sweat had exploded out of Mike's forehead, and he had to brush it out of his eyes with his forearm. "See you later, Dolores!" he called, and rushed for the back door.

Left standing in her room, Dolores felt a little pang of sadness. Was she *never* going to lure him inside? She had tried so many things already, and goodness gracious, he was the *only* man she had ever known to refuse, ever since the fourth grade, when she couldn't do the ciphering or the reading, and the teacher said she was dumb, but then she took the teacher for a walk, and he was such a sweet man and they went to the cow shed and she ended up getting an A-plus in *every* course, for goodness' sake!

But Mikey, she thought, was different. And she so loved Mikey. She would do anything for Mikey.

He was probably upset because that hateful woman who had come to town yesterday was trying to hurt him, Dolores reasoned. Dolores did not know the nasty woman's name, not being good at such things. But gracious goodness, if that nasty woman was trying to *hurt Mikey—!*

Dolores went back into her room and closed the door, thinking about it. If something bad happened to Mikey, she thought, she would never let that hateful new woman get away with it. *No!* Mikey needed help, and that new woman was trying to hurt him.

Dolores went to her bed and sat crosslegged in its center, cuddling her shaggy stuffed doll against her breasts. It made her feel more secure, and better. But she kept thinking about the nasty woman, too, and that was bothersome. Dolores slipped one hand under the mattress and pulled out the needle-sharp Italian knife she always kept there, just in case she ever really got in trouble. She looked at the ugly little blade and held it in her hand, making stabbing strokes in the air and pretending she was stabbing that nasty woman. It felt really, really nice and really, really good. She sat there thinking about it, a baby-woman, her doll in one hand and her stiletto in the other.

For Heck, school started out a disaster and went downhill from there.

The teacher, Miss Prigle, stood tall and straight and black-clad in the front of the room, under the American flag and the picture of the late President Garfield, and started the lessons by calling out spelling words. After that it got worse, the single large room was too hot from the central stove, and Heck's backside got unbearably itchy. When Miss Prigle made him get up and introduce himself and tell all kinds of dumb stuff about himself and Cleveland and all, while the boys grinned insolently and the girls giggled, it was the worst yet.

Recess at ten o'clock was the only thing that saved his life.

They scattered over the rocky, worn-down soil surrounding the high-roofed schoolhouse, and Heck found himself standing around with four other boys roughly his own age. One was named Albert and another was Charles. Heck didn't get the names of the other two.

"You really from Ohio?" Albert asked, as if it was the moon or something. He was a dumb-looking kid with buck teeth.

"Cleveland," Heck agreed.

"Izzat a big place?"

"Mighty big. It's got streetcars."

"Wow," Charles, who was a little younger, and impressionable, said.

"Your sister come to git Mike Kelly?" Albert asked.

"Nope," Heck replied, feeling defensive. "How come you to ask that?"

"She's gettin' him," Albert said. "She filed a lawsuit on him."

"Well," Heck said loyally, "she wants part of the business, an' she's got it comin'."

"My dad was talkin' last night," one of the unidentified boys said,

59

"an' he said Mike Kelly's is the only nice place a man can go for a beer in the whole town, an' your sis is going to mess it up."

"Yeah?" Heck said belligerently. "What else did he say?"

"That's all," the boy shrugged. "Him and mom had a real big fight right after that and I got sent to my room."

"Your mom probably told him how dumb he was," Heck suggested.

"Don't say my dad's dumb, boy, or I'll—!"

"Well, he *is* dumb if he said Katie's trying to wreck Mike Kelly's place, because she ain't. All she's trying to do is fix it up *nicer.*"

"You're really dumb," Albert cut in.

"Says who?" Heck shot back.

"If you don't know," Albert said loftily, "that Mike Kelly has the best beer joint in town, and every man likes him, and people like Ray Root are crooks, then you're the biggest dummy in town, boy."

"I bet you wouldn't say that," Heck countered, "if Ray Root was here right now!"

Albert blanched slightly. "You dang betcha I wouldn't, because people get *killed* at Ray Root's place, boy."

"Aw!" Heck gasped.

Charles solemnly held up three fingers. "Last year. That many."

"I don't believe you," Heck stammered.

"Ask anybody."

"My sister wants to make that place better, *that's all.*"

"What do you mean, that's all?"

"I mean she ain't out to hurt anybody, and she ain't in cahoots with Ray Root, and she's a nice person," Heck fumed. *"That's* what I mean."

"Well," Albert said stonily, "your sister is gonna make a lot of people mad in this town if she hurts Mike Kelly, boy. I'll tell you that. I'll tell you that for danged sure. And lemme tell you this, too: when you're around here a while longer, you'll find *everybody* likes Mike Kelly."

Heck tried to find a rejoinder. He was stumped. Stumped and upset. These people, he thought, *knew the territory.* If they said Mike Kelly was okay, then he was okay. And Katie was *after* Mike Kelly.

Albert and Charles were waiting for him to speak up again, but the smallest boy saved him momentarily.

"Streetcars?" he piped. "What's a streetcar?"

But the thing really bothered Heck, and he was preoccupied through the rest of the morning. He had to do something, he decided finally. If he couldn't convince Katie, then he had to go find Mike Kelly and see if there was some way he could help *him*.

He couldn't just stand by and let Katie mess up things. He had to try to do something to prevent Mike Kelly's ruination, even if whatever he did turned out to be wrong.

Mike Kelly, meanwhile, had cautiously checked his cooker apparatus in the heavy oak still house behind the Roadhouse. The batch was coming up nicely, and might be ready to pour sooner than anticipated. Locking the heavy doors to the shed and walking a safe twenty paces away, Mike paused to light his pipe. The alley was redolent with sour mash fumes.

Life, he thought, was not all bad. Everything would work out yet. Maybe later this morning he would even walk over to the Shady Nook and call on the danged girl and try *again* to be nice to her.

After all, he told himself, she didn't know the country. She didn't know him. The poor kid might be scared—might need some help and guidance. Maybe he had been much too hasty in judging her. As pretty as she was, she couldn't be all bad.

Puffing the pipe luxuriantly, Mike strolled into the back of the Roadhouse.

Shorty Shelbourne met him at the bar, and Shorty's face was the color of old pie dough. "Mike! Mike! Did the deputy find you?"

"Deputy?" Mike asked. "What deputy?"

"The *court* deputy!" Shorty groaned.

Mike stared at his manager, not understanding at all.

"The judge," Shorty informed him, "is gonna call your case—the one that girl brang against you. You're due in court to defend yourself right after lunch today!"

SEVEN

The courthouse was a long, low, flat-roofed building that had been a barracks in better days. The county had bought it from the army and moved it from Fort Forgot plank by plank, reassembling it, more or less, on the north end of Front Street. It was a block from the main area of downtown, which was usually defined by the bank, the post office, and the Roadhouse-Blanscombe's Rest-Kelly's Emporium complex.

Ordinarily, the courthouse was virtually deserted, but today was different. Standing behind a crack in the paper blind of his office window, Judge John Edwards looked at the crowd milling around outside. Men were in the street, men were on the steps, men were on the porch, men were shoving each other around the front doorway, and the din of men's voices boomed through the paper-thin walls from the corridor just beyond his closed office door.

The judge briefly pondered retirement and suicide, in that order, and then turned bitterly to Sheriff Pat Paterson and the others in his office.

"Pat," he snapped, "go out there and restore order."

Pat Paterson, a man of about fifty, blinked, removed his hat, and scratched around in his mane of gray hair. "I don't rightly know how to do that, judge."

The judge lost his temper. "You're the sheriff. I don't have to tell you *how* to do it. I just tell you *what* to do. You get out there and you tell those men I want those halls cleared!"

"They all want to see the trial," Pat Paterson protested. "I can't go out there an' shove citizens around just because they want to see a trial. They got rights, an' I gotta run for reelection next year—"

"I don't care," the judge rapped, "if you have to shoot some of them. I want this place quiet! *Now!*"

Pat Paterson, ordinarily a phlegmatic man, finally recognized the fire in the judge's eye. With a resigned heave of his chest, he turned to the door and opened it. The noise of clamoring voices exploded into the room as he wedged his way out into the mob. A few voices came through the general hubbub clearly:

"When's it gonna start?"

"How come the courtroom's still locked?"

"They in there awready?"

"You tell the judge his ole buddy—"

Paterson's voice boomed, "All right, all right, back up now!"

Judge John Edwards turned his attention from the noise to the others in the room. There were just enough chairs to go around for Mike Kelly, glowering and sweating near the door; his lawyer Bill Busher, the enormously fat senior partner of Busher & Cline; and for the young woman, Katherine Blanscombe, looking pale and pretty in a dark green outfit, and her lawyer, shaky Hugh Corkern. They were a solemn-looking group.

"I don't intend," the judge told them, "to hold a trial today. We're not going in that courtroom and have sixty-two zillion people staring at us while we wash our dirty underwear. We're going to have a hearing. Right here. Right now. In this office. I'll hear arguments and—"

The office door opened. Pat Paterson's deputy, Henry Phizer, stuck his head inside. It looked like the immediate corridor outside was cleared. "Judge, the sheriff said not to worry if—"

Wham! The room rocked with the deep, hollow explosion of a gunshot just beyond the partition toward the front entrance. Mike Kelly jumped to his feet, knocking some books off the shelf beside him. The lawyers stared at each other and Katherine Blanscombe cried out.

The judge knocked his chair over starting for the door. "What the—"

"That's what he said, that's what he said!" Henry Phizer yelled. "He might have to fire a warning shot!"

The judge stopped, his heart hammering. He turned to the window and cracked the blind again. He saw men falling over each other in their haste to get out of the building and onto the porch, the steps and the street. Farther back in the crowd, spectators were shaking their fists. As the judge peered out, Pat Paterson strode stoically out of the front door and stood facing the crowd, his arms folded over his chest, a smoking Colt in his right hand.

"All right," the judge said, struggling to regain his composure. "Go out there and help him, Henry. Try to calm them down. Tell them no trial today anyway. Just a pretrial hearing—a conference, call it. Tell them to go on home."

Phizer nodded and ducked out, slamming the door.

"Your honor," Katherine Blanscombe said, "I don't want a hearing. I want—"

"Young woman," the judge said bitterly, "you're getting far more than you have any right to expect. You have no idea how lucky you are. Don't press your luck."

The girl opened her mouth as if to speak, then frowned and lapsed into silence.

"Everybody sit down," the judge ordered.

They complied, and he thought vaguely how nice it was to have authority somewhere. He thought of Cora. If he had a little more nerve, he thought, a nice batch of rat poison, in the teakettle—

The thought shook him and he discarded it, getting back to business.

"As I understand it," he said, glaring at each of the participants in turn, "what we have here is two partners with equal shares, and they don't agree. You, Mike, are running these places. You, Miss Blanscombe, inherited from your uncle, old Hank, and you want a share of the action."

"I—" the girl began.

"Shut"—the judge said—"up."

She did.

"Now," the judge said, looking at the papers in the folder. "Plaintiff has filed two actions. Mister Corkern, do you want to address the court on these actions?"

Hugh Corkern, white as a ghost, got to his feet. His throat worked. "If the court please," he began, strangled, "plaintiff's action follows the classic pattern of *sequitur,* the first conjoining with the second in casual relationship. In equity, precedent dictates—"

"Spit it out, spit it out!" the judge snarled.

"Yes, your honor," Corkern choked. "Plaintiff's first motion goes to community standards. In determining antecedent action as it precludes—"

64

"Oh, for heaven's sake!" the judge snapped. He looked at the young woman. "You say Mike's place is a public nuisance and you want him shut down. Right?"

The girl looked startled but game. "Yes," she whispered.

"And then you say you want to take over the show. Right?"

"Right," she managed.

"All right. Sit down, Mister Corkern. Bill, what does Busher & Cline have to say about this?"

Bill Busher got to his feet. Observing him move was like watching a ship dock. An elk's tooth glistened on the rounded front of his brocaded vest. He smiled, showing a lot of his own teeth through folds of flesh that gave his face an appearance like that of a half-collapsed balloon.

"Your honor," Busher said, "we think the first charge is ridiculous on the face of it and the second is without foundation. We are prepared to argue if need be. We ask a dismissal of the charge and refusal to hear on the second matter."

The judge studied Bill Busher's face. The fat lawyer was perfectly confident. He didn't, the judge thought, know about Cora.

"Well," the judge said slowly, "the court will not immediately dismiss." Maybe, he thought, some very small nails in the pudding some night—

Startled, Bill Busher nevertheless had his next weapon ready. "If the court will not rule *prima facie,* your honor, then defense requests a postponement of ninety to one hundred and eighty days in order to prepare its case and bring in witnesses from various parts of the country."

Judge John Edwards almost whooped. He could have kissed Busher's fat face.

"Now, your honor," Hugh Corkern was protesting with pale heat, "comes the plaintiff to request more immediate and satisfactory action on the basis that justice delayed is often justice denied, community standards in cases such as Blair *versus* Weatherall, 1878, and the United States *versus—*"

The judge mentally shut him off and let him blather on so he could think about it.

Bill Busher, he saw, had given him a way out.

He had walked in here after the final pep talk from Cora with all the hope and enthusiasm of a four-day-old corpse. The law in this

65

whole area of public nuisance and community standards of morality was foggy at best, so he didn't have ironclad rules to work under. He knew, in his heart, that he ought to dismiss the girl's case against Mike Kelly, but he also knew that if he did, Cora would kill him. So he had been facing the hideous task of finding for the silly little girl.

But he had been hoping faintly that something—anything—would occur that might get him off the hook.

Now Bill Busher had given it to him.

A delay—especially a long delay—would give the girl time to cool down. Maybe, the judge thought, the whole thing would blow over.

At least it got him off the hook right now, and it gave Mike a chance.

Seldom had the opportunity to do nothing looked quite so wonderful.

"—and therefore, if the court please," Corkern concluded in a wild burst of oratory, "we ask, nay, we well nigh *demand,* equal justice at this immediate time and place, under precedents and findings aforesaid!"

"Yes, yes, yes," the judge murmured. "Sit down. —Mister Busher, you can justify—I trust—a lengthy postponement?"

Busher saw the clue. He hove onto his feet again. "Your honor, if we are to defend the reputation of these establishments, we must call witnesses from many areas. Soldiers who once served here but are now in other lands—"

"Right," the judge said crisply. "The court sees that." He looked for his gavel, couldn't find it, folded his hands. "The court finds," he said, "that plaintiff's case requires long-term study and time for both sides to prepare. Defense motion for a continuance is granted. This case will next be sounded on the docket, uh, in the first week of January, eighteen hundred and eighty-three."

Busher grinned. Mike Kelly looked puzzled. Hugh Corkern had the expression of a man who has just walked down the street to find his house missing. The girl rose slowly to her feet, very pale.

"That's five months from now!" she gasped.

"Correct," the judge said. "Defense asked for six months. I believe in compromise."

"But I—"

"Court is adjourned," the judge snapped. He began gathering up the papers while they all stared at him. He was having a hard time keeping a completely straight face. He could hardly wait to get home to tell Cora. She couldn't say he had done the wrong thing. Wasn't she the one who always croaked on about compromise and caution? Oh, it was going to be beautiful. He hadn't ruled for Mike Kelly; all he had done was give the girl a lot more time to prepare a better case, right? Right. Cora couldn't complain. She would be stunned. She wouldn't know *what* to say.

It would be marvelous, telling her solemnly about the fine thing he had done to carry out her wishes.

She would have cats.

Stumbling into the courthouse corridor, Katie was simply stunned. She looked across the hall at Mike Kelly, heatedly arguing with his lawyer in an undertone, and then at Hugh Corkern, who was mopping his wet face with a handkerchief.

"It's not a defeat," Corkern said soberly. "We just have to prepare, that's all. We can win the case—"

"But I can't *wait* that long!" Katie wailed.

Corkern frowned furiously. "But you must. The court has ruled."

"But I don't have that much money! I can't—there's no way to stay here until *next year*, waiting for another hearing, and that dreadful man operating the businesses all that time!"

Across the hall, she heard Mike Kelly say angrily to his lawyer, "—hanging over my dagnab head another five months! It's out of the question!" And then the lawyer talked earnestly to him.

"There's no other choice," Hugh Corkern was telling her softly. "Actually, this is a great victory for us."

Katie looked at the lawyer's strained, nervous face, and almost felt sorry for him. He simply did not comprehend it. How could she make him understand? They had *lost*. She couldn't keep body and soul together until next year. She couldn't stand it, staying here, seeing that dreadful, handsome man running *her* businesses. She had hoped to win, and had gambled, and now she was finished.

Without a word, she turned down the hall toward the doors at the far end. Outside, the crowd milled. Oh, she hated them, she hated all of them; she had lost and they would cheer because she had, they didn't see what a lovely, nice, wholesome place she wanted to make of the hotel and the cafe. They just didn't appreciate fine things. And Mike Kelly had beaten her—in *two* days she was ruined.

She moved numbly nearly to the door, thinking of what she would have to do. They still had the small amount of money hidden in the bag. She would have to pack up again, take Heck right back out of school again, pack up, go somewhere else.

But where? They would have *no* money left after buying more tickets, and there was nowhere to go, she couldn't go back to Cleveland and admit she had been a silly fool—

"Hey!" an angry voice called behind her.

She turned, wooden, and saw Mike Kelly, his face furious, striding after her. His lawyer was in hot pursuit.

"Now, Mike, take it easy!" the lawyer was saying. "You just don't know—"

"Shut up!" Kelly grunted. "You're fired anyway." He stomped up to Katie and glared down at her.

She quailed inside, but fought to look firm and brave. He had to boast now, she thought. He had to rub it in. Oh, how she hated him!

"All right," Mike Kelly choked, his face working. "You win."

Katie almost fell down. "What?"

"I'm not going to run this deal for another five or six months," Mike Kelly raged, "and all the time not know whether you're going to take it from me—all the time have you going around saying it's not a decent place. I might not be the smartest man in the world, but I'm not that stupid. I've got my pride. I'm not going to let you do that to me."

Trying desperately to understand, Katie stared up at him. The towering quality of his anger was a palpable force that swept around her, gathered her up, hugged her fiercely and made her knees weak. She had never, ever, been so terrified or surprised. Or thrilled.

Bill Busher stood behind Mike. "Mike, you're making a bad mistake."

"I told you," Mike said, his eyes never leaving Katie's face, "you're fired."

"You—don't want this to drag out?" Katie asked huskily.

"I won't *let* it!" Mike boomed. "You come to town one day, and the next day I've got this—this cloud over everything. I won't go pussyfooting around, paying big lawyer's fees, asking people to simper around and say what a nice goody-goody I am. I won't beg

68

and I won't come back to court and have people feeling sorry for me—I've worked too hard too long for that."

Hugh Corkern said, "Now see here, fellow, my client is upset, and—"

"Be quiet," Katie told him sharply.

"But I—"

Katie was beginning to tremble as she stared at Mike Kelly. A moment ago she had *known* she was lost. But now it had begun to dawn on her: *Mike Kelly felt he had lost too!* This tremendous surge of hope and elation and excitement and fear and—and—some other emotion—swept through her. Her mouth felt like parchment.

"What is it you want to say?" she asked hoarsely.

Mike made an angry slashing gesture. "You want it? I don't want it like this! I'm not going to spend my life fighting for a *building*. Let me have the fixtures out of the saloon. I'll start someplace else in town. You can have my share of everything else—free and clear—for a thousand dollars."

Katie felt hot tears trying to spring from her eyes. "You'll sell your interest?"

Mike balled his fists at his sides. He was angrier than anyone she had ever seen. He was so angry he looked like he might simply explode at any instant. "It will be yours," he muttered. "The whole kit and kaboodle. I get the bar fixtures, the stuff on the walls, the liquor stock, the pictures, all of that. You pay me a thousand for the buildings, the name, all the rest of it."

Trembling, Katie thought about it. A moment ago she had been sure she was lost. Now she had it all within her grasp. "You could have the bar things," she said. "I have no use for them."

"A thousand for the rest," Mike glowered. "Cash."

"Five hundred," Katie countered.

Hugh Corkern grabbed her arm and turned her around, pulling her a few steps away. He whispered fiercely, "You don't have any money!"

"I can borrow it, can't I?" Katie shot back.

"I suppose you could, but—the risk—"

She turned back to Mike Kelly, and now she was getting her face under control. She felt crazily happy. "Well?"

"Nine hundred," Mike Kelly said, his eyes little furnaces of anger.

"Five hundred," Katie insisted coolly.

Mike took a step toward her and suddenly he was trembling all over. He held a mammoth fist up inches under her chin. "If you were a man," he seethed, "I'd—"

"Mike!" Bill Busher said sharply.

"Six hundred," Katie said.

Mike Kelly turned and drove his fist into the wall. Plaster exploded. Lath splintered. Dust shot out all over the hall. Nails hit the floor. His fist went in all the way past the wrist. He pulled it out and swung around to face Katie again, his hair standing on end.

"I'll go *eight*," he choked. "And if you say seven, so help me, I'll—!"

"Done," Katie said in an explosive little breath.

Mike seemed to sag all over. "All right," he muttered.

"Our lawyers can draw up the papers," Katie said, and her heart was singing.

Mike stared at her with sheer hate. He said nothing.

"How long will you need to vacate the premises?" Katie asked. She was filled with dancing terror as she amazed herself by asking this—by pushing this man this far. What made her do it?

"I won't need long," Mike said. "I won't need long. I'll get it out of there. I know a building I think I can rent."

"Until the weekend?"

"Sooner," Mike said, swaying like a great tree about to fall. "Two days."

Katie took a deep breath and said sweetly, "Mister Kelly, I hope you know that none of this has been personal. It's simply business. And now that we have concluded our negotiations, I hope we can consummate the transaction quickly, and then—perhaps—even be friends."

Mike Kelly's jaw sagged. "Friends?"

"Of course," Katie beamed. "We'll be in competition, but it can be *friendly* competition, in the best American tradition!"

Mike clutched his hands to the sides of his head. He seemed to stagger for an instant with the sheer enormity of his emotions. Then he seemed to get some kind of icy control of himself. He bent forward toward Katie from the waist and fixed her with bright, almost sarcastic eyes.

"Lady," he said very softly, "I am not your friend. I am not even your *acquaintance,* lady. We have a deal and I'll carry it out. You

70

get the money and we have a deal. But we are not friends, lady. I'll tell you what we are. We're enemies. Have you got that? I'm going to sack your apples for you, lady. I'm going to beat you selling beer, I'm going to beat you selling food, I'm going to beat you selling anything else you sell. I'm going to beat you in the morning, I'm going to beat you in the afternoon, and I'm going to beat you after dark. I'm going to beat you six ways from Sunday. You aren't going to have a *chance*, lady. I know this business and I know this town and I know people, and you don't know any of them. Especially people. You get your money and these guys will write the papers and let's sign them right away, fast, this afternoon, because I want to get my stuff and my people out of where they are now, and into a new place, lady, because I can't *wait* to start beating your— beating you."

Katie barely managed to maintain her composure. As often under pressure, she came back waxen-cold. "Very well, Mister Kelly," she replied with no trace of feeling in her voice and her chin high. "It will be fierce competition, then. So be it."

"It won't be competition," Mike corrected her, a light in his eyes. "It's going to be war."

Katie turned and walked out.

EIGHT

Within two hours after the informal sale agreement was made in the virtual secrecy of the courthouse corridor, everybody in Salvation knew about it. Some said Bill Busher had spilled it, and others tended to credit Hugh Corkern. A used wagon salesman who claimed to be close to Mike Kelly said Mike had made a general announcement at the Roadhouse immediately after getting back there from the courthouse, as he started removing antlers and heads from the wall.

No matter. It was news in Salvation when somebody fell off a stepladder, and rumors about distant Indian troubles did get tiresome after so long a time. Mike Kelly selling out? That was *real* news. Clots of men gathered on sidewalks and jawed at each other about it. Housewives clucked with satisfaction behind their chintz curtains. Sheriff Pat Paterson wondered what would happen if there was no law-abiding place in the whole town for the rowdies to go, and the soldiers of Fort Forgot talked about secretly slipping the girls into the barracks and getting them on the army payroll somehow as scouts if Mike didn't open a new establishment.

Among those most interested was Ray Root. He had been among the last to hear because he had spent much of the morning renting a fancy livery rig and getting his hair cut and re-greased. It hadn't been until he went to the Shady Nook to pick up Katie for their "tour of the area" that he had heard what was going on. By the time he got to the courthouse, the hearing was over and the secret of the Kelly-Katie bargain had leaked.

Going back to his saloon to look at his hole card and figure out what Mike Kelly's selling out would mean to his own business, Root found his own place of business occupied solely by two drunk Indians and an old whore with a club foot. It depressed him. Try as he might, he had never been able to build his saloon into more than a marginal operation. He had done all the right things: watered the drinks so he could sell them cheaper than Mike Kelly did, put a switch on the gaming wheel so he could occasionally let somebody win a few dollars for good advertising, had the dancing girls take it all off at the last show each night, and even put a stop to his bartenders' practice of knocking drunks on the head in the alley and robbing them. Even with all this first-class endeavor, his place couldn't touch Mike Kelly's.

Now, however, Mike Kelly was going out of business. Or at least changing locations. It was the big chance, Ray Root thought. He had to take full advantage of it.

Going to the door of his tiny office, Root yelled for his bartender-manager. "Bull!"

Bull Beakman, a shaggy-haired Irishman with tattoos all over his arms, came into the office. "Yeah, boss?" he grunted.

"Kelly's changing locations," Root told him. "We'll get all his business and never let him get it back. Starting tonight, the second

72

drink is on the house for everybody. Put up a sign in front. Tell Amspacher and Frilke I want them to let a few people win a little at blackjack tonight. And have the girls get in early, and *circulate.* Sweep the floor. Clean the joint up a little. This is our big chance."

Bull Beakman blinked and grimaced under the massive shelf of his eyebrows. "I gotcha, boss."

"And Bull," Ray Root added as Beakman shambled out the door. "Yeah, boss?"

"Add another six gallons of water to that barrel of rye out there. No sense losing our heads over this thing."

Leaving the bank, Katie clutched her tiny purse against her bosom as she headed directly for Blanscombe's Rest. There had been a moment when she sinkingly felt she would not get the loan, but the banker had softened under her smile and eyelash fluttering and offer of a first mortgage on the whole establishment the moment the papers were signed. Now, her heart singing, she headed for Mike Kelly's—*her,* she corrected herself—place of business. The sooner the money changed hands, the sooner she would feel certain of her destiny.

A crowd of about a dozen men stood around the front porch of the hotel and the next-door saloon, and some of them gave Katie dirty looks as she walked up to them. She saw that a large pile of items—shaggy stuffed heads, lanterns and those hideous oil paintings —covered part of the porch, and inside was the incessant sound of hammering.

As she started up the steps, Mike Kelly struggled out of the front door, carrying a moose head. As he stopped to put it down, he saw Katie.

"You again?" he said. But it was not an angry statement, only one that carried surprise and regret, quietly.

"I—brought your money," she said, abashed.

He nodded. "All right." He looked tired.

"Can I—come in?"

"It's half yours already, and all yours by tomorrow." Mike turned and walked inside.

Katie hesitantly followed.

The saloon was a shambles already. The tables were all shoved together at one side, and the chairs stacked. Two Indian men were

73

dismantling the gaming wheel. Three bartenders were packing glasses and bottles in barrels. The mirrors were down and the walls stripped. The hammering had stopped.

Katie looked at it all and drew in a sharp, involuntary breath. Mike Kelly frowned at her. "What is it?"

"I—didn't like the—decor," Katie admitted, struggling to come to terms with the feeling of *vacancy* the room now had. "But I see now —it's so bare—"

Mike grunted agreement. "It wasn't bad."

Katie nodded and drew another shallow breath as she watched two of the bartenders work a barrel of glasses over to where others were already waiting to be moved on outside. The walls, without the awful paraphernalia that Mike Kelly had used to cover them, were a faded gray-green, splotchy, with holes in the plaster here and there. The beamed ceiling, without the chandeliers, was ugly and raw and dirty. The floor was wavy and uneven. It was all very empty and sterile and cold.

Mike had, Katie saw now, used every ghastly item on the walls not only to add whatever it was that he had seen as proper atmosphere; he had arranged everything to hide blemishes. Before, even though she had convinced herself that the place was horrible, it had been close and crowded and comfortable and warm. Now it was a barren shell.

Overhead, a plank fell on top of the roof with a loud crash, men's voices sounded up there, and the hammering started again.

"What are they doing on the roof?" Katie asked, suspicious.

Mike shrugged. "It leaks. I'm having it fixed."

"I can't afford—"

"You don't have to. It's on me."

Katie felt a pulse of regret. "Oh, Mike. You didn't have to—"

"I know," Mike grunted, comfortable. Then he frowned and managed to look flinty and irascible. "It's good business. I won't have you saying I sold you defective property."

Katie looked at him a minute, feeling feelings she could not identify. Then, quickly, she got into her purse and handed over the envelope. "There you are."

Mike stuck the envelope in his hip pocket. "Thanks."

"If you need more time, please just say so. I'm in no hurry."

"I went from the courthouse to a place I know down on Straight

Street," Mike said. "I've already got it rented. I'll be out quicker than I said, not slower." He turned and called to the bartenders, "Watch those big mugs! You better wrap 'em up in something." Then he turned back to Katie. "You want to look around while you're here?"

"I—yes," she decided.

Mike nodded. "Okay. You've seen the saloon. The bar stays. It's nailed down."

"You could have it," Katie offered, wanting suddenly to make peace with this man who was inexplicably quiet and gentle, now that she had won.

"Nope," Mike said. "It's yours. I can build me another one." He turned and pointed to the big iron stove against the wall. "Firewood out back. Keep the damper almost closed when it rains. You see the way the door opens? You slide this latch up and then to the side." He patted the side of the stove affectionately, looked preoccupied for an instant, then walked Katie to the little stage. "Doors are back there, if you have entertainment. I figure the piano stays. Look here the way you operate the curtain. It's tricky. You have to hold this rope tight to keep tension on those weights up there."

He showed her. Then, just as quietly, he took her up into the loft, apologizing for his room, and promised to clean it out thoroughly. He told her there was a small outbuilding in back which he would have to take care of later, and she said there was no hurry, no hurry at all.

She could have wept. She was seeing all at once how much the place was part of his life fabric—how deeply he had been into it. And she had taken it from him. She had been cruel, she thought, and mean, and now she was overwhelmed by a remorse her pride would not let her express.

"Next door is the hotel, of course," Mike said, leading her down a hallway and into the garish little lobby beyond. "The, uh, present occupants will be moved by tomorrow. Some are already out."

Katie nodded, looking at the trunks by the front door. She was dazed. He moved with such speed!

"I can show you the rooms now or later," Mike was saying. He patted a door frame. "This is a newer building. Hank and I bought it two years ago. I tore out some walls and rebuilt the floor and put on a new roof. It's solid. It's mighty solid," he added softly.

75

Afraid she was really going to bawl, Katie turned her back on him and moved a few steps down the hallway that led to the rooms. "I don't need to inspect now," she said, trembling. "Later I can—"

There was a swift movement beside and slightly behind her. *"Look out!"* Mike's voice whiplashed.

Katie turned and was staggered as someone—a slender, blonde girl—bumped hard against her. A wicked glint of steel slashed past her eyes and she fell backward against the wall, and then Mike was there, bumping hard into her with his hip and shoulder as he struggled with the other woman. The writhing female figure sobbed and spat words Katie couldn't understand, fighting Mike. Then the long, thin knife clattered to the floor. Mike got his foot on it, managed to hug the girl into submission.

She was blonde, very young and very beautiful, wearing a dusty blue dress, her hair loose, and she was crying.

"I'll kill her!" the girl sobbed. "I'll kill her and then it will be all right, honey!"

"You aren't going to kill anybody," Mike crooned roughly, still hugging the girl to prevent a new attack. "Quit, Dolores. Quit!"

Dolores managed to squirm around to face Katie, who remained numbed with shock.

Dolores spat, "Why do you want to hurt Mikey? Nobody hurts Mikey! If I missed this time, I won't the next!"

"Dolores, quit it!" Mike said more sharply.

Katie, frozen by the surprise, the danger, and the strange pain-thrill of seeing another woman in Mike Kelly's big arms, could only stare, hardly breathing.

Dolores, however, wasn't through. Tears streamed down her face. "Honey, let me kill her! I can kill her, I don't care. They can put me in jail, it doesn't matter. I *want* to kill for you, Mikey!"

"Okay, Dolores," Mike said quietly. "Okay, okay. You don't have to hurt anybody, it's fine, just take it easy. We're moving, but it's okay, Dolores. Calm down."

Dolores frowned at him through her tears. "It's—okay?"

"It's okay," Mike told her comfortingly.

Dolores smiled. "All right, Mikey honey."

"You just go back in your room now," Mike urged gently.

She nodded. "All right."

76

To Katie's astonishment, the girl then turned and meekly went back into her room. The door closed softly, as if nothing had ever happened.

Mike looked at the knife and sighed. "Sorry."

"Who *is* she?" Katie asked.

Mike shrugged. "We found her in town a year ago. Somebody had beat her up and left her for dead. She's not very"—he tapped his forehead—"bright."

"Is she one of the—girls?"

"I'm afraid so."

Katie felt indignation stir. "Don't you think that's exploiting her?"

Mike looked at her with eyes suddenly flinty. "I've sent her away to hospitals twice. Both times she's run away and come back. It's not a very good life. It's the one she wants. I don't pretend to know why. At least here she's protected. Ruby watches out for her. Maybe some women aren't built for any better."

"And I suppose you do enjoy her," Katie said bitterly.

"If you think *that*," Mike shot back, "then I'm sorry for you."

"Perhaps," Katie said stiffly, "we should conclude the tour."

"You may want to see Kelly's Emporium," Mike said, walking on down the hall. "It goes with it too."

Despite the turmoil of anger and jealousy within her, Katie's curiosity got the best of her. "What *is* 'Kelly's Emporium'?"

Mike swung open a door that led to a dirt-floored, slant-roofed annex to the rear. It was dim, and smelled like a barnyard. "This is it," he said.

Wondering, Katie went in, having to duck her head because of the low roof. She saw that the timbers slanted up from the center, and rickety bleachers ringed a central pit. She didn't understand.

Mike's forehead furrowed. "Cock fighting," he explained.

"Oh, my heavens!" Katie burst out in disgust.

Still angry with her, Mike Kelly said nothing.

Revolted, Katie walked down the bleacher stairs toward the pit. She saw that it was deep dust, walled to a height of about four feet with bare planks, stained here and there with dark splotches whose source she did not like to speculate on. Behind the barrier on her side were a series of cages. From one of them, startling her, came a scratching sound.

77

"What on earth—?" she murmured, and bent to look.

A big rooster—a fighting cock—huddled in the cage. A piece of red bandanna was tied around his head, covering his eyes.

"Everybody has picked up his bird already except that one," Mike explained. "It's Jimmy Huddleston's. I don't imagine he'll even come pick it up. It's lost two fights in a row."

Katie rose slowly to her feet, and her old indignation was back in full cry. "You really are a beast," she choked.

"What?" Mike gasped, startled.

"Fighting animals," Katie said, her voice shaky with loathing. "The cruelty of it—the barbarism!"

"Right, right," Mike snapped. "At other places in town they fight 'em to the death. House rules here say the damaged bird loses. There's seldom a kill. But you're right, lady. I'm just a beast. Right." Then, all at once, he was shouting into her face. "Don't you understand *anything?* This isn't Cleveland, Ohio! This isn't a tea party! People aren't very cultured out here! They sweat and stink and get sick and die and fight and make love and have babies and cheat and kill and gamble! That's the way people *are,* you danged fool! Go ahead and live in your dream world if you want, but don't expect anybody *else* to be that stupid!"

Katie froze. "We have nothing more to talk about. Obviously."

In a rage, Mike hurled the door of the cage open and reached inside. "Here!" he yelled, thrusting the cock into her arms with such force that she caught it. "Take it with you! Put it in your hotel room and see if you can make a pet out of it! You watch him! Watch him good! You could learn a lot from him! He's mean and ornery and dirty, just like folks! *Take him!*"

Katie was so startled, and so outraged, that she clutched the bird to her breast and turned and marched out of the arena. She fled down the hall, tears stinging her eyes, vowing she would never speak to him again—would *destroy* him in business—would do *anything.*

She ran half-blindly through the saloon and onto the front porch, stumbled down the steps into the street before the stunned eyes of the hangers-on, and tripped and fell to one knee in the dirt. The rooster sprawled ahead of her, and his blinkers came off. He saw he was free, came up in a shower of flying dirt and feathers, and half-ran, half-flew under the porch. An old hound dog who had been sleeping under there howled in surprise and loped out, running for dear life.

The men were slapping their thighs and falling down, laughing.

Katie scrambled to her feet, picked up her purse, and ran across the street toward the Shady Nook. She had never been so humiliated. She was hurt and angry and frightened, and what made her angriest was the realization that for a few minutes—a very short time, but very real—she had almost liked him—had almost felt something for the horrible, ugly, mean, ghastly, selfish, shouting brute.

She would get him now. Oh, she would get him *now!*

In the saloon, Alvin Singing Duck was unscrewing the base of the gaming board and David Swooping Hawk was morosely sweeping up wood splinters when it happened. Alvin Singing Duck was totally unprepared.

He had been feeling better today. Mike Kelly's move meant extra paid work for him, and had even resulted in Swooping Hawk getting a full day's wages. The tribe could use the money. It would buy some luxuries, like food, that would further take everybody's mind off Swooping Hawk's diatribes and Wakinokiman's absurd prophecy.

Alvin Singing Duck had even begun to feel that his troubles might be over for a while.

Then a door slammed open. As Alvin Singing Duck turned toward the sound, he was astonished to see the woman from the East run through the saloon, right past him, carrying a rooster. She flew out the door and Alvin Singing Duck, stunned, heard the men outside laughing, and the sharp baying of a hound.

Swooping Hawk slammed a forearm into Alvin Singing Duck's chest with crushing force. Swooping Hawk's eyes were ablaze with fierce excitement.

"Did you see?" he hissed exultantly. "Did you *see,* my brother?"

"I saw it," Alvin Singing Duck said, "but I don't believe it."

"Do you know what this *means?*" Swooping Hawk bit off hoarsely.

"She couldn't have stolen it," Alvin Singing Duck muttered. "I don't know if he gave it to her, or—"

"Fool!" Swooping Hawk cried triumphantly, jumping up and down in his furious excitement. "It is as was said! *A fair maiden will carry a chicken.* It is the first portent come true!"

NINE

By late afternoon, Mike Kelly was at his new place of business.

Not that he was open for business yet, far from it. Standing in the jumbled mess just inside the door of the cavernous old hall he had rented, he was wondering if he could *ever* get open again. His bartenders were unpacking glasses and bottles and stowing them on the shelves Mike had thrown up against one wall, and the Indians were trying not very effectively to get the gaming wheel put back together. The girls, in the building next door, were scrubbing floors and walls and throwing paint around like troopers. A few would-be customers were standing around outside, getting in the way of the drovers unloading the last wagon of stuff. Another flatbed wagon was trundling up the street from the corner, bringing the planks Mike needed to start building a new bar.

It would take awhile, Mike thought, but it would be fine.

Striding out onto the porch to meet the wood shipment, he nearly collided with Lieutenant Harley Bumpers, in full uniform.

"You're a little early, if you want a drink," Mike told him.

"My men informed me of this development," Harley Bumpers said, "and I came to check it out for myself." He squinted at the time-blackened planks on the outside wall. "It's true?"

"It's true," Mike admitted.

Bumpers frowned. "Opened tonight?"

"Not likely."

"When? Estimate."

"Tomorrow," Mike said definitely, "on a limited basis. It ought to take a week or so to get the bar built, the stage up, everything in top shape."

"I plan," Bumpers said, after a slight pause to digest the information, "a patrol."

Mike stared at him, not getting any connection at all. He wondered if the life at Fort Forgot had finally scrambled Harley Bumpers's eggs for him. "You plan a patrol?"

Bumpers nodded. "Until your place is in full operation, I want my men busy elsewhere. I don't want them visiting other establishments, being cheated, roughed up."

"What will they do on patrol?" Mike asked.

"Search for hostiles."

"Hostile *Indians?*"

"Naturally," Harley Bumpers said, his eyes snapping.

"Around Salvation?" Mike asked, aghast.

"It's possible," Bumpers said, his hand stealing to the handle of his saber. "It may even be likely, in a situation such as this, where you have, as it were, instability and a fluid outlook, or to put it another way, the responsibilities of command require the utmost care in exercising the various options open to a man with the broadest possible *scope*. In other words, as Grant realized at Richmond, you may not see all sides to it but then of course while various attacks might be presented in theoretical form, the commander's obligation, inasmuch as he is the commander, and the duties of command are manifold and difficult in the best of circumstances, without a broad outlook on all potential hazards, he's without any real series of options and that's often at the very heart of the matter. Whereas three or four possible alternatives might be seen by even a casual observer, but many more obviously exist given a proper perspective, I mean it's a multitudinous panorama of potential givens, when the person at the center of the action, with the action not often clear, and if he doesn't make every attempt to penetrate the complexity with, say, patrols, then, if he doesn't exercise the proper judgment, and if, on the other hand, opposing forces should take the initiative, why, then—"

"I see," Mike said quickly, appalled by the prospect of Bumpers tunneling deeper and deeper into conditional clauses and subjunctive moods. "A patrol in that case is a great idea. Right."

"But when you're back in full operation, that part of the problem is solved," Harley Bumpers added.

"Well," Mike said slowly, "I appreciate that compliment."

"Half my men," Bumpers said, whacking his palm onto the hilt of the saber. "A full-scale patrol, a reconnaissance, as it were, in force.

And unless I miss my guess, unless every ounce of military judgment at my disposal is in error, then *if,* given vigilance, not only will the domestic situation be alleviated, with your new place open I'll have no more worries on that score, because you run a clean business and while the good lord knows we might all wish men to be better, why, if they were, what need would there be for an army?"

Bumpers paused, seemingly startled by the last thought, whatever it had been.

"It won't take us long," Mike assured him.

"Good," Harley Bumpers said, and walked away.

Taking a deep breath, Mike rubbed his forehead. He couldn't quite penetrate why the army was going to send out a heavy patrol, but evidently Bumpers was going to do just that. There was always a chance, of course, that they might bump into hostiles; nobody was exactly certain where Geronimo and his small band had gone, and the mood among Indians generally seemed to be bad. The old fear of what an Indian attack could do to a place like Salvation made a little chill creep up one's back.

But, Mike told himself, any patrol from Fort Forgot would have to fall over the enemy force by accident. They weren't bad troopers here, but they were not exactly spoiling for a fight, either. Some of them had fought the Apaches in the old days, and any man who had ever fought the Apaches did not walk around looking for another opportunity for more of the same.

It would be all right, Mike decided: a hard patrol which would find nothing, and by the time they got back in a week or so, he would be ready for their business.

Turning to the pile of junk on the porch, he bent to pick something up.

"Mister Kelly?" a voice piped behind him.

He turned and saw Heck, the little brother of Katie Blanscombe, standing at the foot of the steps. Heck was frowning with seriousness, his pack of school books slung over his back in a tied length of rope.

"Hello!" Mike grinned. "How was school?"

"Rotten," Heck said. He looked up at the dilapidated old building. "Is *this* where you're gonna have your business at now?"

"Looks like it," Mike said.

"You need any help?"

Mike didn't get it. "What?"

"Help! Do you need any help?"

"Well, Heck, what do you suppose that sister of yours would say if she caught you helping the likes of me?"

"Wouldn't matter," Heck shot back. "I'd be working for a wage. What could she say about *that?*"

"Oh," Mike breathed. "I get it. Working for a *wage.*"

"I can use the money," Heck told him earnestly, "and besides, I've talked with kids today, and some other folks, and—well, I hate to say it, sir, but it looks to me like my sister is *wrong.* —I want to help you, if I can."

Mike looked down at the kid, liking his spunk. It was hard to know what to say. He remembered himself at Heck's age, and the way it had seemed impossible to find a job even for a penny a day, just so you could think you were your own man, and not just a worthless kid.

Heck, evidently mistaking his silence for a negative reaction, went on quickly, "I'll even *ask* her, if you want. But if I can get her to say okay, then I could be here this time every day right after school, and I can sweep and wash floors and windows—you *sure* need windows washed—and I can paint, haul out garbage, if somebody throws up or something, clean it up—"

"You sound," Mike cut in, "like a man that needs a job bad."

"I do," Heck frowned. "And I want to help you—be on your side."

"Not if it means hurting your sister, Heck."

"Looks to me like you'd like to hurt her!"

"Not that way, boy. Not that way."

"I'll ask her," Heck said. "I'll get her to say okay."

Mike thought about it. "If you can get it okayed, what do you think would be a fair wage?"

"I don't know," Heck muttered, scowling and scuffing his shoes into the dirt. "I was thinkin' . . ." He let it tail off.

Mike hid his grin and let the kid stew a minute. Then he said gently, prodding, "You were thinkin'?"

"Well," Heck muttered even less audibly, "whatever you think is fair. I guess that's okay . . ."

"How about," Mike asked, "if it can be worked out, a dime a day?"

Heck's face lit up. "A dime a day! I was thinking a nick—I mean," he said, catching himself and looking down quickly, "a dime a day? Uh, I guess that would be okay."

"Find out what the lady says," Mike suggested.

Heck's grin couldn't be contained. "I sure will!" he yelped, and turned and ran down the street.

Mike watched him go. He wondered if the lady would let him do it. Probably not. He hoped that estimate was wrong.

Then, as Heck vanished around the street corner, hightailing it for the old Blanscombe's Rest location, Mike mentally shook himself and got back to work. It was going to take every cent of his payment for the old place, he reminded himself—and then some—to get this old ruin in shape. The roof had to be fixed, painting inside and out, flooring, the bar, the stage, new windows, new guttering, a privy in back—virtually a new building inside the general outlines of the old.

He was risking a lot on his reputation, figuring people would break their old habit patterns and walk all the way down here. He might be acting like a fool in a lot of ways. But he had to try it. The girl would *not* beat him.

Heck ran into the building that had been Blanscombe's Rest and skidded to a halt. Katie and two ladies he had never seen before were up on ladders, scrubbing at the aged plaster walls, and here and there the walls looked a shade or two cleaner; but there was plaster all over the floor where the rags were knocking down as much wall as they were cleaning.

The whole room, Heck saw, looked like the inside of a very old cave—dark, dank, empty, cold, nasty.

Katie, her face smudged and her hair down limply, managed a smile for him. "Hello, Heck. How was school?"

Why did they always ask *that?*

"Great," he said, figuring a lie might help. "Listen, sis, what would you think of me having a job after school—I mean, a real, *paying* job?"

Katie smiled fondly down at him, her hands in the bucket. "That

84

might be worked out, honey. I can use the help, certainly. Would a penny a day be about right for wages?"

"Not here!" Heck said, realizing his mistake. "I mean—I'd *like* to help you, and I can, nights, and like that. But see, I've already got a job—and it pays a dime a day."

"A dime!" Katie said. "What will you be doing? Killing people?"

"A man down the street," Heck said. "He needs help real bad, and I went and asked him." He decided his sister was looking dubious, and he'd better lather up the story a little. "He said he thought I was a fine young man, showing the initiative to come apply the very first day of school and all that, and he said I can start tomorrow, and I said I was sure you'd let me, because I can help you at nights, too, and this way I'll be, like, making my own salary, and not depending on you. See?"

Katie looked down at him with a funny mixture of love and uncertainty. "I certainly need the help here, Heck."

"Yeah," Heck said urgently. "But this is a dime a day, and I'd be having my *own* job, like a *man!*"

Katie smiled. "And you want to start being a man, don't you, honey."

Heck gave her the little-boy-smiling-stoutly-like-a-little-brave-trooper look. "Gee, sis, yes. I guess that means more to me right now than almost *anything*."

"Well," Katie sighed, "all right, then."

"Wow!" Heck cried, giving her the delighted act, which was not all faked by any means, just exaggerated to make sure she got the maximum benefit from it. "Do you *mean* it?"

"I mean it," Katie said, and really smiled for the first time.

"Gosh! Gee! Then I can start tomorrow!" Heck tossed his books on the floor. "What can I do to help *you* today, sis?"

It was the least he could do, after all.

TEN

On the next day, a patrol of thirty-eight cavalry rode out from Fort Forgot under the command of Sergeant Bobby Biggs. It was his first command and, at twenty-seven, he was determined to make good. Lieutenant Harley Bumpers had said to look for signs of hostiles, and Sergeant Bobby Biggs started looking—hard—the moment the patrol cleared the fort gate. He was determined to find signs of hostiles if it killed him. He led the patrol north, into the roughest part of the mountains. He did not believe in doing things the easy way.

The same afternoon, Katie Blanscombe hired two local men to repaint the outside of Blanscombe's Rest. She knew she couldn't really afford it, but the glaring red exterior just had too many bad associations for her. She told the painters to repaint the building white, like houses were painted in Cleveland, and they secretly thought she was crazy, but did as they were told, starting the following morning.

The two painters were up on scaffolds, about half through with the front of the building, when Alvin Singing Duck walked by, with Swooping Hawk right alongside him.

Swooping Hawk took one look at the building—the top half fresh white and the bottom half the old scarlet—and jumped four feet straight in the air.

"Look!" he hissed, practically tearing Alvin Singing Duck's arm out of the socket. "Red to white! 'Blood will become as milk'! *It is the second omen of Wakinokiman!*"

ELEVEN

The weekend came and went, and it was pretty quiet. With half the soldiers on patrol and most of the others on duty inside the fort, Salvation lost its usual military look. The weather turned hot and Sheriff Pat Paterson jailed a number of drunks. The Salvation *Examiner* carried a quarter-page ad proclaiming:

—THE BLANSCOMBE HOTEL—
—THE QUALITY CAFE—

Under New Management,
With A New Family Policy!

Bring the entire family for
a relaxed and wholesome
meal or relaxation in a
place of comfort and decency
designed for your pleasure.
A Christian Place of Business!

NEW MANAGEMENT—NEW POLICY

K. Blanscombe, Prop.

On Monday, the first day of business, Katie was up at five in the morning to start preparing food, and by eight there were three other members of the Salvation Women's Auxiliary in the kitchen helping her. At lunch, the minister and his wife came, as did Mayor Elihou Stetter and his wife, Fred Jenkinsen the editor of the paper, Judge John Edwards and his wife Cora, attorney Hugh Corkern, two husbands of ladies working in the kitchen, and a pair of slightly bombed waddies who stomped in, took one look at the chintz curtains, and beat a hasty retreat. At the evening supper hour, two younger couples appeared early, a lone old man came in about seven o'clock for a bowl of soup, and the rest of the time there was nobody.

"Don't worry, dear," said of the ladies who had helped, patting Katie's hand after the uneaten food had been thrown out. "It takes a little time to establish customers, that's all."

The hotel had exactly one occupant, a seed drummer staying just overnight between stage connections.

Mike Kelly's new joint, opening formally the same night, started turning people away at 6 P.M. and could still be heard going strong in the early hours of the morning, when Katie lay wide awake, tears of loneliness and worry in her eyes, in the front bedroom of the silent, redecorated hotel.

On Tuesday it rained. Katie prepared considerably less food than she had the first day, and had exactly seven customers all day long, with the result that she threw more away than ever.

On Wednesday, Editor Jenkinsen dropped by before lunch. "The same ad this week, Miss Blanscombe?" he asked briskly.

Katie mustered a brittle smile. "I think I'll take just a small one, Mister Jenkinsen."

"Smaller?" Jenkinsen murmured, peering at her through the thick lenses of his glasses. "Of course. The same copy? Or it could say, 'Continuing our new tradition of elegance and decency in dining,' and then, perhaps, a sample menu and prices? You can't underestimate the value of price information, Miss Blanscombe. Now if I may suggest a layout—"

Katie stopped him by holding up her hand with the thumb and forefinger about an inch apart. "An ad this big, Mister Jenkinsen. One inch. And it can just be the name of our place."

"A card ad," Jenkinsen murmured, crestfallen.

"Yes." Katie held her chin up.

"Fine," Jenkinsen said, recovering. "A change of pace, eh, and then a big campaign for next week again? Good!"

"We'll see," Katie said.

"Uh, Miss Blanscombe," Jenkinsen added, "about the account, there's certainly no *hurry,* you understand, but we printers must pay our bills too, you know, and I, uh, was wondering—"

"I'll pay you Friday, Mister Jenkinsen," Katie smiled coolly.

"Good! —Well, good day, then!" And he hurried out as if he was afraid he would be handed a lunch menu if he stayed another moment.

Katie leaned against the frame of the door that led from dining room to kitchen. She wondered what she was going to do.

Mentally she totaled some of it: to Jenkinsen, $20; for groceries, $70; for supplies, $55; for the tables and chairs—a payment, $30; for deliveries and pickups, $8; for the carpenters, $35; for printing, $11; for painters, $40; for a payment to the bank in another two weeks, $50; for ice, $4; for lamps and oil and napkins and laundry and firewood and all the other things ticketed neatly in her own handwriting in the small metal box behind the counter, at least $100 more.

Debits, immediate—$400.

Income so far—$8.32.

Oh, God.

She looked around the cafe, her heart breaking. The walls, painted a pale yellow, glowed cleanly, and here and there the little pictures of eastern rural scenes added a restful touch, just as she had imagined. The neat, round tables with the red-and-white checkerboard tablecloths stood in perfect rows, the wicker chairs waiting. The counter was freshly painted, spick and span. Even the old flooring, thanks to the red-rough blisters on her hands from the lye soap, gleamed dully, a rich, freshly oiled mahogany hue. The big, airy room was immaculate, and redolent with the aromas of coffee and spices and good, savory food, and at the windows the white chintz curtains were fluffy and nice.

It was just as she had pictured it except for one item: customers.

Well, she told herself as bravely as possible, it was simply as Mrs. Houaser had told her: it would take some time. It was as easy as that. Word would get around. The town of Salvation might be a rough, crude, frontier settlement, peopled mostly by rugged men with little realized appreciation for the finer things. But they would learn. Sooner or late a few of them would come in and see how—how *nice* it was. Then the word would spread. And she would be all right.

She really would, she told herself.

Telling herself also that she had to keep busy, she walked to the front windows to adjust the already perfect curtains. She touched them here and there, thinking how it would be when people started coming in, and she had to hire lots of extra help. *Then* Mike Kelly would be surprised, she thought spitefully, and that made her feel a little better.

Outside, in the slightly muddy street, an empty flatbed wagon churned past, followed by two bearded, muddy horsemen. Two soldiers strolled past on the other side, gazing toward her place of business and talking about it, but then going on. An old man, with no teeth, walked up the street from the left, wearing a stovepipe hat and dark, baggy suit, and carrying a sandwich sign on his back.

GIRLS
GAMES
DRINKS
At Mike Kelly's,

it said in red lettering on a black background.

Katie, reading it, felt her old sense of anger welling up with quick, unbidden tears. The hateful man! She would beat him yet, she would show *everybody!*

But how? Oh, *how?*

It was chilly in the high mountains, and snow flecked the air as Sergeant Bobby Biggs reined up for a moment at the head of the long, ragged line of troopers. They were very far up, and had come out on a brink that looked down perhaps six thousand feet into a far valley. Sergeant Bobby Biggs signaled to his second in command, Corporal Vince Shapiro, who moved up briskly, the hoofs of his horse clattering and sprinkling around chunks of broken granite.

"Dismount," Sergeant Bobby Biggs snapped crisply. "Ten minutes."

Corporal Shapiro turned in the saddle and signaled to the troopers. They tumbled off their horses where they were, many of them simply dropping to lie on the cold, rock-strewn ground. A chill wind whipped the dead trees.

Pulling his spyglass out from under his tunic, Sergeant Bobby Biggs trained it on the floor of the valley below and scanned it for what seemed a long time. His legs ached as he stood against the cold wind, hoping to see a sign of hostiles.

Finally he took the glass down from his eye. "Take a look," he snapped at Corporal Shapiro.

The corporal sighed, took the glass, and swung it once around the panorama. He took it down. "Nothing," he grunted.

"Our scouting mission is nearly concluded," Sergeant Bobby Biggs reminded him unnecessarily. "We turn back here—swing through the river gorge and across the mesa country toward Pinochle Ridge. We ought to be back at the fort in two days."

"Yessir," Corporal Shapiro said, wiping snowflakes out of his mustache. "The men are beat, an'—"

"We have plenty to report," Sergeant Bobby Biggs added darkly.

Corporal Shapiro's jaw sagged. "Plenty to report, sir? Begging your pardon, Sergeant, but we've been out here five complete days. We've crossed four rivers, climbed a half-dozen mountains, drove all night the night before last, almost got in that avalanche, doubled back on ourselves, set lines, climbed up here, and we haven't seen that first sign of *anything!* What do we have to report—begging the sergeant's pardon, sir?"

Sergeant Bobby Biggs turned fierce eyes to his corporal. "Lieutenant Bumpers had reasons for sending us out. If it's one thing I've learned in this man's army, it's that commands are given for a reason. I knew from the start that this patrol was vital . . . my first command, and a vital one. It's important to establish yourself as a leader on your first command, Corporal. Remember that."

"Yessir," said Corporal Shapiro, evidently a little dazed. "But you said—you said we had plenty to report. *What,* sir?"

Sergeant Bobby Biggs's eyes narrowed keenly. "We've seen no campfires."

"Yessir, that's right."

"We've seen no tracks."

"Right, sir."

"We've come upon no old camps, no jerked venison, no signs of hunting, no old campfire ashes, no trails, no signs of Indian ponies."

"Yessir, that's right, sir. We haven't seen a damned *thing.*"

Sergeant Bobby Biggs slammed a gloved fist into his palm. "They're clever—fiendishly clever!"

"*Sir?*" Corporal Shapiro faltered.

"Don't you understand?" Sergeant Bobby Biggs rapped triumphantly. "We *know* there are Indians out here somewhere. We *know* something is going on, or we wouldn't have been sent. But we've seen *nothing!* That proves it beyond a shadow of doubt! These savages are up to something—*they're hiding from us on purpose,* which proves they're up to something *big!* We must return to the post as swiftly as possible to report it!"

On the following day, Thursday, in Salvation, Heck was sweeping the floor and trying to be careful so he wouldn't awaken a man asleep across one of the tables, when Mike Kelly signaled him from the back office. Heck leaned the broom up against the moose head and hurried back to see what was wanted.

Mike Kelly had walked back into his cubbyhole office, and had his feet propped up on the packing box he used for a desk by the time Heck got there. In his shirt-sleeves, with stacks of coins and wads of paper money all over the top of the box, Mike looked to be in high good humor.

"Payday," he told Heck, and shoved a gold piece across the box at him.

"That's five bucks!" Heck gasped. "I don't have no change for *that* kind of money!"

"Bonus," Mike told him. "You've been good help. I appreciate it."

Dazzled, Heck shoved the heavy coin into his pants pocket. "Gee, I guess business has really been good, huh?"

"Not bad," Mike smiled. "Not bad at all. Just don't get to expect a bonus every week, though. You won't always be getting it."

"Yes sir," Heck said. "I mean, *no* sir, I sure won't."

Mike indicated the straight chair beside the packing box. "Take a load off for a minute."

Heck complied, wondering what else was up. He felt flushed with the excitement of all this wealth.

"You're going to school," Mike frowned, "right?"

"Right," Heck said. What was *this* all about?

"But," Mike went on, "you're staying with your sister."

"Oh. Yes sir. Sure. And I help her some at nights."

Mike looked off into the corner very casually. "How's she doing over there? I've heard she isn't getting much business."

"Well," Heck admitted, "she's not doing *great.*"

"Is she—worried about it?"

"I don't know, boy. I mean it's hard to tell with ole Katie. She wouldn't let me know what was going on, if her britches was on fire."

"Watch the way you talk," Mike said sternly. "Let me put it to you this way: How many customers did she have when you got back there last night?"

"Last night?" Heck repeated, trying to remember. "Let's see . . . there was Ray Root, he was there with some friend of his . . . and lemme see now . . . one of them ladies in the club, and her husband."

Mike watched him, waiting.

Heck waited too.

"And?" Mike prodded.

"That's all," Heck said.

"Four customers?"

"Uh-huh."

"Is that, uh, typical?"

"Well, not really. Night before last, nobody came."

"*Nobody?*"

"Just me," Heck said.

Mike frowned and heaved a gigantic sigh.

"She keeps sayin' everything is just fine, though," Heck volunteered.

"Yeah . . . ," Mike grunted.

"Maybe," Heck suggested cheerfully, "she'll go outta business, and then you'll be able to move back into your old spot."

Mike's reaction surprised him. Mike's face clouded over like a bad winter storm coming in off Lake Erie. "Listen, bub, don't talk about your own sister that way! You ought to be rooting for her to make it big!"

"How come for *you* to get excited?" Heck demanded, astonished. "After what she's done to you, boy—"

"I don't *care*," Mike shot back defensively. "But on the other hand, there's room in the town for a good eating place . . . if she wasn't so stupid about the way she runs it, if the boys didn't all feel they had to tiptoe in because they were afraid of getting the floor dirty. . . ." His voice trailed off. Then he resumed, "Of course she *is* stubborn. She'd never change. If it was the death of her. You

93

have to admire that kind of gumption in a woman . . . if she wasn't so nasty all the time . . ." He trailed off a second time, and now stared into the corner again, lost in his own thoughts.

"Should I get back to work?" Heck asked after a while.

"Does Root go over there much?" Mike asked.

"He's been by every day, I guess. I sort of have the feeling he's trying to spark her a little bit."

"Root?" Mike Kelly said bleakly. "Sparking Katie?"

"I guess everybody's gotta spark somebody," Heck observed. "Maybe he wouldn't be such a bad guy if he didn't wear all that grease on his hair. Katie says, leastwise, he's a perfect gentleman—"

Mike's eyes blazed. "A perfect *what?*"

"A perfect—"

Mike's fist crashed on the top of the box, sending coins and paper money all over the place. *"God!"*

"How come *you're* excited?" Heck asked.

"I'm not," Mike snarled. "Now go on and get out of here. Knock off now. A man ought to get off a little early on payday. Just don't let me see you trying to sneak next door to spend any of that!"

Heck stared at him, and then he understood. He felt his face turn crimson, and then he grinned, and then he just turned and high-tailed out of the office. He was tumultuously flattered and embarrassed and surprised all at the same time. He hadn't even thought about going next door . . . until now.

The idea made him feel like a real man.

One of these days, he thought, by gosh—!

He headed home, swaggering.

He didn't even see David Swooping Hawk, one of Mike Kelly's Indian swampers, walk out onto the front porch of the saloon behind him and watch him all the way up the street with eyes that were secretly as cold and calculating and crafty as those of a genuine bird of prey.

Because Swooping Hawk was sure, now.

Going back into the saloon, he began scrubbing again without a word to Alvin Singing Duck. But Swooping Hawk was far too busy with his own thoughts to engage in idle conversation anyway.

Two of the omens had already appeared. Next there would be thunder in a still place. And that was the only remaining omen that had to be awaited, because Swooping Hawk had already seen the wisdom of the fourth and last one, and knew exactly how it would be accomplished.

Watching his chieftain, Alvin Singing Duck, he felt a swift burst of scorn and anger, which he managed to hide totally. Alvin Singing Duck was like a female child, without the blood and sinew of a real man. Alvin Singing Duck did not know real pride. But Swooping Hawk knew. The Tikoliwani band could be led in one more battle— one final outburst of rage that could, in its heroism and beauty, fire every Indian in the land to rise up simultaneously and crush the white man once and forever. They might be many, the white men, but they knew fear. Once the uprising had killed all of them in this part of the country, they would stay away, fearfully, and the red men would again have their own land, daring any intruder to step foot across its bounds. A new treaty could be drawn, not for a pitiful patch of ruined land like Dead Cow Valley, where a few wretched cowards could die, but all this land—*all* this so-called territory— and the ones beyond it.

Thinking of it, Swooping Hawk felt a thrill of anticipation.

The uprising would come, soon. The white men would die horribly. The white men would be filled with fear, and the red men would again rule here.

And he—David Swooping Hawk—would be remembered in the twilight chants of the noble heroes until the end of time.

It was his destiny.

At the cafe, Katie stood near the counter with Simon Jasper, the wholesale grocer. Her fists were clenched in the hidden folds of her dress, and she wanted to scream.

Instead she said quietly, "I assure you it will be paid by then."

Simon Jasper cocked his head downward, obviously embarrassed. "Not that much of a rush, even, Miz Blanscombe. When I said we collect every two weeks, I just meant *ordinarily*. You take longer if you need to. Take another week or even two."

"That's very kind of you, Mister Jasper," Katie said crisply, "but I can assure you that your payment will be in your hands by Saturday."

"Well," Jasper sighed, "we like to see new business in town. The town needs it, you know. We don't want to be unfriendly."

"You're not unfriendly," Katie assured him, wanting again to scream. "Don't worry about a thing, Mister Jasper."

Simon Jasper nodded, as if starting to feel relieved. "Okey dokey, then, Miz Blanscombe. Pleasure doin' business with you."

"Goodbye," Katie said, and ushered him out.

The wholesale grocer gone, she turned back to face her empty cafe. The supper hour was approaching. In the back, her hired girl was preparing the food. The street outside the windows was bathed in a cool golden light, and the sun had already slipped behind the rim of the distant mountains. Men stomped up and down the sidewalks, horses moved, wagons clattered along, the first lanterns glowed in windows here and there. It should have been the time of greatest activity here, when—according to her dreams—every table would have been filled and she would have been rushing about madly to serve them all.

But there was none of that, and she had to face it now: rather than becoming better, business was actually becoming even worse. The good businessmen of Salvation were beginning to notice, too —and had started circling like vultures for their payments.

Katie went around the room, adjusting tablecloths unnecessarily. She was at quite her lowest ebb.

"Evening!" a familiar voice called from the doorway.

Katie turned. Ray Root, smiling broadly, stood just inside the door, his hat in hand and lanternlight glinting off his hair. He wore what she had come to know as his "best" outfit: black suit with wide lapels, lavender flowered vest, white shirt with high celluloid collar and black string tie, an elk's tooth at the end of the chain looped across his lank belly.

"Hello, Ray," she said without much enthusiasm.

Ray Root strode across the room toward her, his black boots gleaming with each step. "I wanted to stop by a moment before going to my business." He looked around, affecting a deep frown. "No customers yet?"

"Not yet," Katie said, and managed a smile.

"While Mike Kelly," Root growled, "takes not only *your* business, rightfully, but half of mine. I tell you, Katie, the only step is for you to pursue your lawsuit against the scoundrel in his new place and operation, and drive him from our midst."

"I've told you, Ray, that I won't do that."

"But if it's a case of your own survival—"

"I won't hound the man," Katie said sharply. Then she thought to add—unconvincingly, she thought—"no matter *how* much I detest him."

Ray Root sighed. "Very well. There may be other ways to deal with him, if it comes to that."

"What do you mean?" Katie asked, alarmed by his tone.

"Nothing," Root said, remembering to put his smile on again. "But also remember, my dear, that my own offer remains, if all else fails you."

Katie was so depressed and confused that she didn't even feel anger at being reminded. Root had told her yesterday that he would be willing to "help her out of her problem" by buying her operation completely.

For $250.

But an offer like that, besides being a final defeat, wouldn't even let her pay all the people she owed. Again the list of debts swept through her mind: a total of almost a thousand now to the bank—

"Katie?" Ray Root said.

"I'm sorry," she said, startled. "I was gathering wool."

"You should gather ye rosebuds," Root said grandly.

Katie couldn't muster any enthusiasm. It wasn't just that she was low today. She knew Ray Root was being just as sweet and nice to her as he knew how, and she ought to be flattered. But two things kept nagging at her mind in dealing with him: the vague feeling that he might, in some way, be trying to use her . . . and thoughts of Mike Kelly.

Ray Root didn't compare well with Mike Kelly, even though Ray Root, she told herself, was a perfect gentleman and Mike Kelly was a disgusting adventurer and a cad.

"Why," she asked Root now, thinking out loud, "does he get all the business while I get none?"

"Habit," Root replied instantly. "Sheer habit. Habit and the fact that many in this town have no appreciation for the finer things, my dear. After all, you offer exquisite cuisine and a thoroughly lovely, wholesome atmosphere, with service by the most exquisite of all, yourself. Mike Kelly offers only base instinctual satisfactions —his girls, loud music, whiskey—all the things one who would frequent *this* establishment would abhor."

"I thought there would be people to appreciate this other kind of place," Katie admitted.

"And there will be," Ray Root said softly, patting her hand between his cool fingers. "You must persist, my dear."

At the door there was a little racket, and Heck burst in. "Hey, sis! I got paid!" Then he saw Ray Root and his face fell. "Oh. Sorry."

"I was just leaving, young man," Root said grandly. He turned back to Katie. "Remember, my dear. If worst comes to worst, I stand by to help in any way I can."

"Thank you," Katie said, feeling frosty. "Goodbye, Ray."

He left, and she thought for an instant about the possibility that his *only* interest was in getting control of this place when she failed and had to meet his terms. But that was a depression-thought, she told herself. She turned to Heck.

"So you got paid, did you."

Heck grinned. "You better believe it, I did!"

Katie enjoyed his enthusiasm. At least things were going right for somebody! "How much did you collect?" she asked.

Heck pulled his hand out of his pocket and opened it. There in his palm was a slightly sweaty $5 gold piece.

"All *that?*" Katie gasped.

"I got a bonus," Heck said proudly.

Katie felt a tug of suspicion. "Heck, you never have introduced me to the man you work for."

Heck's smile began to fade. "Yeah. Well—I will one day, sis. Listen, I better git back to the kitchen and start—"

"Heck," Katie said, "who are you working for? I want to know his name."

"He's just down the street there," Heck said over his shoulder, scurrying for the kitchen.

"Heck!"

He stopped and looked back innocently. "Huh?"

Katie's hands were on her hips. "I want an answer, young man!"

"I better git to work now," Heck parried. "I'll talk to you later, okay?" He gave her a ghastly, desperate little grin.

"Heck," Katie said softly, bracing herself for the worst, "are you doing something . . . wrong for this man?"

"No!" Heck cried. "Gosh, *no!* Mike wouldn't do—"

He stopped, seeing what he had given away.

Katie felt like someone had doused her with ice water. "Mike? —*Mike Kelly?*"

"Aw," Heck growled defensively. "I had to have a job *someplace* —an' he's a good guy—"

Katie dropped to a chair at the nearest table. "Oh, Heck, how could you?"

Heck looked scared but game. "He's a good guy," he repeated stubbornly. "And I like him. I want to help him, Katie, I do. And I need a job, an' he works me real hard, but he's square—"

"But how could you *humiliate* me this way?" Katie cried. "He's my enemy, and he's probably been laughing at me—everyone in town has been laughing at how my own little brother works for Mike Kelly—"

"He's not your enemy," Heck shot back stoutly. "He was jus' talking about you a little while ago, saying how he hoped you'd make it, an' how you'd have lots of business if the guys all didn't feel like they had to wipe their shoes before they come in—"

"What are you talking about!" Katie snapped. "How *dare* you quote that awful man to me!"

"I'm just tellin' you what he said, sis. He *likes* you. I think he feels bad you're doin' so bad. He said you was a real lady and nobody should say bad about you, but he said you're so persnickety around here, none of the men will come in because they're afraid they can't have muddy boots or smoke or cuss or anything—"

"I won't listen to any more!" Katie choked. "You just get to that kitchen, young man! And you're finished working for Mike Kelly as of this instant!"

Heck stared at her, his mouth turning down. "No ma'am, I ain't," he said finally.

Katie was jerked out of her frustrated anger by this surprising response. "What did you say?"

Heck shook his head. "I said I'll help you here. That's what I need to do. I want to do that. But I *ain't* gonna quit working for Mike."

"*I* say you are," Katie snapped.

"Then I guess you're gonna haf to chain me," Heck said softly.

"Are you really defying me this way?" she asked unbelievingly.

"I don't want to, sis."

"Then do—"

"Huh-uh. I'm sorry. But I got rights too. He's a nice guy, sis. He's not mad at you, even after all you've done to him. And he's *right* about this place." Heck gestured at the walls. "Guys in this town are rough and tough! They don't *know how* to appreciate a place like this! But you just sit here, expecting them to change, instead of changing your own self to meet them halfway!"

"That will be quite enough," Katie said coolly.

Heck looked at her for a moment, then turned and walked to the kitchen. He turned back at the door. "But I'm working for Mike," he said gently.

Katie put her face in her hands. It was the ultimate mortification. And now, on top of that, Heck was disobeying her. And she knew, somehow, that this was no idle disagreement; he was becoming a young man. There were points beyond which he would not be pushed, now. He would have his way and there was nothing whatsoever she could do about it.

She might be at a point, she thought, where she couldn't do anything about any of her problems. A phrase crossed her mind from a poem somewhere. She loved poetry. It gave her the words for where she was now—in a slough of despond.

Tremblingly straightening the tablecloth at the table where she had been sitting, she got to her feet. She went to the front door . . . the empty front door. She was crying again, which she had been doing a lot of, and felt very sorry for herself.

Outside, in the evening gloom, a group of men were standing along the far sidewalk. A young black man, wearing bright yellow trousers and red suspenders, was walking along, picking a battered banjo. His grin seemed to shine in the dark. The men clapped their hands appreciatively, keeping time.

Katie sighed. Mike Kelly was a beast, but he was *right*. The men of Salvation only understand *awful* things—darkie music and girls who showed their legs and loud singing and everything else that was rude and uncouth.

But then a sudden thought struck her like a thunderbolt.

It was so simple and so obvious that she was stunned.

She considered it—rejected it—grabbed at it again.

It was ridiculous!

She asked herself: *Are you going to quit—or fight?*

100

The very thought of a different kind of fight—with some odds on *her* side, for a change—made her skin heat. Mike Kelly might have all sorts of advantages, but my God! there was one advantage *she* had—and she hadn't been using it!

Fired by the ideas that were coming now, she turned and looked at the cafe, its quiet cleanliness—its purity. It was just perfect, and it was taking her to bankruptcy.

Across the street, the banjo player was strolling on.

Katie took a deep breath and made up her mind.

She ran out of the cafe and across the street, startling the men watching. She caught the black man by the arm. He was young and looked anxious as he faced her.

"Didn't mean harm, ma'am," he said.

"Would you like a job?" Katie asked.

"A *job?*" he echoed incredulously.

"Come on," Katie snapped, and started dragging him across the street.

"I don't rightly know, ma'am," the boy—for he was not over sixteen—complained half-heartedly. "I might have me a job sometime soon over to Mister Root's—"

"You've got a job here," Katie said firmly, "now." She pulled him inside the cafe and ran to the little, dusty stage, hauling at the curtain ropes. "I want you to get up there and play like crazy, understand? Fast! Loud!"

With that, before the startled young musician could argue, she reached up to her puffed dress sleeve, grasped the material firmly, and ripped it, tearing it off to bare her arm. She repeated the process with the other sleeve, then, angry with herself for her reluctance, pulled the prim collar loose, too, letting the blouse slip open to the creamy valley of her breasts. She tossed her belt aside so the dress would billow, and hopped up on the stage.

"Do you know 'Hometown Girl'?" she asked.

"Yessum—"

"Play it!"

He started picking. The sound of the banjo filled the room and echoed out into the dark street.

Katie, her face hot, began to sing, "I want a hometown boy, 'cause I'm a hometown girl—"

101

Heck and the kitchen lady appeared in the back door, looking like they had been shot. Katie waved and started singing louder, swinging her arms and moving her hips a little. She had had ballet, hadn't she? She had had singing lessons, hadn't she? And she was a *woman,* wasn't she? Let Mike Kelly match any of *that!*

Wondering if she had lost her mind or just her morality, she felt a little thrill as she saw men's faces at the windows in front. She waved gaily. "Come in!" she called, laughing at their expressions. "Come in, you darlings!"

By nine-thirty, Mike Kelly knew something was going on. Half his tables were empty, and business was getting worse by the minute.

He sidled up to the bar. "What's going on?" he asked Shorty Shelbourne.

"I dunno," Shelbourne muttered worriedly. "But something is."

"I'm going to go check around," Mike decided.

Outside it was warm and still, with a few stars overhead. The usual saloon lights glowed here and there, but the entire street seemed quieter and less active than usual for this time of night. Frowning, Mike wondered again what was going on.

He strolled up to the corner, saw nothing unusual, and cut through to Main Street, heading toward the area where he had previously done business.

When he was more than a half-block away, he heard the banjo and the men's voices.

"What the hell!" he muttered, and hurried.

The street in front of the cafe was crowded with parked horses. There was a *line* of men waiting on the front porch and down the sidewalk. Those lucky enough to be waiting by a window were peering inside, nudging each other, and grinning.

Inside it sounded like the biggest kind of night Mike had ever had there when he owned it.

Unable to believe it, Mike walked up onto the board sidewalk, went by the line of men, and peered in over the shoulders of those waiting in the doorway.

The place was packed. The air was so dense with cigar smoke that it was difficult to see to the far wall. At every table, every chair was filled. Mike saw Heck and at least four women rushing around with platters and cups and trays of food.

And up on the stage—*up on the stage,* Mike spotted Katie.

He almost dropped with shock.

She had the Negro banjo player, and he was grinning and whanging the banjo like a madman, and Katie, her hair streaming wanton and loose, her collar open, her arms bare—her *skirt* off and she in her pantaloons, showing a tantalizing flash of leg—was singing and dancing. She moved—dipped—swirled her shoulders—*kicked!*

The kick was too much. The kick was something Mike had no way to handle emotionally or intellectually. His mouth fell open and he stared. Maybe it *wasn't* Katie.

But it was—it was, and she looked beautiful, was laughing and having a *hell* of a time, obviously, and the men were roaring such approval that nobody could possibly be hearing much of whatever it was she was singing.

Mike closed his eyes. He couldn't even start getting it together in his mind. Katie? *Katie?* He opened his eyes again.

Katie.

"Don't shove, buddy," one of the men in the doorway growled.

"Sorry," Mike managed.

Inside, the banjo player hit a batch of fast chords, Katie held her bare arms high, and the song ended. The crowd roared, men applauded, stomped their feet and banged each other on the back, nodding their pleasure.

Katie held her hands out for quiet, and within seconds the room got so still that even Mike heard her voice when she spoke.

"Thanks, boys," she laughed. "I'm going to take a little rest now—"

They groaned.

"Just a few minutes," she promised, her eyes sparkling, "and then I'll be back, you darlings!"

They cheered as she hopped down off the stage. Several of them tried to grab her as she flipped between tables on her way toward the kitchen, but she laughingly got away and went out of sight.

Mike started to push inside.

The man in front of him turned. "You try to dish in in front of me, buddy, and I'll bash your mouth in!"

103

"Okay," Mike snapped, and turned away.

He went down the sidewalk to the alley, around the side of the building, into the rear alley, and through the familiar dark to the rear entrance to the kitchen area. The door stood open and he walked in.

Four old men were running around like maniacs, two cooking, one dishing, and one washing plates and silverware. Heck was just going out the front door with a laden tray of steaming food. Katie stood at the side counter, her face and arms filmy with perspiration and her color high as she scribbled furiously at a list.

"We're going to be out of everything," she said to no one in particular. "It's going to take a wagonload in the morning—" She looked up, saw Mike, and stopped cold.

Mike, his pipe jammed between his teeth, glowered at her.

Katie, surprising him again, put her hands on her hips in a pose that he could only interpret as downright saucy. "Well, Mister Kelly!" she flipped. "You didn't have to come to the back door!"

"About the only way I could get in," Mike growled, walking across to her side.

"And what brings you around?"

The closeness of her—the bare arms, open throatline and those pantaloons—drove Mike over the edge. "What the hell do you think you're doing?"

"What do you mean, what am I doing?" Katie fired back. "It's obvious, isn't it? I'm having a good time!"

Mike winced. "You're not having a good time. This isn't your kind of a deal. Look at you—half bare, jumping around, making a fool of yourself—"

"I'm not jumping, Mister Kelly. I'm dancing. And I'd hardly call it making a fool of myself. What I'm making of myself is *rich*."

"It's indecent," Mike blurted.

Katie's eyes widened. "Oh, *my!* Look who's talking about decency, now! Don't tell *me* about decency, sir! I'm simply making sure my customers enjoy themselves, and you can see it's working. That's the real issue, isn't it! I've got a lot of your customers out there—"

"You know danged well that's not it!" Mike flared, grabbing her arm, which even in his anger he distantly knew was silken soft and warm, and did things to him inside. "You aren't *like* this, Katie.

104

And you could get yourself in a bad fix, those are rough dudes out there—"

Katie pulled away sharply. "You're the only one who's gotten free with his hands so far, Mister Kelly! I'll thank you to keep them to yourself."

"Listen to *reason*," Mike groaned. "You're a *lady*. You—"

"Precisely," Katie clipped. "And if a lady wants to dance and sing and call her customers darlings—and if it works—it's her business. Now I'll thank you to leave. We're awfully busy here."

"You're disgracing yourself," Mike argued.

"I'm having the time of my life," Katie shot back. "Now *go!*"

"You won't—listen to reason?"

She stamped her foot. *"Go!"*

"Katie—!"

"Do I have to scream for help?"

Mike stared at her, wanting to hit her. Or kiss her. Or something. God, he didn't know *what,* he was all mixed up, he had never seen her like this, but one thing was the same: she was still like a seven-ton chunk of ice, ice now encased in fire, and he couldn't budge her an inch. He couldn't get through at all.

His shoulders slumped.

"Okay, Katie," he said thickly.

She held his eyes, hers blazing.

Mike turned and walked out of the kitchen.

Walking slowly around in the dark, past his as yet unmoved still house and to the side alley, he returned to the street. The line in front was almost as long as before. Word was spreading. Not that much happened in Salvation these days; Katie Blanscombe was the most exciting thing that had happened since the old brewery had burned down.

Mike started back toward his own place.

It was incredible. He couldn't figure it out, couldn't come to terms with it. *Katie!* Acting like that! He was horrified and shocked and disgusted and so sexually stirred up he didn't know what to do, all at once. Did she live just to mess up his life?

Back at his own place, he found about a dozen customers sitting around morosely, getting drunk. One of them stone sober was Ray Root, surprisingly standing at the bar.

Mike walked over.

"You saw it?" Ray Root asked.

"I did," Mike said, and signaled for a beer.

"What do you think?"

"I think," Mike said wearily, "that we just got into a whole new game. I think it's real big trouble."

TWELVE

Ray Root was up well before dawn. As a matter of fact, he had never been to bed.

Sitting in the dark in his deserted saloon, he dropped the stub of his cheroot to the floor and ground it under his heel. He was so tired he could hardly see straight by now, but the desperation was as high and keen in his bloodstream as it had been all night.

He had spent the night thinking.

Katie Blanscombe, he knew now, was not the blessing she had promised to be. Far from it. His business last night had hit an all-time low. He had figured she would take a little of Mike Kelly's trade, and so muddy the waters that only the smaller places, like this one, would really profit. Then when she was foundering, Ray Root had figured he would eventually get to buy the buildings she was in, and open a first-class joint of his own.

Last night's new developments had shot that hope out the window.

Now it was clear that he had to do something, or he was going right down the pipe.

He was willing, at this point, to do anything short of murder, which wasn't morally repugnant to him but unfortunately seldom worked. The problem was that he couldn't come up with a decent plan.

He had to find one or he was ruined.

While he was sitting there in the dark, a side door opened. His early cleanup man, an old war veteran named Billy Jack Simpson, shuffled in, put his buckets and mops against the wall, and went to the bar to light lanterns to work by. He had lighted three when he turned and spotted Ray Root. He nearly jumped out of his skin.

"Beggin' your pardon, Mister Root, sir," the old man stammered, his toothless jaws working. "Didn't know anybody was in here this early."

"Okay, Billy Jack," Root muttered. "Go about your business."

The old man looked around. "Hey, they kept it purty clean las' night." He was pleased.

"They did at that," Ray Root snarled.

"New liquor shipment come in yet?" Billy Jack asked as he began mopping.

"Not yet." Not that it would matter much, unless something was done.

"Guess Mike Kelly feels lucky," the old man panted as he mopped, "havin' that still house out ahint where he usta have his biness. I walked by there yestiday an' it's real fragrant . . . *real* fragrant. Must be cookin' off the second or third time, just about ready."

Ray Root cocked a leg over the corner of the table and bit the end off another cheroot. "If he ever has enough customers to use it again."

The old man evidently didn't hear. "Guess he'll haf to drain it off purty quick now. Exhaust valve must be plumb open, the way it smelt. Git dangerous if the weather turns hot an' it cooks much longer in there."

Ray Root lighted the cheroot. He wished the old man had been late this morning. It was a shade early for this kind of time-wasting talk. Maybe if he kept quiet, the old man would shut up.

"I worked in a distillery back in Bourbon County a hunnert years ago, seems like," Billy Jack Simpson rattled on as he worked, splashing water everywhere and doing more harm than good. "Sure gits touchy when you run 'er through second or third time that way."

Root continued to try to ignore the wheezing voice. He had to find a way to *stop* Katie Blanscombe now, he thought for the hundredth time. He had to get her out of business. Then, if he could get the buildings, Mike Kelly's business was disrupted slightly and there would be a chance. But how to get Katie out of it?

"Seen a big rig back there in Bourbon County onct," the old man droned on, "got too tight, too hot. Figger the valves stuck somehow. Blew sky high. It was some dinger, I can tell you."

In Ray Root's mind, his goal and the old man's irritating talk began to get all mixed up with the fatigue. Had to get her out of there . . . valves and cookers . . . blew sky high—

The old man began to hum an old war song.

Ray Root dropped his cheroot as the idea dawned on him.

Sweat burst out on his forehead.

Crazy! Too dangerous! No time to get somebody else to do it, but he couldn't trust anybody else anyway!

Springing out of the chair, he strode to the window and looked out. The street lay waxen gray in the first pearl light of false dawn.

In another thirty minutes it would be too late for cover of darkness, at least for today. People would be up.

But nobody was up now, nobody was around, the alleys would be empty. He could go out the back door—

He shrank from it. What if it went wrong? What if he got caught? What if—What if he didn't do it, though—how long did he have to stay in business otherwise?

When you did something, Ray Root told himself, you just up and did it. Delaying helped nobody . . . and there was always the chance that even this morning Mike Kelly would go to the old place and disconnect the apparatus. That would end that.

The very thought chilled Ray Root to the bone, and decided him.

Stubbing his fresh cheroot in a bucket, he yawned loudly and started for the door. "Going to bed, old man," he called back, as a cover. Did his voice shake?

Billy Jack Simpson nodded and hummed his song and mopped on.

Katie awoke a little after daylight, turned over, moaned because she hurt in places she hadn't even known she possessed, and sat up in bed. Some more parts of her anatomy sent in distress signals. She got to her feet and wondered if she was going to be able to stay there. She laughed painfully. She had never had proper sympathy for professional dancers.

Slipping on her robe at the cost of some new aches, she walked down the empty hotel corridor, rubbing her back. She tapped on Heck's door. "Rise and shine!"

"Aw!" Heck groaned inside.

Katie laughed again. "School! And we have lots to do later, after you've helped that *other* businessman try to make ends meet!"

"Okay, okay," Heck grumbled, and she heard his feet hit the floor.

She washed and dressed quickly, noting through the window that it was already a cloudless, warm day. It would be hot by afternoon, she thought. She would make a huge vat of tea for lunch, and send over to the ice plant for enough ice to make it painfully cold in every glass.

It was a far cry from other mornings she had known here, she realized as she went downstairs. For one thing, she hurt all over, and was *tired* instead of just disgusted and beaten. For another, she felt wonderful.

A third difference confronted her when she walked into the cafe.

The curtains were crooked at all the windows, the tables had been moved around in helter-skelter disorder, a chair had been broken, the serving counter was piled three feet high with dirty dishes of all kinds, and the floor—her beautiful floor—looked like a herd of muddy elephants had marched across it. There was mud on the floor, and also cigar butts, cigarette shreds, pipe tobacco ashes, chunks of spilled food, dirty napkins, dropped silverware and empty tobacco sacks and miscellaneous trash. The room reeked of smoke and sweat and stale food.

To Katie, it was the most beautiful sight she had ever seen.

Humming one of the old songs they had made her sing six times last night, she waltzed to the counter, winked at the mountain of dirty dishes, and went on into the kitchen. She unlocked the lower cabinet and took out the cigar box and the coffee can. Both were stuffed with money—paper money, silver, gold, all denominations. In the chaos, some customers had been short-changed and others had probably gotten too much in return. Toward the end, it had almost gotten completely out of hand as everyone was dog-tired, and the men kept stomping in and filling the tables, grinning docilely for their food and entertainment.

But it didn't matter, Katie thought happily. She had to find more help today, she had to clean, she had to shop, she had to get all these empty boxes and bags out of here and burn them in the alley, and she had to run to the bank—amazing fact!—and deposit much of this money.

She had a mess on her hands, but she also had taken in more than two hundred dollars.

Putting the money back in the cabinet and locking it there for the time being, she tied up her hair and looked around. Where to start? She had to go find more help—lots of it—but it was too early for that because most people were still asleep and Salvation was quiet. She decided to clear a path through the disarray of the kitchen, anyway.

Hauling empty boxes and containers into the alley, she began tossing them into a pile for a bonfire, remembering to keep the fire well away from Mike Kelly's still apparatus shed. Glancing at the shed, she reminded herself that she simply had to ask Mike to move it within the next few days. The fumes were a constant irritant to her, reminding her of him.

But at least this morning, for some reason, the fumes were not nearly as strong as they had been other days. That was nice.

Poor Mike, she thought as she piled trash and made repeated trips out with more. He had looked so *funny* last night! And she had put him in his place, all right. She could think of the scene with something like fondness now, which was odd. But maybe it was because she felt so wonderful about the entire world this morning.

Nothing could stop her now, she thought, and the world was a marvelous, bright, happy place. She had enjoyed dancing and singing and being a little—well—naughty once her first fear got over. That had surprised her. But she wasn't going to think about it too much. She told herself she had been much too serious much of her life, and now she was going to have a fine time.

Going back in to fix Heck's breakfast, she felt like singing, and even though she was slightly hoarse from all her singing last night—which gave her voice a little sultry quality that she secretly rather liked—she went right ahead and sang anyway, banging pots and pans in counterpoint.

Heck came into the kitchen a few minutes later, eyes puffy from sleep, grouchy as he always was first thing in the morning.

"What's all the racket?" he complained.

"That's your sister singing," Katie laughed.

"Do you *have* to?"

"I do," she replied flippantly, "because I'm happy!" And she planted a kiss on his forehead.

110

Status report on the still (7 A.M.):
Contents: 194 gallons
Analysis: 137 proof (second run)
Temperature: 80 degrees and rising
Pressure inside kettle: 26 psi and building
Apparatus pressure rating: 40 psi
Pressure release valve: fully closed

At eight o'clock, Mike Kelly was in his saloon, raging.

Shorty Shelbourne told him cautiously, "It's just a fad, Mike. She'll have business a few days, and then everybody'll come back."

"We're fighting back," Mike seethed. "We'll have to improve everything. We can't count on her losing the customers she started last night."

"It's just a fad, I tell you," Shorty Shelbourne repeated, mopping the bar. "Hell, her food ain't even that great. It's good, but not—"

"*What?*" Mike, who had started to calm down a little, whirled on his bartender.

"I mean," Shorty Shelbourne said, realizing his mistake, "it's not like she was *established* in Salvation, and—"

"When," Mike asked bitterly, "did *you* go over there last night?"

"Well," Shorty Shelbourne muttered defensively, "I got a supper hour, you know, and a man's gotta *eat,* I mean—"

Mike slammed a fist on the bar. "That does it!"

"Where you going?" Shorty Shelbourne called after him.

Mike whirled back on him. "Get a new sign painted and put it on that guy today. 'Second drink on the house at Mike Kelly's, new entertainment nightly.'"

"What are we gonna—"

"Just do it!" Mike bawled, and charged for the upstairs.

Up there it was quiet as a tomb. Still raging, Mike went to Ruby's room door and tapped softly. In a moment Ruby, her face doughy from sleep, cracked the door and peered out at him.

"It's the middle of the night!" she complained.

"Ruby," Mike snapped, "I want to know if any of the girls can sing."

"Sing?" Ruby echoed, dazed. "How should *I* know?"

"I want a show tonight," Mike told her. "I want one of the girls

111

to sing. We'll build a stage right away. I want one of the others to do some kind of a dance. Then—"

"Do they take their clothes off?" Ruby asked.

"No. Well, not a lot of them."

"If they don't take their clothes off, I don't know how good anybody will think their dancing is."

"*Make* them good," Mike rapped. "Get them up. Find out who can sing and who can dance."

"*Now?*" Ruby looked startled.

"Now," Mike replied. "And start rehearsing whoever you pick."

"I can't make a girl a good singer or dancer just like that!"

"You don't have to do it just like that," Mike retorted. "You've got all day."

Ruby's face set. "Don't you think you're getting in a little too much of a panic over a little cafe down the street?"

Mike pointed his finger at her. "Ruby, you run your business and I'll run mine, okay?"

"Okay," she said dubiously, "but it won't work."

"Get them up," Mike ordered. "Make them sing and make them dance. Start rehearsing them. I'll pay them extra if they bring a crowd in tonight. Tell them I'll make big stars of the winners. Tell them whatever you have to, to get them trying. I'll be back after while, and I expect to see the winners practicing on that stage then."

"You're crazy," Ruby said heavily. "You've gone crazy."

Ignoring her, Mike charged down the stairs and outside.

The street was not very crowded yet, and the sky overhead was crystal, with the sun already hot. A slight breeze sifted dust along the street, coming from the south. It would get hotter. Mike churned past the livery barn, the feed store and the deserted old grainery, cutting across the vacant lot at the corner, heading for the newspaper office on Second Street.

He had gotten to sleep by telling himself he would handle it this morning, but he had awakened early, and raging mad. It wasn't bad enough she had to come here and run him out of his property. It wasn't bad enough she had to be cold and hateful and cute. Now she had to be acting like a woman. It was the last straw. She was going to see how the Irish could really fight when they set their minds to it.

The front door of the paper was open, but editor Jenkinsen was in the back, behind the counters, bent over a type form, laboriously shoving pieces of metal into a page that looked too jammed already. He looked up sharply, blinking through his thick glasses, as Mike stormed in.

"I want to buy an ad," Mike announced.

Jenkinsen smiled and wiped his inky hands on a towel. "Fine, fine. Of course you have that six-inch ad this week, Mike. What week were you considering?"

"This week."

"I'm afraid that's impossible," Jenkinsen frowned. "Why would you want an ad when you've already got one? Of course it pays to run more than one ad sometimes . . . if I could just convince some of our merchants here how advertising pays—"

"I don't want the ad I've got," Mike cut in. "I want a big one."

Jenkinsen blinked some more. *"This* week?"

"Now. In today's edition, the one that always comes out on Friday."

"I can't get it in, Mike. The paper's full. I don't have hardly any news in it now, except on page one, and all the other pages are already on the press." He pointed toward the flatbed with the page forms gleaming blue-black on the bed.

"Look," Mike snapped. "Price is no object. I've got to have an ad. A big one."

"Well," Jenkinsen said thoughtfully, "I suppose I *could* sell you page one . . . I've got some news I sure wanted to print, but I guess if it's important to you, and you'll pay the price, the news could wait another week or two, nobody else will print it anyhow—"

"Give me a pencil and paper," Mike said, "and I'll write out what I want it to say."

It took awhile to work out the wording, and then it had to be changed because Jenkinsen was out of one kind of type. By the time they were finished, it was almost ten o'clock. Then Mike went by the general store, listened to some of the men talking about Indian rumors, and didn't get back to his own place of business until about 10:15. He was still all fired up with his competitive plans.

Up on the stage in his saloon, Ruby had three of the girls practicing. She was playing the piano for them. Dolores was singing in a tiny little contralto that Mike couldn't even hear with the room empty, and Jeanette and Elizabeth were dancing with all the grace of camels.

113

They stopped when they spotted Mike, and looked unsure of themselves. Mike managed a taut grin and waved to them.

"Keep it up!" he called. "You're doing fine!"

"Are we doing all right, Mikey?" Dolores called back plaintively.

"Great," Mike said. "Just great!"

He went toward his office, feeling depressed again.

> *Status report on the still* (10:30 A.M.):
> Contents: 194 gallons.
> Analysis: 138 proof (second run)
> Temperature: 88 degrees and rising
> Pressure inside kettle: 35 psi and building
> Apparatus pressure rating: 40 psi
> Pressure release valve: fully closed

Salvation was fully awake by this time, or as fully awake as it ever got. It was morning recess at the school, where people like Heck felt the day had already been sixteen hours long.

"My mom," one of the boys in the circle was saying, "said you couldn't trust anybody no more, with your sister changing her place from what it was to a place for rowdies."

"Yep," Heck said cheerfully. "But we sure did the business last night, boy."

"My mom says she'll never go near the place now."

"How many times had she been there before?" Heck shot back.

"Well, none . . . yet. But she said she *might* of gone, only now she won't."

"I guess that's what my sis did," Heck pointed out. "Traded off all the folks that *might* of come some day for the ones that'd come in right now, money in hand."

"I heard the place was packed," another boy said.

"It was, boy," Heck assured him proudly.

"You gonna change from Mike Kelly's?"

"No!" Heck said. "I'm gonna work both places."

"If they're both busy, you think you can?"

"Sure I can. Why not?"

The older boy shrugged. "Looks like you'd want to choose a side."

Heck thought about it. He was pleased as punch with Katie. He had never guessed she had it in her to act as she had last night. On

114

the other hand, the sneaking suspicion had been growing that maybe his companion's observation was truer than he liked to think. He was *tired* today. Working both places had been easy when Katie had no business and he didn't really have anything to do but play checkers with Mrs. Swanson. More days like yesterday, though, and it would kill him.

He hated the thought of quitting Mike, though. Mike had been awfully good to him. You didn't just quit a friend because your sister needed you. But on the other hand you didn't let your sister down for a friend. It was hard.

"Hsst!" one of the boys hissed. "Look! There he goes again!"

The boys all looked. Along the road, peering toward them, went a young, lean hungry-looking Apache; he wore a combination of white man's and Indian's clothing, Levi's and a Stetson, but moccasins and a blanket-adapted sort of shawl over his bare torso.

The boys watched him stride along, his face turned toward them for a few paces. Then he turned eyes front and walked on up the road and out of sight behind some trees and shrubs.

"I don't like the looks of *him,* boy!"

"You see how he *looked* at us?"

"Aw," Heck grunted, "that's one of the guys that works for Mike. His name is Swooping Hawk. He's okay."

"He was past here yesterday," one of the boys pointed out nervously. *"Twice."*

"He's okay," Heck insisted. "He's asked me some stuff about the school—when we go, when we get out, things like that. He's just interested."

"Why?" one of the boys asked.

Heck shrugged. "Maybe he'd like to learn to read himself, or something."

"When an Apache shows interest in you," the oldest boy murmured, "I think you're smartest if you figger it for a bad sign."

"Baloney," Heck grinned. "He's okay, I tell you. I've talked to him lots. He don't smile and he acts sort of funny sometimes, but he don't mean no harm."

"I hope you're right," one of the boys said fervently.

"Sure I am," Heck chuckled.

For his part, David Swooping Hawk was content for the moment. He was just checking. Having assured himself that the target white boy was in school, as he should be, Swooping Hawk went back down the side street and returned to Mike Kelly's.

Inside, some of the white squaws were on the stage acting very strangely. The sign painter was sweating over a new board to be carried up and down the streets. Alvin Singing Duck was in the back, washing glasses.

"Where have you been?" Alvin asked as Swooping Hawk entered. "Do you think I want to do all your work?"

"I had an errand," Swooping Hawk said with great dignity.

"Then forget it now and get busy," Alvin said irritably. "I have the whole drainboard filled with glasses. Start drying them."

"It is beneath my station in life," Swooping Hawk said.

"Then you will be fired," Alvin told him, "and you'll have to go back to Dead Cow Valley."

Swooping Hawk thought about it. He couldn't leave now, when the portents were nearly concluded and his plan was so near fruition.

"I shall dry the glasses," he said loftily. "But I shall not stoop to putting them away."

At noon, Hugh Corkern, having had no business at his law office all morning, decided to have a beer. The nearest place for one was Ray Root's, so that was where he went.

Only three other men were at the bar when he shambled in, and one of them was Ray Root himself. The gambler looked slightly disheveled and tired, his hair was mussed, his eyes were bloodshot, and he was looking at his watch.

"You look like you had a night of it," Corkern smiled, signaling for a beer.

"Me?" Ray Root said, startled. "Why do you say that? Of course not. You're mistaken. I feel fine. Slept all night, didn't get up until just a little while ago." He closed the cover of his watch and put it back in his pocket.

Hugh Corken shrugged. If a witness in court had protested that vociferously, then according to the correspondence course, you were supposed to bore in, certain he was lying. But this wasn't in court, so he ignored it. "Nice day," he observed.

"What?" Root said, startled again out of a reverie.

"Nice day."

"Oh." Root frowned. "Yes."

116

"Hot."

"Um."

"Going to get hotter, I guess."

"Um."

"Probably hottest day of the year."

Ray Root turned on him. "See here, Corkern, what are you driving at?"

"Driving at?" Corkern said, astonished. "Nothing!"

Root stared hard at him.

Corkern grinned and raised his beer mug. "Cheers."

Root turned his head, as if listening for something. He rubbed his eyes and then he took his watch out again, flipped the gold cover open, and studied the hands.

"Expecting someone?" Corkern asked.

"No!"

"Sorry," Corkern said, stiffening.

"See here," Root offered. "I'm—a little edgy today. Don't know why. I appreciate your patronage. How would you like to have a few hands of low-card?"

Corkern grinned. "I'm awfully broke, Ray."

"We can play for pennies," Root urged. "Come on. We'll sit right down. Just a few hands. Take our mind off our troubles, eh?"

Corkern shrugged and followed Root to a corner table. The gambler broke a new deck of cards and shuffled them up and down, evidently feeling for the factory marks. Corkern dug into his pocket and got out a dollar, all he felt like losing.

"Here we go," Ray Root said with ghastly cheerfulness as the cards leaped like quicksilver from his pale hands.

Corkern sighed and leaned back, not even trying to watch where the cards were coming from. They could be coming from the top of the deck, the bottom, the sleeve, or Root's left ear, and he wasn't nearly quick enough to catch it. It was only a dollar anyway.

On the first hand, after consulting his watch again, Root absently bet four cents, Corkern called, Root dealt, and Corkern won. Corkern also won the next two hands, then Root won two, and then Corkern won nine in a row. Root, checking his watch four more times, lost three more in a row, won two, lost three, won four, lost six, won one and lost three.

117

To his amazement, Corkern won almost four dollars in less than an hour.

"I'd better be getting back to my office," he said finally, unable to believe his good luck.

Ray Root, putting his watch away again, looked at Corkern's money and seemed to realize for the first time that Corkern was winning.

"One more hand?" Root asked. "All or double?"

"I have to get back," Corkern hedged.

"We'll just cut the cards," Root pleaded.

Corkern thought about it. Root was acting very, very odd. A sucker seldom won enough money to be encouraged to stay in the game. Now it seemed that Ray Root had just figured out what had been going on, and he was watching Corkern with bright, greedy eyes that said he badly needed one more chance to cheat and get his four dollars back.

"What do you say?" Root grinned.

Corkern sighed, took out his original dollar, pocketed it, and left the other piled coins on the table.

"One cut?" Root said.

"Fine."

Root shuffled the cards in a bright blur. "Cut," he said, slapping the deck onto the surface.

Corkern cut. He got the jack of diamonds.

Root cut the ace of hearts.

"Amazing!" Root smiled. "My luck finally changed." He raked back his money.

"Have to hurry," Corkern smiled, getting to his feet. "See you later."

"Yes," Root said, but his voice already has an abstracted tone again, and Corkern looked back to see him closing his watch still another time, and frowning into the distance as if *listening* for something.

It was very weird, Corkern thought, wending his way back to the office. Ray Root wasn't like that. What was going on?

At the cafe, meanwhile, Katie had found two old men to help in the kitchen. The front area was roughly cleaned up and the kitchen was humming into shape. The lunch crowd had begun to arrive, many of the same men who had been in the night before, but strangely subdued in the daylight, talking among themselves and smoking as they waited to be served.

"Gonna sing for us today, Katie?" one of them, a grizzled ex-miner, asked as she served them.

"Tonight," she beamed at him. "All right?"

"I'll be here," he promised, winking.

"You'd better be, you old darling!" she flashed, and hurried to the kitchen.

Out in the alley, a seemingly safe distance from the still house, all yesterday's trash blazed in a large bonfire. The light breeze carried the heat waves toward the still house.

> *Status report on the still* (1 P.M.):
> Contents: 194 gallons
> Analysis: 139 proof (second run)
> Temperature: 113 degrees and rising
> Pressure inside kettle: 44 psi and building
> Apparatus pressure rating: 40 psi
> Pressure release valve: fully closed

At the fort, the patrol had returned.

Lieutenant Harley Bumpers, puffing a long black cigar, pacing his office, his hands clasped behind his back. Clouds of smoke gushed around him. He kept his head down and frowned fiercely. He had seen U. S. Grant doing this in pictures.

On the other side of the desk, Sergeant Bobby Biggs stood braced.

"You fear the worst?" Harley Bumpers snapped. "Explain."

"Well, sir," Sergeant Bobby Biggs said stiffly, "it's not easy to explain—"

"Try," Harley Bumpers said curtly.

"Yes, sir." Beads of sweat glistened on Sergeant Bobby Biggs's face. "We proceeded north and west, sir, through Easy Man Pass and then up into the highlands."

"No signs of hostiles there?" Harley Bumpers snapped.

"No, sir."

"All right. I thought not. Continue."

"We camped that night northeast of Baxter Wells—"

119

"Good campsite. Good choice, Sergeant."

"Thank you, sir. We—"

"Hostiles?"

"No, sir."

"Proceed."

"Yes, sir. The second day took us through Mesa Blanco Canyon and into the mountains beyond—"

Lieutenant Harley Bumpers tensed. "Hostiles sighted there?"

"No, sir."

"Oh. All right. Continue."

"As a matter of fact, sir," Sergeant Bobby Biggs burst out, "we had no contact with hostiles at any time on this patrol."

It was a blow. Harley Bumpers had felt *sure* there was activity. He stared hard at Sergeant Bobby Biggs, meanwhile thwacking his own boot with his map pointer. "When you say 'no contact,' you mean no skirmishes. What about signs of hostiles?"

"None, sir," Sergeant Bobby Biggs said.

"I find that hard to believe, Sergeant."

"Yes, sir," Sergeant Bobby Biggs said.

Harley Bumpers turned to the giant local terrain map behind the desk and whacked it so hard with his pointer that two colored pins fell out. "I sent you *here*, Sergeant, and *here*—and up *here*—to reconnoiter hostile strength. I recognize difficulties, we all have these in such situations, to be clear about it, I should point out that an expedition of this nature traditionally involves complexities and situations where things are not what they might seem, because the obvious often appears as otherwise in view of, and using the insights springing from, later events, while these are not often helpful in the immediate present as opposed to the recent past, as any of the classic military histories clearly indicate in classic pattern, notably the Roman campaigns in Gaul."

Sergeant Bobby Biggs's face was sickly with perspiration now, and very pale. "Yes, sir," he said, strangled.

"It's not helpful to be negative," Harley Bumpers snapped. "The positive approach. Positive action at all times. Positive outlook. Positive movement." He paced back and forth, hands clasped behind his back, then whirled on Bobby Biggs. *"No* hostiles?"

"No, sir!" Sergeant Bobby Biggs said sharply. "No *signs,* sir, but I believe that's the most significant finding of all."

Harley Bumpers narrowed his eyes. "What?"

"Well, sir," Sergeant Bobby Biggs gasped, "we know, sir, that there are Apaches in those mountains. There have always been Apaches in those mountains. The whole land used to *belong* to those Apaches, and—"

"It never belonged to them," Harley Bumpers cut in. "That's muddled thinking, Sergeant. This country has always belonged to the United States of America. It was simply here waiting for us to come exercise our God-given right to it. These savages were, as it were, *nature's custodians,* watching over our land until we could get here in due course and take control of it. Have you got that, Sergeant?"

"I hadn't thought of it that way, sir—"

"Think of it that way! It's the only way. It's the army way."

"Yes, sir."

"Now. You started to say something."

"Yes, sir. We didn't see any Apaches, sir. But I believe they're there."

"Why?" Harley Bumpers barked.

"Because we didn't see them, sir."

Harley Bumpers was bitterly disappointed. He was convinced there was something afoot. He had seen more of the Tikoliwani Apaches in Salvation, for one thing, and the reports showed troubles elsewhere. It had been quiet here: too damned quiet.

The phrase had a nice ring to it, so aloud he said, "Things have been too quiet here, Sergeant. Too damned quiet!"

"That's it, sir!" Sergeant Bobby Biggs agreed.

"What?" Harley Bumpers said, baffled again.

"Sir," Sergeant Bobby Biggs said, slapping one hand on his fist and forgetting he was at attention, "we know they're out there . . . somewhere. But we didn't see them. What does that mean? Sir, it means they're hiding from us! And what does *that* mean, sir? Sir, it means they're up to something!"

It took a moment for this logic to sink in. Then, as it became clear, it also became music to Harley Bumpers's ears.

Not that he was looking for trouble. But he had *guessed* something was in the wind, and this theory tended to verify it. Which made him feel good.

Also there was the matter of the official correspondence on his

121

desk. His recommendation for promotion to captain had been turned down. Again. Reason: "Lacks command experience of large military forces."

So if he was ever to be promoted, he had to command more men.

The only way to command more men was to *get* more men.

You got more men in the army by getting yourself under fire.

Now, if Sergeant Bobby Biggs's theory was correct, Harley Bumpers might be about to come under fire from the maneuvering, hidden-out hostile Apaches. If *that* happened, he could urgently request reinforcements . . . and he would command the reinforcements . . . and then after he won the battle and killed all the Indian women and children, et cetera, he would have not only larger command experience, but a great victory to recommend him.

Harley Bumpers could practically feel the heavier braid on his shoulders already.

He began pacing again. "If you're correct in your estimate of their intent, Sergeant—and you may be, you may be—then I believe we are faced with a variety of options dependent upon their course of action, but needless to say, the initiative must be ours at all times, the savages can't stand that, even if we must necessarily sometimes react. In other words, the problem is in anticipating them. Now. We can expect a diversion, I think, of some kind, it's useless to try to imagine what that might be, they're devilishly clever in these matters, but when it comes, it will come and we'll recognize it as such. To look at it more positively, they will certainly strike some-where first in a way that will be confusing to us. But we have to be ready to respond. We have the Tikoliwani band in Dead Cow Valley. An obvious threat to us. The Tikoliwanis must be dispersed and/or neutralized, and that's top priority. Second. An attack is certain to be made upon this post itself, in some form or fashion, but the trick in fighting these people is to attain greater mobility than they themselves have, that's the ticket, you see, because they take maximum advantage of theirs while too often we tend to fight the static fight. Therefore we have to consider that. To put it another way, Sergeant, we have to (a) move on the Tikoliwanis in Dead Cow Valley, (b) maintain alert in the north, (c) set up a situation of mobile tactical unvulnerability around this post, and four, advise higher headquarters without delay, not necessarily in that order."

122

Sergeant Bobby Biggs blinked several times, but looked dumbfounded. He said nothing.

"Dismissed, dismissed!" Lieutenant Harley Bumpers snapped irritably. "Oh! Good work, Sergeant! Good work! Close the door on your way out. Speak to no one about this!"

The sergeant, still dazed, left the office. The door closed behind him.

Lieutenant Harley Bumpers fell upon his charts and manning tables, plotting his strategy to meet the attack he felt *sure*, now, was coming.

> *Status report on the still* (3 P.M.):
> Contents: 194 gallons
> Analysis: 140 proof (second run)
> Temperature: 129 degrees and rising
> Pressure inside kettle: 81 psi and building
> Apparatus pressure rating: 40 psi
> Pressure release valve: fully closed

It was really miraculous that the old rig had lasted as long as it had, but to everything there was some practical limit.

The still reached its practical limit at exactly 3:03 P.M.

It blew.

THIRTEEN

The explosion was violent. The apparatus shattered in several places virtually at the same time. The pressurized alcohol shot in all directions, spraying. Some of it hit the bonfire, ignited, and splattered on the rear wall of the cafe. Two drums of coal oil, standing against the back wall, had loose covers; flaming droplets fell into the coal oil. The two drums exploded with far greater violence than the alcohol had.

No one saw this precise sequence of events, and to everyone it seemed different.

Katie was in the kitchen, helping wash dishes. The first thing she knew, there was a hollow popping sound and then a bright orange flash outside the back door and then a fantastic thunderclap that shot black dust and smoke in a rolling cloud across the alley. Every pot and pan on the wall came down, the rack of dishes tipped and went over, and the back wall of the kitchen collapsed inward. Then Katie found herself on the floor against the inside wall, and the other women in the kitchen were screaming and she had a bright, salty taste in her mouth and thick red fluid on her hands and she was hurt and she smelled smoke and there was fire.

"Out this way!" she cried, scrambling to her feet. She grabbed Mrs. Silvers and pushed her through the doorway into the serving room. "Come on! Out the front way! Hurry!"

There was a great roaring sound in the building. Smoke was getting more dense by the moment. Coughing, Katie found one of the other women and pushed her into the front area, and saw the third one a pale ghost in the smoke as she went through on her own. Katie glanced toward the back door—but there was no back door any more, just a sheet of blinding orange-yellow flame.

Staggering into the serving room to the front, she saw through the thinner smoke that the other three women had run toward the street door. She followed. The four of them burst out onto the front porch.

Men were running from all directions. Several of them skidded to a halt at the steps just as Katie and her helpers got out.

"What happened?" one of the men yelled.

"I don't know," Katie coughed. "Explosion—fire—in back—"

"Godamighty!" another yelped. "Look at that smoke!"

More men were coming on the run. Somewhere an alarm bell clanged.

"You better git clear!" a man yelled, taking Katie by the arm and pulling her into the street.

"You have to stop it," Katie pleaded, dazed. "Put it out—stop it—it's in the back—"

"It ain't just in the back," the man grunted, pulling her across the street.

She let him take her. The street was already chaos: one of the town wells was only a half-block away, and men had appeared from everywhere with buckets, and somebody was pumping like mad, and a bucket brigade was getting organized. Three men ran past Katie and into the alley; they had a long ladder and axes. Somebody ran into the cafe, vanishing into smoke that now billowed from the doorway, but he stumbled right back out again, his arm shielding his face. Katie was separated from the other women, and stood alone, transfixed by her horror. Great clouds of dense black rose up behind the cafe and hotel buildings. Somewhere glass was breaking. She thought she heard a series of smaller explosions.

By now another long line of men was forming to her right, toward the corner where spigots came out of a rock formation built around the only street terminal for the town's skeletal pipe system from the river. The spigots gushed water and men filled buckets, but their line was ragged and had holes in it, and men were running singly with buckets, spilling more than they carried.

There was no order to any of it, Katie saw. The bucket brigade from the well pump was extending down the alley toward the back. The spigot line's men were running and simply throwing the water anywhere they could on the front of the hotel. The smoke was worse overhead, covering the sky.

A farmer drove a covered wagon down the street into the melee. His horse was fighting the reins and men scattered, yelling. From somewhere, Sheriff Pat Paterson came running and waving his arms.

"Get that thing outta here!" Paterson yelled, and kicked the horse in the slats.

The wagon careened on down the street.

Paterson started pointing and yelling orders. So many men were shouting, the roar of the fire was so loud, and so much was going on that nobody seemed to notice him. His hat fell off and he bellowed, red-faced. Katie could hear only the bellow, not the words.

The clanging she had heard earlier was suddenly closer now, and she turned to her left and saw, beyond the chaos of the street nearby, a pair of running black horses hauling a tall, red-painted wagon that looked for all the world like a spinner top with huge handles on the top. The ungainly rig skidded around the

125

far corner, almost tipping, and knocking off two of the men who clung to its sides. The driver laid on the whip and men ahead of it scattered. The clanging came from a bell on the front.

It was a *big* piece of equipment, and as it crashed up the street and started skidding to a halt, Katie saw it was a fire pumper with volunteer firemen clinging to it. Some of the men wore suits, others work clothes, one only long underwear and a red hat. She stepped back involuntarily as dust billowed from the brake-locked wheels and men started tumbling off.

One of the men ran straight at her. She recognized Mike Kelly. His eyes were at pinpoints and his bright hair stood on end. "What happened?" he barked. "How did it start? Where?"

"I don't know," she gasped, overwhelmed by the sheer physical *presence* of him, because she had never seen him quite like this. "In the back—something blew up, and then—"

Mike turned to the pumper, where men had started uncoiling canvas hoses and unbolting ladders off the sides. *"Get some people out back and see what it's like there!"* he bellowed. *"Get a ladder on that roof!"*

Men sprang to obey his orders. Three of them rushed to the front of the hotel with an extension ladder, slammed it against the front, breaking out a window in the process, and began hauling the extension rope.

Mike Kelly ran to the pumper and jerked an ax off a bracket. He rushed to the ladder and jumped on it, starting up with dazzling quickness even as the others were still extending the top section. By some sort of miracle, Katie saw, everything was getting co-ordinated: the bucket line on her left was dousing the one-story buildings beyond the cafe, and men were on the roofs there. The other bucket line extended inside the hotel and buckets were being passed in swiftly if raggedly. Mike, meanwhile, scampered up the ladder and leaped off onto the high roof. Its pitch was sharp, but he went up like a man possessed and disappeared over the top after being silhouetted for a fraction of a second against the ugly, billowing smoke beyond.

Katie leaned against the pillar of the store porch, knowing she couldn't do a thing. She felt sick inside, and powerless. She didn't know how bad it was, but it was very bad, possibly disastrous.

The volunteer firemen had their two hoses uncoiled. Three men

126

on each end of the pumper climbed up onto the bed and unfolded long wooden handles and began pumping them up and down, working as teams against one another. Another fireman threw a long toggle on the side of the unit. Men grabbed the hoses and held them upward. Water sprayed out of the brass nozzles. It looked like pitifully little water against such a fire.

Mike Kelly appeared at the crest of the hotel roof again, came down the slope sliding on his hip with such speed and recklessness that Katie bit her hand, sure he would plunge over the edge. His feet caught in the drainpipe, stopping him. He got to his feet and began chopping frenziedly to enlarge the hole. More chunks flew and shingles flew all over the place.

"Get one of those hoses up here!" Mike roared. *"Bring it up the ladder!"*

The men on one hose shut off the valve, and one of them started up the ladder with the nozzle end. Katie, craning her neck to watch Mike, saw when his ax bit through the roofing to the inside. He pried a board loose and some smoke came out from underneath. He began chopping frenziedly to enlarge the hole. More chunks flew out and sailed into the street, hitting people below. Then the man on the ladder got to the top with the hose, Mike grabbed it and started spraying water all over the roof, and the second man worked at enlarging the hole to the attic below. Smoke gushed out of the roof beneath Mike's feet with every hammer-blow of his companion's ax.

The first sound, like a distant clap of thunder, had made a few kids in the classroom turn their heads toward the windows, but Miss Prigle had put an end to *that* in a hurry with a rap across the knuckles of the boy in the front row and a threat of detention. But within two or three minutes the distant sounds from town were unmistakably exciting, and Heck, like the others, was unbearably curious. Then someone banged on the back door of the school and Miss Prigle hurried to answer it.

A man was standing outside, Heck saw. The man said something to Miss Prigle and she stepped outside, drawing the door shut behind her.

Naturally the class exploded into sound and confusion. Spitballs started flying. Somebody threw an eraser. One of the girls, Milly

127

Stracent, cried out because somebody had stuck her pigtails in an inkwell. Heck started making a monster spitball out of four sheets of writing paper.

The back door slammed, Miss Prigle strode back up the aisle, two of the boys fell down returning to their desks, and eraser dust sifted off the big blotch on the blackboard where the missile had hit after missing its intended target.

For once, Miss Prigle faced them with something like emotion on her face, although it was evident she was fighting to hide it.

"All right, children," she said, her voice quaking just a bit. "The noises you've heard come from town. There's a small fire in a business establishment on Main Street."

Several kids started talking at once.

"Silence!" Miss Prigle's voice whiplashed.

They obeyed excitedly.

"Our standing orders in such circumstances are that the class will remain in the building," Miss Prigle said.

Everybody groaned.

"You could only hinder fire-fighting, or possibly be injured, if you rushed right down there," she explained icily. Then she paused and the tip of her pink tongue touched her lips, which was a shock because nobody had ever figured her for a tongue or other internal apparatus.

"Heck Blanscombe?" she murmured.

Heck jammed the big spit wad into his desk. "Yessum?"

"It appears the disturbance is at your sister's cafe. I'm sure it isn't serious. However—"

"At our place!" Heck cried, on his feet and scattering books on the floor.

"Be careful," Miss Prigle told him. "But you may go to see, since it's your sister's and she may have need of you."

Heck turned, aware of the wide-eyed stares of everybody in the room. But for once he didn't much care. He ran.

He charged directly out the back door, leaving it flapping open, tore across the side yard, jumped the hedge, and ran fast down the side street, his shoes thumping in the warm, deep sand. *Fire,* he thought despairingly, *at our place!*

He crossed the little creek bridge and streaked past the first houses, then cut into the next street, running full out, already out

128

of breath but feeling like he was positively flying. He could see black smoke over the buildings, and could hear all the commotion.

At the corner he saw somebody running the other way—directly toward him. He had just an instant to make out the blue pants and leather sandals and blanket-made shirt and wide-brimmed hat, and then the figure swerved *right* at him, and before he knew what was going on, the figure's arms reached out and swooped around him, knocking him entirely off his feet and then catching him roughly before he could fall.

"Leggo!" Heck yelped, fighting as the strong arms got a better hold. "I gotta go help fight that fire!"

The man turned him, and he looked into the face of Swooping Hawk, the crazy Apache from Mike's place, and Swooping Hawk's face looked like his name, for a change, very cold and excited, with dark eyes blazing.

"What's the idea!" Heck yelled at him, and tried to kick his shins. "Let *go* of me, you big dummy!"

Swooping Hawk's big hand moved sharply, and pain exploded in the right side of Heck's brain, and the last thing he was aware of, as he plunged into black unconsciousness, was very great irritation and surprise.

Katie watched in horrified fascination.

She hadn't moved, and it seemed like hours, but she knew it was only minutes.

The fire was out of control.

On the roof, Mike was still pouring water into the chopped holes, but the smoke obscured him at times now, and every window of the hotel had been broken out by the intense heat within. The frenzied activity on all sides seemed only chaotic, meaningless. Katie stood dazed, her thoughts a jumble.

She didn't know how it had happened, and that seemed terribly important. If she could wrench it into some kind of *sense,* somehow, she could deal with it—come to terms with it.

But she didn't understand, couldn't cope. She remembered the blast and flash in the kitchen, the sudden heat and smoke—but could hardly recall how she had gotten out of the building. It was all mixed up.

The blast had been behind the building; this much she knew.

It had seemed to spurt flame. Had the bonfire done it? But there had been nothing in the bonfire to explode; she knew this because nearly everything in the trash burner had been put in it by her own hands.

Something else, then, had blown up. But what could it have been? *Why* would it have happened?

Watching the flames roar through the building, she was filled with a sense of horror and loss. She was struck, too, by a sense of bitter irony: a day earlier, it might have seemed less a loss, perhaps almost insignificant, because *then* she had been failing. Now she had just begun to see how the cafe could be a success, had gotten up this morning so happy and exuberant and sure of herself again.

The fire looked horrible, but she tried to convince herself that there was a chance part of the place could be saved. With this in mind, she forced herself to try to look at the activity around her with some semblance of rational analysis. *Hang on, hang on,* she told herself. *Watch and hold onto your senses.*

The fire was worsening by the moment. Windows in the hotel were filled with smoke, plumed dense clouds of it. The cafe was gone—flames gushed out of the front windows, driving men back, and they had turned their efforts to the buildings on either side. In the street near Katie's position lay four men being worked over by some of the wives who had appeared; they had been overcome by the smoke and flames. The smoke was everywhere now, dense and choking, and heat, too, seared Katie's face as she stood watching, seeing everything go.

On the roof, two of the men with Mike ran for the ladder and came down so fast they appeared to be falling. Katie heard more shrill screams. Looking toward Mike's position, she cried out herself: bright red tongues of flame now gushed from the roof in a dozen places, all around Mike's tall figure.

"Get down, Mike!" she screamed, but the general din swallowed her voice.

He seemed to ignore everything—the smoke, the fire leaping magically higher all around him with each ticking second. Men on the ground poured a feeble stream of the other hose toward him, but it fell short, vaporing in the fire that now began to leap from second-floor windows. The roar and crackle of the blaze was deafen-

130

ing, and Katie saw a chunk of the front wall give way, and inside was a sizzling inferno of skeletal timbers blazing and falling.

On the roof, Mike Kelly continued fighting it. Watching him, Katie felt a thrill of admiration and fear such as she had never known. It was as if he would not *let* a fire beat him, as if he couldn't imagine it beating him. The roof was half in flames, the blazing building below roared, things were falling down, men were shouting at him, and he stood up there, spraying the hose into the holocaust.

Oh, get down, Katie impored mentally. *Get down! Get away! Don't make me lose everything else and you too!*

Something inside the cafe ruin—she couldn't imagine anything being left—blew up. The front wall fell flat into the street, shooting tons of sparks and fire everywhere. Staggered, she fell back against the front of the store, and was aware for the first time that the firefighters with buckets were now dousing *this* side of the street, and the wall that caught her was soaked with water.

The hotel structure grumbled and seemed to sway.

"Mike!" Katie screamed.

Up on the roof, obscured by smoke and leaping flame, Mike Kelly suddenly made his move. A portion of the roof had simply disappeared, fallen into the blazing ruin below. He tossed the hose clear and it snaked in the air, falling toward the pumper and the men scattering. Then he ran for the edge. The roof started to go completely. He jumped—sailed out through the smoke, vanishing for an instant, and then falling—sickeningly—

He hit the bare dirt street on his feet and rolled head over heels.

He sprawled.

Katie ran.

Several men reached him first. They had him sitting up. His face was blackened by smoke, he had lost most of his eyebrows, his shirt smoked where the men had beaten out a fire in it. But as Katie tore through the men to fall on her knees at his side, his eyes opened—amazingly bright and pale against his dark skin— and he looked up at her.

"Oh, Mike!" she sobbed, throwing her arms around his neck. "Oh, *Mike!*"

"I'm all right," he choked. "I'm okay—"

131

A gigantic cracking sound—then a series of them—tore everyone's attention back to the hotel.

A single dazzling sheet of boiling black-red flame and smoke from top to bottom, it *leaned* on its foundation.

The roof collapsed and disappeared.

Then, with a deep, throaty sigh, the building gave up the ghost. The side walls went first, tumbling inward, and then the front wall caved in, going backward into the blinding brightness of the fire within, and for a split-second the air was filled with fiery debris, and then the rubble hit the ground within the flames, a fireball seemed to burst upward, making a kind of mushroom cloud, and the hotel—like the cafe—was simply—gone.

FOURTEEN

With the fire clearly visible from Fort Forgot, Lieutenant Harley Bumpers was beside himself. He already had the entire fort in an uproar, men running everywhere, horses being saddled and lined up, ammunition being checked out, the battle flag going up the staff. In his office, at attention, stood his adjutant, his four platoon leaders and his two staff officers.

"Men," Harley Bumpers rapped, pacing up and down, "this is it. The savages are making their move against us, and whereas rapid movement, as rapid as tactically possible, I believe almost instantly in this case, as you see from my initial orders. Now." He turned, picked up his pointer, and whacked the map. "We have reason to believe there's hostile activity up here to the north, but that's a day's ride from here, and clearly the pressing danger is to our south, where we know the location of hostiles—*here.*" Wham! The pointer hit the chart in the middle of Dead Cow Valley.

"The Tikoliwanis will move," Harley Bumpers said. "No doubt about it in my mind. Their plan, as I see it, is a classic pincers drive, the Tikoliwanis to delay and then move north, onto Salvation"—he swooped the pointer northward toward the fort—"and the unidentified hostiles to the north coming *this* way"—the pointer swooped south from the top of the wall and toward the fort—"to join an attack by tomorrow night."

Harley Bumpers faced his men, who stood ramrod straight, silent, their eyes bulging slightly over their tight collars. Ah, he thought, they were good men, and now they might all go down in history—they and he—together. *The Bumpers Maneuver,* they would call it in the textbooks in years to come . . .

"Our mission," he resumed, whacking the chart again near the fort, "is to destroy their tactic. The fire in town is obviously tied in with their scheme in some way. Probably they expect us to lend assistance, and be busy with that when their attack comes. Well men—I tell you here and now: we are not helping Salvation! The tactic will not work! We are going to respond with mobility, speed, range, attacking power, surprise and cunning such as those devils have never seen before!

"Here," Harley Bumpers said, lowering his voice, "is the plan. Platoons A, B, and D will leave within the hour under my command. We will swing north, so if observed we will appear to be heading toward the mountains. Once in the canyon we will swing *west,* and then *south,* setting up positions by nightfall *here.*" He punctured the chart with the pointer-tip in three locations, the south, east and north ends of Dead Cow Valley.

"C Platoon and Support Company," he resumed, "will move into the town itself and dig in on the north bank of the river. I am convinced the seeming activity to the north is part of their grand scheme, and that the pincers are to link at the river and then come northward upon the town and hence the fort. But our attack at Dead Cow Valley will eliminate one pincer arm, while the forces at the river will hurl back the other pincer due to the element of surprise. We'll attack in Dead Cow Valley shortly after dark, and, having completed that mission, swing north again to reinforce those troops at the river, perhaps even before the savages can mount that arm of their plan."

He paused, out of breath, and stared at the chart. It stared back. He turned to his key men. They stood at attention.

"Questions?" he barked.

133

"Sir?" said Sergeant Manners, D Platoon.

"Yes, Sergeant?"

"How will we attack in Dead Cow, sir?"

"The same way George Custer did it to Black Kettle on the Washita," Harley Bumpers replied. "Complete surprise. A single sweep through, while they're sleeping or preparing their fiendish plans."

"Sir?"

"Yes, Sergeant?"

"Sir, the Battle of the Washita included killing all the women and children—"

"It happens sometimes," Lieutenant Harley Bumpers scowled. "The greatest single factor in such an operation is surprise, and surprise lends itself to confusion, while it should be clear to everyone that the confusion is more theirs than ours, but I can assure you our intent is not a massacre, Washington is very sensitive about that these days, but the sweep will be at *night,* gentlemen, allow me to remind you of that, and given a hostile situation and the need for quickness, I would say when in doubt, the answer is obvious on a kill-no kill decision."

Sergeant Manner's mustaches drooped. "You mean, sir, we kill the women and children."

"The army, Sergeant," Harley Bumpers shot back, "does not *want* to kill women and children! If the tactics make it necessary, then of course tactics come first, but if those women and children don't want to be killed, then they shouldn't run the risk of being there in the first place!"

"Sir?"

"*Yes,* Sergeant!" Harley Bumpers was losing his temper.

"Dead Cow Valley is where they're *supposed* to be."

"That's *their* problem!" Harley Bumpers roared. "*My* problem is defense of this country!"

Sergeant Manners blinked and fell silent.

"Other questions!" Harley Bumpers barked.

"Yes, sir," Second Lieutenant Swelcher said. He was a youthful, pale man from Virginia, one of the very newest on the post.

"Proceed," Harley Bumpers said, glad to get Sergeant Manners off his back.

"If A, B, and D go to the valley," Lieutenant Swelcher said

slowly, "and C and Support go to the river—who stays here at the post?"

"Good!" Harley Bumpers snapped. "Good analysis! Excellent question! The answer, Lieutenant, is that you are to remain here with one squad."

"Me? With *one* squad?" Lieutenant Swelcher was stunned.

"Housekeeping," Lieutenant Harley Bumpers said briskly. "This post is invulnerable. With anyone at all inside to make sure roof fires are extinguished properly, no attacking force could possibly make an entry. That will be your job, Lieutenant, you'll pick a squad of men, you'll remain here in command in my absence, you'll fire the cannon if you see any evidence of potential difficulty, although I see none whatsoever, the men at the river would hear such a shot and respond accordingly, and inasmuch as my own position by, say, three o'clock tomorrow morning will also approximate the river, with the southern pincer removed, then I see no reason for it."

Lieutenant Swelcher stared unbelievingly, but said nothing.

"Other questions?" Harley Bumpers snapped. He looked at his men.

No one spoke. They stood at attention, their eyes blazed with the effort of looking confident and unworried.

"All right, then!" Harley Bumpers commanded. "Lieutenant, select your squad! Sergeant, sound formation! All troopers, full dress! Form up! Sound the roll! Divide the forces! Corporals report! Sound 'Boots and Saddles'! Check all walls and approaches! Battle flag to the gate! Man the tower! Prepare to mount! Prepare to ride! Dismissed!"

In Salvation, smoke hung low in a gray pall over everything and everyone. The fire fighters had gotten it under control, and only a small band of men inside the store to the east of the ruined hotel were still working at a frenzied pace as they doused a stubborn blaze inside a wall. The street was a tumult, and Katie, numbed still by all of it, stood back from the smoking wreckage with Mike Kelly on one side of her and Hugh Corkern on the other.

"It was so *fast*," she choked.

"It was an explosion," Mike Kelly said. His face was blackened, his eyes white sockets in the smoky fatigue. "There was coal oil

135

back there, and then the still went." He hung his head. "I should have drained the still yesterday."

"It wasn't your fault," Katie said quickly.

"I didn't help any."

"You did all you could."

The pumper had run out of water, and one of the volunteers —the old man clad only in his long handles—clambered up to the seat and clucked at the horses. They tugged the big unit slowly off from the smoking ruins, hauling it across the street and hard against the hitching racks. The old man jumped down and hustled back to where most of the other workers were using buckets now to soak the places in the great pile of charred wood and rubbish that still seeped smoke. Sheriff Pat Paterson kept shooing onlookers away, with the result that there was a large crowd at the end of the block in either direction.

Hugh Corkern awkwardly put an arm around Katie's shoulders. "It doesn't have to be the end, Miss Blanscombe."

Katie felt like laughing bitterly. "Of course it's the end! I have no money left—no credit—nothing!"

"The town pulls together at times like this," Corkern said. "The bank will provide more money. I feel sure of that. An extension on your present note, too, I'm sure. And—"

"Oh, what's the use!" Katie burst out. "I'm beaten!"

"Here now," Mike Kelly growled. "What kind of talk is that?"

"*True* talk," she told him.

"You just got started in good shape," Mike pointed out solemnly. "What he's saying here makes good sense."

Katie started to argue, but then just didn't even feel like the effort. She simply closed her eyelids on the tears and shook her head.

"We're going over to my place," Mike said gruffly. "What you need is a drink."

"I don't drink," Katie said feebly, but let his strong arm propel her down the sidewalk.

"It's time to start," Mike grunted. "You need it."

With Hugh Corkern tagging along, they went around the parked pumper and down the street, the smoke still dense. The crowd at the corner seemed to be boring into Katie with their silent eyes, but

136

they simply gave way without words to let them pass. Mike steered Katie through and into the quieter, less smoky street beyond.

A few shocked bystanders stood along the edges here, and the street dust was soaked in great patches where the pumper unit had spilled part of its load on the way to fight the flames. But with her back turned to what she knew lay behind, Katie could almost have imagined it as a normal day—what little of normalcy she had known in Salvation.

"How did it *start?*" she choked.

"I told you," Mike said huskily. "The still—the coal oil—"

"But they don't just blow up! I have to know *how!*"

Mike's arm around her shoulders tightened slightly. "Does it matter?"

"Yes," Katie whispered. "Oh, yes. It matters a great deal."

"You'll start again, either way," Mike told her.

She stumbled along, allowing him to lead her, and she felt sure he was wrong. She would not come back from *this,* she thought. Not the way she felt now. Everything was lost, all of it. There was no property now, no money, no supplies.

She wondered if she had started the battle with Mike Kelly because she wanted the property—or because she was afraid. She remembered how frightened and upset she had been when the stage brought her and Heck into Salvation—how rude and ugly everything had appeared, and how disappointed she had been in everything. Had she seized upon a struggle with Mike Kelly because it gave her a path to follow, one on which she didn't have to think about where she was, and how silly she had been to come this far alone?

She had been a fool, she thought.

So many ways a fool.

Fighting Mike had been wrong. She had just seen him risk his life trying to save her buildings. Of course, she told herself, he would have done the same for anyone . . . or he might have reacted because he had helped build the hotel and cafe, and thought of it as still partly his.

It was not, however, his property any more. She had seen to that, she told herself bitterly. She had taken it from him and then destroyed it. She had been so smart and so wise and so—so priggish.

137

Priggish: yes. Acidly she told herself she had to face this. She had been so damnably sure that her uncle would never have allowed gambling, drinking, uncouth women in the hotel. But now— as a result of last night's success and the shock of this disaster— she saw that the way her uncle and Mike Kelly had been running the places *might be the only way to survive in this town.* They had been right and she had been wrong, *all* wrong, and now she had let it all be destroyed. For nothing.

"I've been such a fool," she whispered, her voice quaking.

"Don't talk that way," Mike snapped. "It wasn't your fault, and you can rebuild!"

"No."

"It's like Hugh, here, told you: people pull together."

"But I deserved what I got," Katie said, holding tight to the tears trying to get through.

"It was an *accident,* Katie! Stop talking that way, now!"

"Yes, but—but I was wrong all along—"

"We'll have that drink," Mike told her grimly, "and talk about it later."

"All right," she sighed. "But I ought to just face the fact that I'm finished."

"You're *not* finished!"

"I don't understand," Katie said. "You *wanted* me to go out of business. Now I *am* out—and you're being nice!"

Mike kept his face to the front, but his profile revealed a thousand worry-wrinkles all over it. "Nobody likes to win *this* way. I didn't approve of what you were doing, but a man doesn't want to beat a lady by *luck.*"

"Is that what bothers you?" Katie asked shrilly. "Beating me only by luck?"

Mike whirled on her, his haggard face tightening, and they might have had another fight right then and there except for the interruption.

"Miss Blanscombe?" the woman's voice called behind them.

Katie turned to see the school teacher, Miss Prigle, hurrying out of the crowd at the corner.

"Miss Blanscombe," Miss Prigle said sincerely, patting her hand, "I can't *tell* you how sorry I am!"

"Thank you," Katie murmured. "I—"

"I do hope I did the right thing with Heck," Miss Prigle gushed. "After your man, Mister Kelly, came to the school and told me what you had said, I of course kept the other children in the classroom until regular finishing time, but I knew Heck might be able to help in some way, which was why I let him leave immediately—"

"Wait!" Katie said, suddenly getting a horrible icy feeling inside. She turned to Mike. "Your man went to the school?"

"We got the alarm," Mike frowned. "I sent Shorty Shelbourne over there to let Miss Prigle know, so she could keep the kids away—"

"But you let Heck *leave?*" Katie cried, turning back to Miss Prigle.

"Yes," Miss Prigle said, baffled. "I thought it—" She stopped and looked around. "Where *is* the little rascal? Surely he hurried directly to your side!"

Katie stared at Miss Prigle. Then she looked up at Mike. Her stomach had turned to ice.

"I haven't seen him *at all,*" she said softly.

The front gates of the fort stood wide open, and the troops rode out in a long column, two abreast, their guidons at the head. Once outside the gates, the column broke in two, and the larger half moved smartly to the right, heading out across the open field to skirt Salvation on the west. This band of men quickly vanished over the little hilltop, while the other swung to the left, moving out of sight to the east as it entered the brush.

Dust sifted down out of the air in the silence of the nearly deserted fort.

One of Lieutenant Swelcher's eight men slowly plodded the gates closed and dropped the bar into place. The plopping sound of the bar carried sharply, echoing from building to building inside the stockade, emphasizing the heavy silence.

Lieutenant Swelcher stood in the middle of the compound alone.

One of the men walked up smartly and saluted.

"Gates secure, sir!"

"Very well," Lieutenant Swelcher sighed. "One man at the gate. One in each of the four towers, be armed and watch smartly. The other two men will police the grounds, then prepare our rations."

"Yes, sir," the soldier, who was a corporal, said. "What about me, sir?"

"You'll be my orderly," Lieutenant Swelcher said, and then, realizing how bad that sounded for the only noncom left on the post, "and also acting adjutant and designated commander if I should be forced to absent myself from the post."

"Yes, sir!" the corporal said smartly. He was a grizzled old veteran, and looked immensely pleased with his newly assigned status. "Do you have immediate instructions, sir?"

"Yes," Lieutenant Swelcher replied. "Make sure the men are in position and carrying out their duties. When satisfied, report to the headquarters office. I'll be in Lieutenant Bumpers's office."

"*Yes,* sir!" the corporal yelled, and saluted so smartly that he looked like he had a spasm, then turned and rushed off, double-time.

Lieutenant Swelcher sighed again. He turned and walked to the headquarters in the near-perfect silence. Pausing on the porch a moment, he looked back at the settling motes of dust in the compound and the long stain of smoke against the sky over Salvation.

It was, he thought, insane.

He went into Harley Bumpers's office, sat down at Harley Bumpers's desk, rummaged through the drawers, and poured himself a stiff belt of Harley Bumpers's brandy.

There was no hostile activity to the north, Lieutenant Swelcher thought. There was no hostile activity to the south, either. There was no hostile activity anywhere except in Lieutenant Harley Bumpers's imagination. The fire in town, likely as not, was an accident.

But the troops were out—*gone*. And unless Lieutenant Swelcher missed his guess, the larger body of them were on their way to a massacre.

It was good brandy.

Lieutenant Swelcher thought about West Point. He wondered if this was what he had been training for. He remembered how the people back home had made a very great fuss about his being fortunate to get into the Point, being a Virginian, this near the War. They had told him he had an obligation to the entire South, and so forth.

He had worked hard at the Point.

But not for this.

He poured another glass of brandy.

It was *very* good brandy.

There was a tap on the door.

"Enter."

The corporal came in and had another of his saluting fits. "All secure, sir!"

"Sit down, Corporal," Lieutenant Swelcher said. "At ease. Relax. Have a drink."

The corporal grinned nervously as Swelcher poured.

"What's your name, Corporal?"

"Higginbotham, sir."

"Higginbotham, do you believe hostile Indians are in this area?"

"By the lieutenant's leave, sir, the commanding officer gave instructions, and I've been told, sir, the commander's information is usually—"

"Higginbotham."

"Yes, sir?"

"Do you believe there are hostiles about to attack us? Come on!"

Higginbotham frowned. "No, sir, I don't, sir."

"Neither do I," Lieutenant Swelcher sighed. He peered into his brandy snifter and then held it up toward Higginbotham. "To your health."

"But I ought to be *looking* for him!" Katie protested as Mike steered her into his saloon. "We don't know where he is, and—"

"And he might be right here, I told you!" Mike replied gently. "Just sit down at this table a minute while I check around."

Katie, appearing in shock, obeyed as he led her to a table against the side wall and pressed her into the chair. She looked pale, shaky, withdrawn. Mike felt a new pang of sympathy for her. She had taken more than most had to accept already today, and now the problem with Heck.

Still on his feet, Mike looked around his saloon. There were men at only two tables: a trio playing stud poker on the far side, and two waddies drinking beer near the bar. At the bar itself, four men stood separated from one another, nursing their drinks. Mike was surprised to see that many on hand; with the fire out, the town was starting to struggle back toward an uneasy normalcy.

He had been hoping he would find Heck, but the kid was no-

141

where in view. That was bad, he thought. Where could he have gone? It was baffling, and something about it had already made a sour ball of worry form in the pit of Mike's gut.

He gave Katie a faked smile. "Sit tight. I'll check around."

She nodded, wordless.

Walking to the bar, Mike looked for Shorty Shelbourne, but didn't spot him. Bernie was on duty, and came over to Mike, frowning. "You okay, boss? You're covered with smoke and crud—"

"Is the kid here?" Mike asked softly.

"Who?"

"The kid. Heck."

"Naw, I ain't seen him. But Shorty's in the back room, and—"

"Thanks, Bernie." Mike strode back to the table.

Katie raised her eyes to him. The pain made him wince.

"Is he here?" she asked hoarsely.

"Doesn't look like it," Mike said. "But that doesn't mean anything. You know how kids are. He'll turn up."

"Where could he have *gone?*"

"I don't know. Maybe he got mixed up in the crowd. Or he might have figured you were somewhere else, and went off hunting for you." It was a stupid line of reasoning, Mike thought despairingly: weak, without logic, and totally unconvincing.

Katie clearly was unconvinced. She put her face in her hands and bowed her head.

"Aw, look," Mike grunted. "It's going to be all right!"

Katie shook her head mutely.

Mike resisted what was suddenly a potent impulse to reach out to her—touch her hair—try somehow to comfort her. In the aftermath of the fire, his body was going weak on him: his knees shook and every joint ached. The plunge from the roof had jarred him from head to toe.

But that didn't make much difference. What mattered was the great pulse of despairing futility that swept over him as he looked at Katie, seeing her like this.

She had seemed so tough and strong, and it was still numbing to witness her downfall, see her hurt and weak and woman-like in worry and distress. He had almost forgotten that women were like this, Mike Kelly realized. He had lived so long among men, treating the girls who worked for Ruby as remotely as possible, to avoid possible messes and complications. But now he was confronted with a *real* woman, one he had imagined he despised only a few hours ago, and he was flummoxed. He wanted desperately to do something for her, stop the pain, make things all right again. He wanted this so badly that he felt almost truly desperate.

"Heck's going to turn up," he told Katie huskily. "Then you'll tan his bottom for him, and get mad at *me* again, too, and everything will be back to normal around here."

Katie looked up quickly, trying to laugh through the tears. "If that were just true!"

Mike grinned at her and turned at the sound of a door slamming. He saw Shorty Shelbourne come out of the back storage room. Shorty spied him at the same time.

"Mike!" Shorty called. "I got something to tell you—"

"Bring a bottle over," Mike called back. "And glasses."

"No, listen: you better come over—"

"Bring it!" Mike said sharply, and turned back to Katie. "A drink will do both of us some good."

Katie shook her head. "He might have run to the fire—seen it—run inside—"

"Do you think Heck's stupid?" Mike countered.

"No!"

"Well, what makes you think he'd run into a fire, then?"

"If he didn't, where *is* he?"

"He's around," Mike said, as if dismissing her worries.

But the hell of it was, she was *right*. The kid should be here. Shorty brought a bottle. He looked hot and excited. "Mike—"

"You seen Heck?" Mike broke in.

"No, but—"

"Look around for him."

"Mike, I got something to tell you," Shorty said, pouring the drinks.

"Can it wait?"

Shorty met his glance, and Mike saw it couldn't, whatever it was. "It ain't the kid, nothing like that," Shorty added. "But—"

Mike waved him silent and turned to Katie. He held the glass up for her. "Drink this down. It'll burn, but you'll feel better."

She shook her head weakly. "I don't want it—"

"Drink it and I'll be right back!"

143

She nodded and tried to sip the fiery whiskey.

Mike walked quickly to the bar with Shorty, who led him to the back end where no one was around.

"What is it?" Mike bit off. "Did the kid—"

"Naw, I really ain't seen him, Mike, but listen: you know that one Apache swamper we got, Alvin?"

"Yes," Mike grunted, puzzled and unable to make a connection.

"He's in the back room, there," Shorty said. "I got Charlie watching him. He got bashed over the head by somepin really hard, it looks like; he's jus' comin' around. And that other Indian buddy of his—Hawk—he's noplace to be found around here at all!"

"What the hell—?" Mike muttered.

"You wanna talk to ole Alvin?"

Mike hesitated, glancing toward Katie, who was still trying to gag the liquor down. He felt his first responsibility was to her. But his mind was in top gear and he thought he saw the glimmering possibility that Alvin—and the disappearance of his buddy and Heck—might in some insane way be tied together.

"Go sit with Katie," Mike told Shorty. "Be nice, dammit! But don't let her out of your sight. I'll be right back."

"You gonna ask ole Alvin what's going on and what happened to him?" Shorty asked.

"You," Mike snapped, "better believe it."

FIFTEEN

Alvin Singing Duck held the towel to the side of his head and tried to cope with the pain. He had just sat up on the floor, with the white man bartender watching him stoically, and he was badly confused.

The door of the storage room opened and Mike Kelly, his hair on end, came in swiftly. He closed the door behind him and came over to squat beside Alvin.

144

"Alvin, what the hell happened?" Mike muttered. "Lemme see that." He raised the edge of the towel off Alvin's wound and winced as he saw it. "That's going to have to be sewed, man!"

Alvin Singing Duck nodded, which cost him additional pain. He was trying to remember precisely how it had happened and what it meant—and what he had to do about it.

"What happened?" Mike Kelly demanded for the second time.

"I don't know," Alvin Singing Duck lied.

"The hell you don't!" Mike snapped. "Now come on!"

Alvin rocked on his haunches and thought about it. The situation had taken him badly by surprise, and now, unless he missed his guess, David Swooping Hawk had really made a mess of things. Swooping Hawk had to be stopped—somehow—and it was up to him as chief to do it.

The trouble was, he didn't know if he could handle it.

But could he tell Mike Kelly any of it? He was, after all, a white man.

"Now look," Mike Kelly said, a growl in his throat. "Katie's place has been burned down. Her kid brother—you know him, he's the one that worked here, Heck—has disappeared. You've been whapped alongside the head, and your buddy Hawk is missing too. It's not all an accident, buddy. What do you know about it?"

Alvin Singing Duck allowed himself a little groan to make it seem he was still out of it mentally. He had to have time to think, and he half-expected Mike Kelly to do the white man thing and bash him on the *other* side of the head.

But Mike surprised him, as he often had. "Look, Alvin," he said gently. "I know you're hurt. Just tell me what happened. I'll take it from there. Then you can go get yourself sewed up. Whatever the trouble is, you've been good help here, and a good man. I'm not about to let anybody get to you again."

As shaken as he was by Hawk's attack, the words of kindness came as a soft shock to Alvin Singing Duck. He looked up at Mike and felt a genuine pang.

Mike nodded as if he had gotten some signal. "You want to tell me alone? Okay." He turned to the other man. "Go on out front. Close the door behind you."

The bartender nodded and walked out. The door closed, and Alvin was alone in the storage room with Mike.

145

"Now," Mike said encouragingly.

Alvin Singing Duck let out a sigh as he decided there was no way but to tell him—and trust him.

"David Swooping Hawk has wanted war," he said thickly. "He would be chief of the Tikoliwani band, and take our people on the warpath. I have been against this."

Mike Kelly's eyes narrowed and he nodded. "You're making sense. Your people wouldn't have a chance—"

"I knew this," Alvin Singing Duck said. "I asked Wakinokiman, our wise man, for signs. Wakinokiman gave us portents for when our people would again make war on the white man."

"Portents?" Mike muttered.

"A fair woman would carry a chicken," Alvin said wearily. "Blood would become as milk. There would be thunder in a still place. A child as our prisoner would bring us strength."

Mike Kelly frowned deeply. "Doesn't make any sense!"

Alvin allowed himself a thin smile. "I think Wakinokiman saw war would ruin us—wipe us out. He made portents impossible of coming true."

"But now this Hawk is doing it anyway," Mike pointed out.

"The woman you have fought, who had the other place you owned, carried a chicken," Alvin pointed out.

"The cock from the pit," Mike groaned.

"And she painted the hotel white, when it was red—"

"Oh, good lord," Mike groaned again. "That's blood becoming milk—and then the explosion—*hell!*—it was my *still* back there—thunder in a still place—!"

"David Swooping Hawk came to me in the confusion after the explosion," Alvin went on. "He said three portents had come true. He said he was going to make the fourth come true at once—"

"He grabbed Heck, to have the child prisoner!"

"—I saw this," Alvin went on, "and tried to stop him, but he hit me with something."

Mike sank back onto the floor, sitting there with his legs drawn up. His face was blank. "So *now* he's hightailed out there to get your people and start on the warpath!"

Alvin Singing Duck hung his head.

"He's got to be stopped," Mike growled, "and we've got to save Heck."

"It is as you have said it," Alvin agreed.

"The question is—"

The door banged open. Shorty Shelbourne stuck his head inside. "Mike!"

"Not now, Shorty!" Mike snapped.

"Yeah, but listen! Jamie Barnstable was just up by the fort, and he says danged near every trooper in there has rode out someplace! There's only a couple of soldiers left in the whole place!"

Mike Kelly got to his feet. Alvin Singing Duck struggled up, too. How had the soldiers heard of it? Had Hawk made some attack this swiftly? But that was impossible—

"You don't know where they went?" Mike was asking.

"Nobody knows—nobody would say—"

"Stay with Katie," Mike ordered sharply. "I'll be out there in a minute!"

"Should I tell—"

"No!"

Shorty Shelbourne went out again.

Mike turned back to Alvin Singing Duck. "Look. You know where the doc's office is. Get down there and tell him I sent you down to get your scalp sewed up. Tell him you hit it on a box or something. If he gives you any trouble or tries to delay you, come on back here and I'll send Shorty back with you. It shouldn't take more than a few minutes. I'll explain to Katie what's going on, and get somebody to watch after her, and then I'll get a couple horses. You and I have got to get out there to Dead Cow Valley and stop this thing before it gets *completely* out of hand."

"David Swooping Hawk is desperate now," Alvin pointed out. "He will do anything."

"We've got to stop him and we've got to save Heck," Mike Kelly shot back. "*I'll* do anything right now, myself."

Alvin nodded.

"Go," Mike urged. "You can cut out the back way."

Alvin obeyed. He went to the rear door and slipped into the alley. Even here, smoke clung to the air. The late afternoon sun made the sky overhead a color of old bronze.

Alvin started down the alley. He was dizzy and the pain was exquisite, but he was thinking swiftly.

It was not a white man's battle now, he told himself. Mike Kelly

147

was a good man, but if a white man walked into Dead Cow Valley once David Swooping Hawk had returned to tell of the fulfillment of the omens, the white man might die instantly—only serve as the final catalyst to the outbreak.

No, Mike Kelly could not go to Dead Cow Valley.

Which was, Alvin Singing Duck thought, as it should be.

Going back there—and stopping David Swooping Hawk—was *his* job, as chief.

It was very simple and true.

Alvin Singing Duck cut through from the alley to the street. He examined the situation. A few men stood at the far corner, talking about the fire. Four horses stood tied to a rack very near Alvin's position. They looked like good horses—capable of a long run.

As he walked to the horses, Alvin Singing Duck felt another wave of vertigo and nausea. He yearned to do it as Mike Kelly had said— let someone else fight this battle.

But he shook off the desire as best he could, and squinted his eyes hard to get the world back in focus. He was the leader of the Tikoliwanis. It was his struggle, and his alone. If his people were to be saved from fleeing headlong into their own destruction now, and if David Swooping Hawk was to be stopped, it was rightly up to the chief.

Up to him.

Alvin Singing Duck untied the best-looking horse and shinnied up into the unfamiliar saddle. White man's saddle; white man's horse; and the fate of the Tikoliwani resting on the sagging shoulders of a chief who had tried to be as white men, to save his people.

It was not favorable, Alvin Singing Duck thought.

But it was what he had to do.

Picking the shortest, deserted way, he headed the horse out of town, digging in his heels and urging the big bay to a full, shattering gallop.

"Go ahead. Finish drinking it down."

Katie shook her head and pushed the glass back toward Mike Kelly. "I can't. That's enough. Have you found anything about Heck?"

Mike had just come back to the table, his face chalky. Now, as

148

his mouth tightened in response to her question, Katie knew he *had* learned something . . . not good.

"I've got a lead," Mike hedged.

"Tell me," Katie pleaded.

"Well, it isn't much and I think everything will be fine—"

"Mike," Katie said hoarsely, reaching out her hand to grasp his forearm . . . arm with thick, pale masculine hair like fur on it, affecting her somehow even in this moment . . . "Mike," she repeated more firmly, "I'm not a baby. I'm not weak. I've acted weak. I'm not. I've fought you, haven't I? I haven't—collapsed today, have I?"

Mike Kelly met her eyes and flushed. "All right. I think I know where Heck is."

"Tell me."

He told her what Alvin Singing Duck had said.

Katie listened with sinking horror and fear, but something—her own pride, perhaps, or knowledge that she simply *couldn't* break down now—kept her rigidly under control and silent even though her vision faded and became blurry once or twice.

"I've sent him to get stitched," Mike concluded. "When he gets back, we'll go out there. We'll stop them and get Heck back."

"I'm going," Katie said.

"No."

"I'm *going*."

"*No!*"

"But I—"

"You're staying here," Mike told her firmly. "You'd only mess things up. It's going to be dangerous . . . maybe. Or maybe not. I mean—I don't want you to worry. But you're doing what I *say*. You're staying here, and you'd better not tell anybody what's going on. We don't need a panic in Salvation right now, on top of everything else."

Katie thought about it as she stared into his eyes. She saw worry and pain there—but strength, too. She saw she had to do as he said. It was the only way.

"All right," she choked.

Mike's face went slack with surprise. "You *agree?*" he said.

"I know you're right," Katie told him. She was very near going

149

all to pieces, and so her voice was taut with the effort it took to maintain control. "If Heck can be saved, I know you're the one who might do it, Mike. I know that. But oh, God—he might be dead already—!"

"No!" Mike hissed, holding her arms. "Listen to me, Katie. *Listen!* He isn't dead! He isn't going to be! I'm going to go get him out of there!"

Katie stared up at him. He seemed very big and strong and sure, and that was what she needed now, strength—someone to lean on. She was helpless. She knew that. She had never really been helpless before. All she could do was obey, and hope to God that Mike Kelly could handle the crisis. All she could do was stay out of the way.

It was a mighty comedown for the high-and-mighty young woman who had smirked as she signed that wire "K. Blanscombe," she realized.

It was probably what she deserved.

But Heck didn't deserve it. If there was fault, it was all hers. And now she had to rely on Mike, or she would bear the guilt as long as she lived.

She said aloud, "I'll do whatever you say, Mike."

Mike nodded. "I'm going to take you into the other building. Ruby and the girls can watch after you."

Katie recoiled. "I don't want to go in there with them!"

"You said," Mike reminded her gently, "you'd do what I asked."

"Why should I go in there, Mike? I don't understand!"

"Because," he explained, "you have no place else."

She moaned. She had almost forgotten.

"No one is going to hurt you," Mike went on, easing her toward the door. "I guarantee that. I want you where I know you'll be safe. Ruby will watch over you. You can trust Ruby."

"All right," Katie sighed. "Whatever you say—"

Behind them, a voice sang out: "Mike!"

Katie froze, her nervous system jangling.

Mike turned sharply.

Shorty Shelbourne hurried across the room toward them, his face twisted like that of a man with an entirely new set of problems.

"A bunch of sojers is digging in down at the river!" Shorty informed them.

"What *for?*" Mike asked.

150

"How should *I* know?"

"Is it worse?" Katie cried. "Does it mean Heck—"

"I don't know," Mike grunted. "Probably it doesn't have any connection." He frowned, seeming to make some decisions. "Go to the barn, Shorty, and get my horse. Rent one for Alvin. Bring 'em around—"

"Alvin won't need no horse," Shorty cut in.

"Why?" Mike shot back.

"Hell," Shorty Shelbourne said. "He took off on Jerry Smith's horse a couple of minutes ago, and lit out of town. I thought maybe you'd told him he could, but I'll tell you one thing: Jerry is madder'n a hornet about it."

Katie's heart turned over. "What does it *mean,* Mike?"

"Nothing," Mike said, obviously lying. "It's all right—"

"Can you still find Heck? Does this ruin things?"

Mike got hold of himself and propelled her toward the doorway. "I'll get it straightened out," he said darkly. "Come on. I'm taking you to Ruby."

"Has everything just gone *crazy?*" Katie cried.

"Yeah," Mike said. "You might say that. But it's going to be okay. I'll take care of it. Just don't you worry."

Katie almost laughed hysterically. Heck was gone, the Indians were going on the warpath, everything she owned was gone in the fire, the soldiers were digging in, and Mike's own plans were already awry before he had gotten to set them in motion. But he was trying to protect her; he was trying to make her feel it would be all right because he would cope.

Trust me, he was saying.

She wanted to. The very act of trying to trust him—letting him hold her fate in his hands—added to the weakness in her legs. The feeling was very complex, and not entirely unpleasant despite everything. She had, after all, no choice. She was in his hands now, entirely, and if he failed—whatever mad scheme he was going to try—she was lost along with him.

Maneuver, General Robert E. Lee had written, was the secret of good tactics.

Lieutenant Harley Bumpers was a great admirer of General Robert E. Lee.

At the head of his column out west of Salvation about four miles, he reined up and spread the chart across his saddle. He was in the foothills immediately east of Rudder Mountain, and by comparing landmarks with spots on the chart, he saw that he could now cut through the foothills by Doberman Pass, reach the desert floor beyond, swing swiftly southward and cut back through the ravine country to hit Dead Cow Valley from the west, or he could proceed somewhat eastward, through more rough country, and then swing eastward and attack from *that* direction.

From behind in the column where it twisted back into the heavy brush, much of it out of sight, rode Sergeant Manners. Mustaches twitching, he reined up beside Harley Bumpers.

"Instructions, sir?" he snapped, saluting.

Harley Bumpers thought about General Lee.

"We'll proceed southeast," he said crisply.

"Sir, I assumed we would go through the pass—"

"Right," Harley Bumpers said. "But wrong."

"Sir?"

"If we go that way," Harley Bumpers explained, "we'll move through open country. We could be spotted, and if that happened, the element of surprise would be lost, which is the element anyone knows is a necessity on this type operation, whereas the reverse could only become situationally impossible in short order, because as I have often noted in similar combat situations, and you can study this for yourself, Sergeant, in studies of Vicksburg, for example, with the Arkansas Post diversion by McClernand. Now. We'll move ahead and attack from the east when we arrive."

"Sir," Sergeant Manners said slowly, "we'll be into unfamiliar country—rough country—in darkness."

"Precisely," Harley Bumpers said.

Sergeant Manners said nothing.

Harley Bumpers looked ahead, seeing, through a little rent in the trees, the rolling, jagged terrain they would use. It was a darkening chaos of pines, junipers, boulders, gullies, ravines, dense wood, little hills, cliffs and dead-end canyons.

"Excellent for maneuver," he said aloud.

"Sir?" Sergeant Manners said.

"Nothing," Harley Bumpers said.

"Sir, it will be dark in less than two hours."

"Correct," Harley Bumpers said. He raised his arm grandly. *"Forwhaard,"* he bellowed, and swung his arm, *"ho!"*

The sun had tipped behind the hills to the west of Dead Cow Valley by now, and in the early evening twilight Heck sat on the ground near the little campfire, taking it all in and scared half out of his wits.

He wasn't really hurt, although he had a whale of a headache. He had even been conscious when David Swooping Hawk had carted him into the sprawling complex of teepees, dugouts, hide-drying racks, fire pits and barking dogs. His position over the front of the pony, draped in front of Hawk like a sack of grain, hadn't been the best for making observations, but he had realized what a sensation their arrival had caused.

Now he was tied near the fire, and just about all the young men of the tribe stood ringed around the immediate area, muttering excitedly among themselves as Swooping Hawk and three other braves had it out.

Swooping Hawk stood to Heck's left, beyond the small fire. In the twilight, the fire glinted in his eyes, making him look truly crazy as he faced the three others, standing shoulder to shoulder and facing him.

"The portents have come to pass!" Swooping Hawk said exultantly. "This is proven, and here is the child who will give us strength! We must prepare for immediate attack!"

"You say this to us," one of the braves muttered. "But where is Alvin Singing Duck? He is our chieftain and we must hear his wisdom on this matter, for he was against it."

"The omens have come," Swooping Hawk snarled. "What does it matter about Alvin Singing Duck? But I will tell you. One portent not given us by Wakinokiman is that of Alvin Singing Duck. —For he is dead."

The three braves facing Swooping Hawk appeared staggered by the news, and a groan went through the men ringing the campfire.

"Dead!" one of the three gasped.

"I saw it," Swooping Hawk shot back. "He was killed by a white-eyes even as the omens had come to pass. We were leaving together, Alvin Singing Duck and I. A man shot him, seeing that we were in haste. Alvin Singing Duck fell. I knelt beside him. His last words were, 'Tell my people it has come the time. Tell them to make war.'"

The men around the fire grumbled and nudged one another angrily, and Heck felt a distinct chill.

"This is true?" one of the braves said huskily.

"It is as I have told it," Swooping Hawk said somberly.

The brave who seemed the least certain turned slowly toward Heck. "You saw this, boy?" he asked.

"No," Heck choked.

Swooping Hawk said sharply, "You would question my truth?"

The brave ignored him and walked over to squat beside Heck. His face was sober and worried. "You saw Alvin Singing Duck die?"

"No," Heck said. Then he cleared his throat, and his anger came through. "And I dunno if it's true or not, but I'd believe *that* so-and-so about as far as I could throw the London Bridge!"

"*Ai!*" Swooping Hawk cried, and grabbed a knife from his belt. He took a step toward Heck.

"No!" the other brave said, standing between Swooping Hawk and Heck.

"He will *die*," Swooping Hawk grated.

"He is of little consequence now," the brave said quietly, with dignity. "First the issue of war must be decided."

"Alvin Singing Duck told me to lead his people!" Swooping Hawk shouted. "I am ready to lead them into war against the white-eyes! We must move swiftly, tonight!"

Some of the men around the fire grunted agreement, and a few stamped their feet. Others—Heck noticed hopefully—looked decidedly lukewarm about the whole performance.

The brave standing in front of him was one of the lukewarm ones. "Swooping Hawk, you bring us grave news and strong words. The fate of our nation may hang in the balance now. We must hear from our wise man!"

"Wakinokiman?" Swooping Hawk said. "There is no time! We—"

"If we make war," the other brave said, "it will be by the wisdom of Wakinokiman—for was it not he who gave us the portents?"

Swooping Hawk looked strangled. He struggled against his rage. He walked around, kicking at the dirt, brandishing his knife. Heck thought for a sickening instant he would attack him yet.

154

Then Swooping Hawk seemed to get it together again. He turned and faced the three braves beside the fire.

"So be it," he said heavily. "Let us hear from the wise man himself that Alvin Singing Duck is dead, and the time for war is at hand."

David Swooping Hawk shot Heck a glance that would have killed if it could, then held out his arms toward the sky and pronounced:

"Bring Wakinokiman to the tribal fire!"

At the river, Mike Kelly stared incredulously at Lieutenant Slade. The troops had dug in now, their earthworks raw in the fading rays of the sun, and the horses were rope-corralled back near the woods. Farther back, campfires glowed and troops moved around as the night meal was prepared. Mike knew that sentries were posted beyond the temporary camp, keeping everyone from Salvation away from the area; he had gotten there just as the line closed.

"An *exercise?*" Mike repeated. "You're out here for *practice?*"

"Yes, sir," Lieutenant Slade, a dark man with a bushy beard, said guardedly.

"I think you're lying," Mike said.

"I have instructions, Mike," Lieutenant Slade said in a gentler tone.

"There's a kid with the Tikoliwanis," Mike grated. "A white kid. Alvin Singing Duck is trying to save him. I've got a right to know what's going on!"

Lieutenant Slade's face stiffened. "You mean a kid was taken to that Apache camp?"

"That's what we think," Mike snapped. "I'm heading out there now."

"I'll have to swear you to secrecy," Lieutenant Slade said.

"You've got it, you've got it. Now what's going *on?*"

"Lieutenant Bumpers is taking a patrol to Dead Cow Valley. He's planning to attack after nightfall."

Mike took the news like a gunshot in the midsection. "Attack the Tikoliwanis? *Why?*"

The lieutenant shook his head. "Maybe he heard about the kid you spoke of—"

"Impossible."

155

"I don't know then. He talked about hostiles—"

"There'll be hostiles, all right," Mike said bitterly, walking back toward his horse. "My God! If he attacks the Tikoliwanis, he'll slaughter them! Every Indian in this country will go on the warpath again!"

"That's what he plans," Lieutenant Slade said.

"And Heck will be right in the middle of it," Mike said, suddenly seeing that part of it too. "And Alvin!"

"What are you going to do?" Lieutenant Slade asked.

Mike swung into the saddle and touched the saddle boot to make sure his carbine was in it firmly.

"Catch Alvin," he grunted. "And then stop that other idiot's plan. And then get those Tikoliwanis out of that valley before *your* idiot can move on them. *God!*"

Lieutenant Slade frowned under his service cap. "Can I help, Mike?" he asked sincerely.

Mike looked down at him and thought about it.

"Yes," he said finally.

"What?"

"Stay here," Mike told him. "Don't do *anything*. Provide one single spot of sanity in this whole crazy mess!"

Then, before the lieutenant could reply, Mike spurred his horse away.

He splashed across the shallows of the river. It wasn't just Heck's life now, he thought, or even Alvin's. It was the whole Tikoliwani band—and maybe the whole of Salvation.

All riding on him, maybe—a saloon keeper carrying a carbine he hadn't even fired for two and a half years.

Mike wished desperately that it were someone else—someone more competent.

But he was the man.

He spurred the horse south.

Far out ahead of Mike, Alvin Singing Duck clung to the neck of his horse and rode like the devil was after him. He was dizzy and sick and his head was bleeding again, badly. But he kept urging the horse faster.

He was almost there.

156

SIXTEEN

The smoke and pitted glare of the campfire in his old eyes, Wakinokiman squatted in the cooling earth with his people all around him, respectfully silent, waiting.

Wakinokiman reached inside the warm folds of the thin old blanket shrouding his naked body and took out his leather bag of entrails, the tied mouse bones, and his other materials.

He held them in his withered old hands, warming them, muttering the incantations. Nearby, David Swooping Hawk and the others stood tense, watching. Wakinokiman pretended to be unaware of them.

Allowing his hands to spread, he cast the entrails, bones, teeth, pebbles, bits of fur and dried animal flesh into the deep sand between his knees.

He looked down at them.

There had been a time, countless seasons earlier, when these things spoke to Wakinokiman, and spoke truly. He had been much younger then, the whole broad land had belonged to his people, the buffalo had been nearby in abundance, and the people from the sky lived close, and whispered to young braves and maidens in the still perfection of the night.

But that had been very, very long ago. It was all different now. Once Wakinokiman had been able to recite the sacred words and stare at the symbols and feel *knowing* come from some source outside him—or from something within himself; which it was, he knew not, and had often pondered. He had been able to read in the symbols the truths of what had been and what was to be, and this knowing had been his life.

But that had been very, very long ago.

157

Now he hunkered in the dirt, staring only. They had come for him tonight suddenly, finding him in his tent with his new, sixteen-year-old wife, and had brought him here hurriedly.

The symbols in the dirt before him said nothing.

Wakinokiman stared at them.

He knew he had to come up with *something*. It was the second time he had known this, the first being when Swooping Hawk and Alvin Singing Duck had asked for portents of war.

That time, too, Wakinokiman had seen nothing in the symbols. But he had long ago learned that a wise man was often wise for the things he did *not* know, and for his ability to cope with this. So Wakinokiman had given them portents that were impossible of coming true, and in so doing had averted war, which was the course of wisdom.

But now they said the portents *had* come true. They said Alvin Singing Duck was dead. They said it was the time for war.

Wakinokiman took a deep breath and wished he were still in the sweet dark with his young bride's hot-smooth body against him. He needed her warmth. He did not know the course of wisdom here.

But they were waiting. Swooping Hawk was waiting, and he was a very dangerous man. Wakinokiman had to give them some new reading.

What would it be?

He could not tell them to make war. They would be destroyed. He knew this.

But he could not tell them the earlier portents had been false. He would be killed. He knew this, too.

"Well, old man?" Swooping Hawk said impatiently.

Wakinokiman began to ad lib.

"The birds move in the air," he intoned, "as men cannot sail. The fish in the sea has powers denied us. Yet the Tikoliwani shall endure and have control of the birds in the air and the fish of the sea and the rivers."

The crowd muttered approval and stamped their feet.

"The time for change draws nearer," Wakinokiman continued, encouraged but still trying desperately to figure a way out. "Earlier signs have come to pass, and yet nature is not yet ripe. I say to you in riddles. A young chief shall lie dead. A child shall be among strange people. There shall be outrage and a stirring of old blood."

158

He was doing badly. They were waiting for it to get clearer. If he got any clearer, he was in bad trouble. He pretended to stare at the symbols again, and leaned far forward to place his ear against the ground, as if to listen.

Amazing—he *did* hear something.

Through the ground came a reverberation that was unmistakable: the sound of a horse's hoofbeats—and not very far off!

Wakinokiman sat up again, figuring he might have a way out.

"Yet the spirit of the dead young chief is in the land," he intoned. "The spirit shall appear among us very soon, perhaps in a form we know, perhaps in another, and this shall lead to a great parley which could require of the Tikoliwani many moons for its fruition."

David Swooping Hawk cried bitterly, "Singing Duck is dead! Your saying this time is false, Wakinokiman! He cannot return, and we cannot delay! We must ride at once, we must go to war and kill the white men before—"

He stopped, his face suddenly going slack.

Through the night air came the sound of the running horse.

The men circling the fire muttered and nudged one another and turned toward the fast-approaching rattle of the hoofs on hard earth. Someone pointed. The noise grew swiftly—the rider was only a few hundred yards away, coming directly for the fire at a pell-mell pace, and David Swooping Hawk stood transfixed, engraven by the firelight, and the circle around the campfire broke open as the rider thundered into view out of the murky dark.

The rider charged directly through the scrambling men, reining up wildly at the edge of the fire so abruptly that gravel and dirt flew like a little magic cloud of crimson—

And swinging lithely out of the saddle, and running forward—his head and face covered with unmistakable blood—was their very dead young chieftain himself, Alvin Singing Duck.

"It is he!" someone cried.

"It is his spirit, as Wakinokiman has foretold!"

Wakinokiman sighed. Sometimes it paid to have a little luck.

The sun was fully gone now, and stars twinkled in a pitiless black night. The moon would not be up for two hours.

At the head of his column, Lieutenant Harley Bumpers urged his horse through a seemingly endless ocean of sticker bushes. The

159

thorns and thistles tore at his pant legs and occasionally sprung back to whack him on the arms. Great trees stood inky on all sides, and to the right beyond the trees loomed the deeper darkness of a cliff. The path they were following was going steadily downward into even more impenetrable darkness.

Harley Bumpers's horse stopped abruptly, having come upon a deep gash in the earth. Harley Bumpers could not see the bottom, but he heard water trickling down there somewhere. He hesitated a moment.

Sergeant Manners galloped up, accompanied by the sounds of thorns tearing up his pants. "Instructions, sir?"

Harley Bumpers took a deep breath as he looked around. "We will proceed to the west."

"West, sir?" Sergeant Manners gasped. "The cliff—"

"Right!" Harley Bumpers snapped. "Good catch, Sergeant! I meant to say *east*."

Sergeant Manners saluted.

Lieutenant Harley Bumpers turned his horse to the left. He heard the grinding of metal and chunking of leather straps and stamping of hoofbeats and muffled cursing of men being torn up by the stickers behind him. Grasping the reins more firmly, he guided his mount along the ragged, eroded edge of the chasm, then swung more to his left as he spied a great old shattered rock formation directly in his path. At this point he had left the chasm, and felt better. He allowed the pace to pick up slightly, with the result that he was almost swept from the saddle when his horse moved in under the trees.

Catching himself, Lieutenant Harley Bumpers reined up again. He looked around.

He was in a woods.

He couldn't see a thing in any direction.

Out of the inky blackness behind him, Sergeant Manners galloped up again.

"Instructions, sir?" he rapped.

"Just a readjustment of course, Sergeant," Lieutenant Harley Bumpers said crisply.

"Yes, sir."

"We will swing back to the south here—through that opening I think I see in the woods."

160

"Yes, sir."

Harley Bumpers started out again. The horse moved between the trees, dodging them even when a man couldn't see them until it was too late. The column behind was strung out, and Harley Bumpers imagined he could hear them on three sides at once.

It was going well, however, he told himself. *Maneuver:* that was the ticket. No one would be able to outguess his course at this point. Things were going very, very well. He was moving with cunning and complex maneuver. He congratulated himself.

The column moved out of the woods and onto hard rock. They had descended further into the canyon or whatever it was they were following. Lieutenant Harley Bumpers could hear water again. It sounded like it was ahead of him. He turned to the right and was back in sticker bushes again. The cliff over there looked vaguely familiar. Lieutenant Harley Bumpers turned left and then right, maneuvering all the time.

He was hopelessly lost.

The liquor, as little of it as there had been, was so unfamiliar to Katie that she was now just a little dizzy. The feeling wasn't very pleasant; she only had the distant suspicion that she was blocked, somehow, from feeling quite as frightened and tense as she would have under ordinary conditions. She stretched out on the large feather bed in Ruby's ornate bedroom, trying not to look up at herself in the mirrors on the ceiling. Ruby entered without knocking.

"You have a caller," Ruby said, "and ordinarily I wouldn't let him set foot in the place, but maybe you want to see him."

Katie sat up nervously. "Who is it?"

"Ray Root." Ruby's lip curled in disgust.

"Oh, I don't want to see him!"

"Good." Ruby started out.

"Wait," Katie said, relenting. "I suppose I *should*—he's tried to be a friend."

Ruby shrugged. "It's up to you, dearie. I can run him off."

"No," Katie decided. "Can he visit me here?"

"Why not? You want me to come in too?"

"Yes," Katie decided. "Ask him to come in, Ruby, but you stay too. Please."

Ruby nodded and closed the door.

161

Getting off the bed, Katie went to the wall mirror and looked at herself, straightening her dress and arranging her hair. She looked like a ghost, but she didn't care . . . much. Ray Root was among the last persons she wanted to talk with right now, yet she felt she owed him civility if he was going to the trouble of visiting her here.

Oh, Heck, she thought. *Where are you? Oh, Mike!*

The door opened and Ruby came back, bringing Ray Root with her.

Root glanced around, spotted Katie near the window, slicked a hand over the grease on his hair, and came over to her. "My poor dear girl! I've been looking for you since I returned to town a while ago and learned the terrible news!"

Katie deftly avoided his arms, especially the one with the oily hand. "Thank you, Ray. It's good of you to call."

Root sighed heavily and adjusted his elk's tooth. "The least I can do . . . the very least. This is a tragic day for all of us." Then he turned and scowled at Ruby. "You're staying?"

"Yes," Katie said. "I think it would be more . . . proper."

"Of course, of course," Ray Root said. "Tell me, my dear, is there anything at all that I might do to help you?"

"It's a little early to say," Katie smiled wanly. "Right now I'm just worried about Heck—and Mike."

"Yes, yes, naturally," Root agreed. "How did the fire start, my dear? Do you have any idea?"

"No," Katie admitted. "There was an explosion."

"Perhaps," Root sighed, "the still."

"You were out of town when it happened?" Katie asked.

"Yes. I own some land east of here. I rode out to inspect it. I was missing during the entire conflagration."

"You know about Heck?"

Ray Root scowled. "I've been informed, and I will say that I trust and hope that nothing untoward has occurred."

Katie nodded and said nothing. She was trying to be nice, but she wished he would hurry up his expressions of sympathy and leave.

"It's no time for business," Root went on heavily. "But I want you to know, my dear Katie, that those of us who believe in Salvation, and in you, will spare no effort to assist you in getting back on your feet once more." He took her hand and spread it, palm up, in his. "We are already beginning a campaign to raise funds to help

162

you, my dear, and I want you to have this small beginning from me personally."

He pressed something into her hand.

Startled, she looked down.

It was an oily five dollar gold piece.

"There will be more," Ray Root assured her. "Everyone wants to see you back in operation. I speak sincerely."

"Thank you," Katie murmured, wondering what she would buy with five dollars.

"I only wish," Root went on, "that I had been in the vicinity to know of this terrible happening. I know everyone did their utmost, and yet I have this feeling deep within me"—he struck his chest— "that somehow I might have been of assistance, had I just been in town."

"That's awfully nice, Ray," Katie said. "They did all they could."

Ruby, who had been standing off to the side listening carefully, suddenly said, "You must have left town pretty early today, Ray."

"Yes, yes," Root sighed. "Shortly after dawn."

Ruby watched him narrowly, her expression one Katie couldn't read. "And you went directly out of town and just got back a while ago?"

"Yes," Ray Root sighed again.

"Do you know what?" Ruby snapped. "I think you are a damned liar."

Root's head snapped back. "What? I say, Ruby, don't—"

But Ruby, hands on hips, had fire in her eye now. "You know what else I think? I think you just couldn't resist the fun of coming up here and twisting the knife a little, you no-good—"

"Ruby!" Katie gasped. "I don't understand!"

"No," Ruby growled, "I guess you couldn't, honey. But let me tell you about it." She glared at Root again. "You said you left town just about dawn. That's what started me thinking, buster, because I was standing in my back window this morning, and it was full sunup, and *I saw you going down the back alley!*"

"You're mistaken," Ray Root stammered. "I haven't been—"

"It was you," Ruby shot back. "It was *you*. And I'll tell you a couple other things I've been figuring out since I tumbled to *that* lie, buster! Number one, you had something sticking out of your coat pocket that I didn't recognize. But you talking about the still just

163

now helped me put it together. It was *a wrench* sticking out of your coat pocket, wrapped in a newspaper. And you had been on down that alley, and into the next one—messing with Mike's still!"

"Insane!" Ray Root choked.

"Is it?" Ruby retorted.

Root turned to Katie. "My dear, I hope none of this has any effect on your thinking. The woman has obviously made a disastrous mistake!"

But Katie was putting it together too now, and she felt a burst of insight that turned her icy with growing anger. *"Is* it a mistake, Ray?" she asked coldly.

"But of course! I wasn't *near* the alley! I wasn't *near* that still! If I had been, wouldn't you have seen me from where you were working in the—"

Root stopped, and his face tightened as he saw what he had revealed.

"See?" Ruby yelled. "See?"

"I was inspecting my land!" Ray Root choked, back-pedaling for the door. "This is ridiculous! I have witnesses! Why should I blow up the still? I was miles from here—"

"You might have been when it went off!" Ruby bawled. "But all you had to do was close off the valves and make it cook itself!"

"And you wanted the property," Katie chimed in, seeing it through the shock. "When you couldn't buy it—and when you saw I might be able to make a go of it—"

"This is the thanks I get for trying to help!" Ray Root shouted. "I've never been so humiliated! I'm leaving, and I won't try to help you again, my dear!"

"Ray," Katie said, "stop!"

But Ray Root, acting out his outrage, grabbed the door handle.

He was going out of the room—maybe get away—and Katie *saw* now that it was true: he had done it.

"Ray!" she cried. "I said to stop!"

Root flung the door open. Ruby, on the far side of the room, started forward to try to stop him. But she was going to be too late.

Katie grabbed the nearest thing at hand—and threw it.

The nearest thing happened to be a brass figurine of a nude girl carrying a pail of water.

The figurine bounced off the back of Ray Root's head and crashed to the floor.

Ray Root made a little moaning sound and dropped right on top of the figurine.

"My God!" Katie screamed. "I've killed him!"

Ruby, her face grim, stepped over Root and started out the door.

"Where are you going?" Katie choked.

"I'm going to do something I thought I'd never do, dearie," Ruby said thoughtfully. "I'm going out and find me the sheriff."

SEVENTEEN

Trussed up and unable to do more than squirm with excitement, Heck was as bowled over as any of the Indians when Alvin Singing Duck exploded into the war meeting. The way Alvin Singing Duck *looked,* his clothing torn and spattered with blood, his head and face covered with it, his eyes bright sparks in a face graven with pain and determination, he could have convinced anybody he was as much dead as alive.

Heck, however, seeing Alvin stumble and almost fall as he started toward David Swooping Hawk, figured a ghost would have been in better shape. Alvin Singing Duck was alive, all right; the question was, how long would he stay that way?

There was no time for speculation.

The throng around the scene was still muttering and gasping. David Swooping Hawk, his face torn beyond all resemblance to itself by surprise, stood rooted for a second as Alvin Singing Duck held out an arm and pointed at him.

"So you go *this* far to have your war," Alvin Singing Duck cried.

Somebody in the crowd wailed, "It is his spirit! Wakinokiman has forseen it!"

Swooping Hawk crouched, his eyes like coals. "You're too late now. The portents have all come true and we stand ready to make war."

"I am the chief," Alvin Singing Duck snapped back with a force that surprised Heck. "There will be no war."

The brave who had been arguing with Swooping Hawk stared at Alvin Singing Duck; his eyes bulged. "Are you a spirit?" he choked.

Alvin stared at him an instant, then returned his gaze to the crouched Swooping Hawk; but Heck could see that Alvin was puzzled and didn't understand what he had ridden into.

Heck sang out, "The old man said your spirit would come back."

Swooping Hawk whirled and hissed furiously, *"Silence,* little white-eyes!"

His barely controlled fury was so great that Heck shrank back. But Alvin Singing Duck, he saw, was nobody's dummy; Alvin had gotten the picture.

Alvin turned to the brave who had asked if he was a spirit. "If you see a man, Running Deer, then believe me a man. If you see a spirit, then believe it as you see it. I have come back as Wakino-kiman foretold. I have come back to say we cannot make war at this time, or *all* of us will go to the spirit ground."

Wakinokiman, huddled under his blanket on the ground at Heck's right, near Alvin Singing Duck, raised his head. "Heed his words!" the old man called out clearly.

Swooping Hawk, at Heck's left and very close to him, shouted bitterly, "It's a trick! This is no spirit! I was mistaken that he was dead! But he is still weak and cowardly, unfit to lead the Tikoliwani. Our only path is the path I have told for you!"

"No," Alvin Singing Duck said, and as he spoke, he stood straighter, with whatever effort it must have cost him, and Heck got a deep chill at the sudden majesty and force that seemed to radiate from what had been, a moment before, a small man who was badly hurt and ragged.

Alvin pointed toward Swooping Hawk. "There will be no war," he said with the utmost gravity. "You have planned against your own people and your own leader. You will leave the Tikoliwani."

The men around the fire muttered, and the mutter had the sound of approval.

"Don't listen to him!" Swooping Hawk screamed. "He's no spirit!"

166

The Indians grunted and stamped their feet in the dirt, clearly disapproving of Swooping Hawk.

Swooping Hawk read this. His face went livid. With a single furious movement he started forward. Magically there was a long knife in his right hand.

"I'll show you he's no spirit!" he shouted hoarsely. "Spirits cannot die!"

He charged Alvin Singing Duck.

What might have happened otherwise, Heck would never know. But Swooping Hawk virtually leaped over him in his wild burst of frustrated rage, the knife high. Heck saw Alvin Singing Duck start to take a step backward—saw it would be too late—heard the startled outcry.

Heck, doing it on instinct, shot out both his lashed-together legs.

Swooping Hawk crashed over them and plunged headlong into the little council fire. Fiery sticks and embers exploded. Smoke gushed. Swooping Hawk screamed and scrambled back to his feet, madly intent on only one thing, getting Alvin Singing Duck. Swooping Hawk charged again.

Then something smashed into Swooping Hawk's shoulder or arm with a hideous *slapping* noise. Bright red erupted from his arm as he was spun completely around. Instantaneously came the close crack of a gunshot.

Swooping Hawk fell to the ground, writhing. Alvin Singing Duck stood like a statue, face slack with surprise, and only now Heck saw that he, too, had a knife in his hand.

The others had all turned toward the sound of the shot, which had been nearby. Silence dropped totally over everyone for an instant as a lone rider appeared out of the dark, his horse walking. The man was a white man, and looked like a ghost himself, he was so pale. He had a carbine in his hands which still released a little wisp of gray smoke from the muzzle.

Heck had never been so glad to see anybody in his life.

His voice split the silence: *"Mike!"*

Shaky from the nearness of it, Mike Kelly walked his horse into the fire circle. On the ground, Swooping Hawk groaned and looked up at him with eyes that brimmed hate and pain. Mike saw at a glance that the wound was not too bad. He turned his head and saw

167

the Tikoliwani men all around him, their faces impassive, mute. He didn't know if he had saved the day or committed suicide. He saw Heck tied on the ground, but didn't have time to give him so much as an encouraging nod. He looked at Alvin Singing Duck, who stood before him like a vision out of an old battle, bloody, unsteady on his feet, a knife in the right hand that dangled at his side.

But it was not the same old Alvin who swept out for him.

With enormous dignity and care, Alvin Singing Duck walked slowly to the side of Mike's horse and held up his hand, the palm open, in a gesture of friendship.

"Welcome," he said, his voice very quiet, but carrying.

Mike took the cue and swung wearily out of the saddle. He hurt all over. His legs, once they supported his weight, felt like water.

With that, the silence broke. Everyone started yelping, shouting and talking at once.

Alvin Singing Duck held up his arms for quiet, and got it.

"Bind this man," he ordered, pointing to Swooping Hawk. "See to his wounds. Do not harm him."

Several men rushed forward to obey.

Mike, the army on his mind, squeezed Alvin's arm. Leaning close, he whispered urgently, "Get a few scouts out around the valley. Tell them to watch and come hollering if they see anything. I'll explain later."

Alvin Singing Duck gave him a startled look, but briskly snapped the orders. Others were taking Swooping Hawk away, and two men were helping Wakinokiman to his feet. Another had released Heck, who stood pale and scared, rubbing his thong-raw wrists.

"Boy was I glad to see *you!*" Heck gasped. "I never—"

Mike grabbed him with one arm and hugged him close. "Later, son. I've got to talk to Alvin, and right now."

"What is it?" Alvin asked. "I have to talk to men here, make sure they accept me again. Swooping Hawk had friends—"

"And you need medical attention," Mike rapped. "I know that. But we've got to talk some place, and right now. This is a bigger emergency than anything else, Alvin!"

Alvin studied his face a moment, then turned to another Indian standing beside him. "Running Deer, can we use your—"

"Of course," Running Deer said. "Come."

168

Relieved, Mike kept Heck under his arm and followed Alvin toward one of the nearest teepees. It was a big one, and when they went inside, it was gloomy with smoke from a tiny chip fire. Skins lined part of the walls and in the back of the place was movement— two or more women, crouched in piles of skins, watching.

Alvin squatted by the tiny fire. "What is it, Mike?"

"The army," Mike said, "has gone crazy. Harley Bumpers has a bunch of men dug in at the river south of Salvation. He thinks you or somebody else is on the warpath."

Alvin Singing Duck nodded. "He must have heard something of Swooping Hawk's talk—"

"It doesn't matter why," Mike cut in impatiently. "More important than the soldiers at the river, Harley has a big patrol out here somewhere right now—in this area."

Alvin stiffened. "And—?"

"I think he's planning to attack this camp."

"But this is our treaty land! We're *supposed* to be here!"

"The Cheyennes were supposed to be where they were a few years ago, too," Mike said bitterly. "It doesn't mean a damned thing if some fool says he has to make a preventive attack, or whatever they call it. I don't know what's gotten into Harley, but he's *scared,* he must be. He's got these troopers out here somewhere, and as nearly as I can figure out, he's planning a sweep through here some-time tonight."

Alvin's blood-caked face twisted in disbelief. "But I've stopped Swooping Hawk. I can maintain peace."

"Maybe that doesn't have anything to do with it," Mike said, hating the fact that he had to try to understand insanity like the kind he was dealing with. "Maybe poor Harley sat up there in Fort Forgot and read dispatches on trouble elsewhere, and just got sick in the head. Maybe he wants glory. Maybe he wants a promotion. Maybe somebody gave him some bad information. Who knows? It doesn't make any difference *why.* It's crazy, I know that. But you've got to react *right now,* or your people are going to be—wiped out." He had almost said they would be sitting ducks.

Alvin Singing Duck bowed his head. It was quiet. From outside came the voices of men excitedly talking about the things that had already happened.

Running Deer, standing inside the teepee flap, muttered darkly, "The army will never let us have peace. Perhaps, in that, Swooping Hawk was right."

Alvin Singing Duck raised a havoc-ridden face to Mike's. "It is as he has said. I have tried. But if what you say is true, and the army comes, they will find my people ready."

"Oh, now, wait—" Mike began.

"No," Alvin Singing Duck replied with great dignity. "Only this place remains to us, of all the world we once knew. We do not seek war, for I know how it must end. But if the army comes, it will find us ready. We have some weapons. I will tell my people to make preparation, hide the women and children among the rocks—"

"Aw, Alvin!" Heck broke in despairingly. "Why don't you jus' go someplace else an' let 'em have the stupid valley?"

Alvin Singing Duck turned sad, suddenly old eyes to Heck. "There is no place left for us. This valley is the poorest in the land. When there is no worse place for the Tikoliwani, the white man will *kill* the Tikoliwani. That has been said by people like Swooping Hawk. I did not believe it. But now I see that it is true."

Running Deer, still at the doorway, said briskly, "I shall call a tribal council."

Alvin nodded somberly. "I shall tell them of Swooping Hawk's treachery, and of this new teachery by the white man's army. When the army comes"—he took a ragged breath—"the Tikoliwani will be ready."

"*Wait* a minute, Alvin!" Mike groaned, grabbing his arm.

Alvin pulled away gently, but with force, and his eyes were as cold as the night sky. "You have tried to be a friend, Mike. Take the boy. Go. After I speak to my people, it may be too late for you— as it will be too late for us."

"You don't have to fight them!" Mike argued. "You can get everybody to pack up as fast as they can. I can lead all of you back to town. I know how to get everybody around the soldiers at the river. I know exactly where they are, and they'll be half asleep anyway; they know Harley's plan is nuts. We can get into town. I can put up the whole damned tribe inside my saloon and hotel. It'll be crowded, but you can all get in. I've got some grub. You can bed down. *Then* how the hell can Harley say you're on the warpath, when the whole bunch of you are right in town, my guests?"

Alvin Singing Duck smiled sadly. "There is a time when running does no more good."

"Yes, but you can get some time, and Harley will see—"

A sudden burst of voices outside the teepee broke off his words. There was yelling and the stamp of feet and men calling back and forth to each other.

Alvin Singing Duck jumped to his feet and went to the teepee opening. For a second, Mike had the sickening thought that the attack was already in progress and everything was lost.

He went to the opening behind Alvin, and peered out between Alvin and Running Deer. Heck shoved at his legs, trying to see as well.

Three of the Tikoliwani, on foot—evidently some of the scouts Alvin had just sent out—had come excitedly back into the fire area. They had a horse—a cavalry horse—held by three ropes noosed around its head. One of the braves carried a rifle, one a handgun and belts, and the third was brandishing a long cavalry saber.

The former owner of all this equipment sat forlornly in the saddle of the horse, hatless, pale, and encased in a cocoon of ropes that held him prisoner.

Lieutenant Harley Bumpers.

One of the three scouts walked proudly up to the teepee and hurled the saber to the ground at Alvin Singing Duck's feet. "We went west in the valley," he announced with fierce pride, "and there we found this one riding alone. We took him!"

"What the hell?" Mike muttered.

Alvin, as surprised as anyone else, judging by his expression, gestured briefly. "Bring the captive inside."

As the men unroped Harley Bumpers to get him down, Alvin strode back into the teepee. *"There's* your chance for escape!" he spat at Mike. "The army is already here, and the attack is at hand!"

"Wait a minute, Alvin," Mike argued. "I don't know what the hell is going on here, but this is no attack. *You don't send your commanding officer in to get captured as the start of an attack."*

"What would you have me do?" Alvin shot back bitterly. "Give him welcome with food and a celebration?"

Running Deer hissed, "We can *kill* him as a warning of our strength."

171

"Wait and see what's happened!" Mike urged. "That's all I'm asking! Something is screwed up or he wouldn't be here *alone,* don't you see that?"

The commotion was right outside the entry to the teepee, and time for discussion had run out. Alvin Singing Duck lowered his head, deep in thought. Then he looked up. "Your idea?" he asked.

"Let me find out what's going on, that's all," Mike pleaded.

Two of the braves brought Lieutenant Harley Bumpers into the teepee. He still had ropes around his chest and arms. He looked around fearfully, saw Mike.

"Mike!" he gasped. "Am I ever glad to see *you!* I—"

"What are you doing here, Harley?" Mike shot back.

Lieutenant Harley Bumpers hesitated, evidently having a lot of trouble coming to terms with what must have been a long series of shocks. He licked dry lips and shot Alvin Singing Duck a frightened glance. "Well, now, as part of routine maneuvers—"

"Forget that," Mike cut in angrily. "I know and they know *exactly* what you've been up to."

"What I've been—up to?"

"You've got a command out there someplace and you've been setting up an attack."

"Not exactly," Harley Bumpers stammered. "As a matter of fact—"

Heck piped up, "They're thinkin' about cutting off your head, boy! You better tell the truth!"

Harley Bumpers sounded strangled. "My—*head?*"

"An' *eat* it, maybe!" Heck added, as if he were enjoying himself.

"Oh, by *Jove!*" Harley Bumpers choked.

Mike almost enjoyed his obvious anguish, but there was no time to savor it. "So you'd better be straight with these people, Harley."

"Yes," Harley Bumpers managed thickly. "Yes. Well—"

Alvin Singing Duck was unable to contain himself any longer. "Where are your men? What plan is this under way?"

"My men?" Harley Bumpers repeated, dazed by it all. "Yes . . . my men . . . my command . . ." By what appeared as a shuddering effort, he got himself under a semblance of control. "Well," he said more firmly, more like the old Harley, "reports have misled us. Yes. We were given to understand war preparations were being made.

172

Item: hostile signs north. Item: the explosion and fire in town. Item:—"

"You'd better get to the point," Mike warned him.

"I moved my command out," Harley Bumpers said. "The plan was to come south, with adequate maneuver to cover any observation, of course it goes without saying that our intent was not hostile in itself, the army does not initiate action against those at peace, but as a variety of tactical histories inform us—"

"Where are your men?" Mike cut in. "Can you still stop the attack?"

Harley Bumpers looked around at each of the people in the room. "I—I led the command through the deep cover, maneuver is essential, of course, but unfortunately, in times of combat readiness there can be unforeseen quirks in the tactical fluidity of the general operation, and my intent was to bring the command near the valley, you see the wisdom in this, of course—the tactical wisdom, I mean, but in the course of maneuver, sometimes command becomes separated from troops, which is not always a serious situation, that is to say basically impossible. At Antietam, as I recall"—

"Harley," Mike cut in impatiently, "where are your men?"

—"three brigades, without combat officer leadership"—Harley continued, his eyeballs rolling in his head."

"Harley, *where* are your *men?*"

—"could happen to anybody, a good officer leads his troops, and if, because of difficulty with terrain, darkness, other factors—"

"Oh, for God's sake," Mike suddenly burst out, feeling a huge impulse to laugh.

Harley Bumpers, Alvin Singing Duck and the others stared at him.

"I get it," Mike grinned. "I *get* it!"

Harley Bumpers stood mute.

"You got lost," Mike told him. "You got out in front of your patrol, you turned left and they turned right—and you came staggering into the valley, here, trying to find your own column!"

"You oversimplify!" Harley Bumpers cried. "Tactical difficulties may seem ludicrous at times to the civilian, but in the field—"

Suddenly feeling like he wanted to whoop with glee, Mike took Alvin's arm and unceremoniously guided him toward the back of the great teepee.

173

"Is it a trick?" Alvin whispered.

"No," Mike whispered back. "Harley has blown the whole operation. It's beautiful. We have him exactly where we want him. Listen: let me keep going a minute, and I think we're out of this whole mess."

Alvin Singing Duck frowned. "To let them attack another day?"

"No! Listen. Will you let me try this idea?"

Alvin thought about it a moment and nodded.

Mike turned and walked back to the forlorn lieutenant. "Harley, you got lost."

"Tactics provide confusing moments," Harley Bumpers said. "However, ground rules can—"

"Harley," Mike said gently. "You got *lost*. Just admit it, okay?"

Lieutenant Harley Bumpers hung his head.

"And now," Mike said, feeling almost sorry for him, "your whole command is out there someplace, equally lost, thrashing around in the dark."

Lieutenant Harley Bumpers raised pained eyes to him. "I'll be stripped of command. I'm ruined."

"Not necessarily," Mike grinned.

"Not—?"

"You'd better talk seriously with this man, here," Mike told him, nodding toward Alvin Singing Duck. "It can go two ways now. You can be a prisoner and maybe get your head cut off, like Heck said, and the Tikoliwani, who know this terrain like their own hand, can go out in the dark and chop your command into mincemeat. Or you can talk to Alvin, here, and make a deal."

"A—deal?" Harley Bumpers said huskily, the faintest glint of hope in his eyes.

"Everybody makes mistakes," Mike told him. "God knows you made a *serious* one. If I were Alvin, I'd want your head. I'd want to kill all your men and just run crazy. But the army would hear about it and send *ten times* more men down here; it wouldn't be 'Fort Forgot' any more. The cavalry would hunt Alvin's people down and kill every last one of them. Nobody would gain anything."

Mike took a long breath, making sure the argument had time to sink in on Alvin Singing Duck, too.

He resumed heavily, "So maybe everybody stands to gain with a deal. What I suggest is this: you and Alvin talk; come to an understanding; no more army attacks, ever; not on the Tikoliwani; a guarantee in writing, a new treaty; a better deal for these people. And what you get in exchange is this: the story of what happened tonight won't leave this tent; Alvin will get some of his people to take you back out there and get you back with your troops; you'll tell them you wanted to avoid bloodshed, so you sneaked in and attacked the village single-handed, and won a new agreement."

Harley Bumpers protested weakly, "No one would believe I came in here alone. I—"

"But you did," Mike reminded him softly.

"Yes," Harley Bumpers said, startled. "I did, didn't I."

"You wanted to avoid bloodshed if you could," Mike told him, "so you heroically rode in here alone and confronted the Tikoliwani. You and Alvin talked. The parley was good. You had a position of strength, with your troops in the field nearby, but Alvin had strength, too, in being warned. Tit for tat. You reached a new agreement."

Harley Bumpers was trying to absorb it, and some color showed in his cheeks. His eyes darted around. "Yes, I see that—a way to avoid a battle, and bring better peace—"

"The Tikoliwani can lead you back to Fort Forgot," Mike suggested, "and you can file your reports. Nobody knows but us here. You win. Alvin's people win. You maybe even look a little bit like a hero."

Harley Bumpers closed his eyes. "Yes. I see it." He looked at Alvin Singing Duck. "I agree!"

Alvin, for his part, had been listening intent and nodding. But now his eyes were hard. "It is good," he said heavily. "But there truly must be a new treaty."

"Yes, yes!" Harley Bumpers said eagerly.

"It will be written," Alvin said.

"Yes, of course—"

"This valley," Alvin Singing Duck went on, "is a bad place. The new treaty will give us the lands to the east, where there is better water and woodland and wild game."

Harley Bumpers looked stricken. "I can't just give away government land!"

"It is government land," Mike reminded him. "Military commanders have been authorized to make local treaties for approval in Washington; you know that. It will give these Indians a decent place

175

to live, and it will bring permanent peace here. You can do it, Harley!"

"Yes," Harley choked, his face glistening sickly with sweat. "I can—*yes*. I accept."

Alvin Singing Duck nodded solemnly, and then, as Mike saw it, really began to press his luck.

"My people need money," Alvin said. "That means work. There will be a contract which says my people supply meat for the post."

"All right!" Harley Bumpers gasped. "That's fine, I'm awfully sick of beans anyway, and—"

"Reparations," Alvin added.

"Repa . . . ?"

"Two wagons of food for my people," Alvin Singing Duck said. "And one barrel of whiskey. Payable before the end of the week."

"But everyone will *know* I gave in if we give you that."

"You give it voluntarily," Mike suggested gleefully. "As a symbol of the friendship of the new treaty."

Harley Bumpers stared at him as if his heart would break.

"It is good," Alvin Singing Duck said.

Lieutenant Harley Bumpers stood stoop-shouldered, a beaten man. He was trapped and he knew it. Watching him, Mike really did feel sorry for him now . . . a little.

"It will be a great treaty," Mike suggested gently. "It will set a new precedent in the West. It will probably go down in the books as *The Bumpers Agreement.*"

Harley Bumpers looked up sharply. *"The Bumpers—"*

Mike nodded solemnly.

Harley Bumpers took one more deep breath. "I accept."

"All of it?" Alvin Singing Duck asked, as if unable quite to believe it himself.

"Yes," Lieutenant Harley Bumpers sighed.

Mike turned and squeezed Heck's arm. They were home free.

EIGHTEEN

It was late midmorning when Katie finally awoke, lost in the vastness of Ruby's huge feather bed. For a moment she was so groggy that she was disoriented, but then it all flooded back: the way she had helped catch Ray Root, Sheriff Pat Paterson's arrival and taking Root into custody, the hours of tossing hopeless as she tried to sleep despite worry about Mike and Heck—and then the commotion outside, the cavalry marching back through town in tumult in the darkness, her rushing downstairs, seeing Mike—with Heck in his arms—stride into the saloon.

Jumping out of bed, Katie hurriedly washed and dressed, and, after tying her hair up quickly, crept out of the room and down the hall.

She expected everything to be different, somehow.

The saloon was deserted. Shorty Shelbourne was behind the bar, mopping. The front door was closed. No one else was around.

"Morning," Shorty Shelbourne grinned at her.

"Where is everyone?" Katie demanded.

"Still asleep, looks like. You're the first one up."

"What time is it?"

"Almost ten," Shorty said, after consulting his pocket watch.

Katie, deflated, stood by the bar trying to think what to do next.

"Want some coffee?" Shorty Shelbourne asked.

The friendly gesture cheered her and she gave him a smile. "If it's not too much trouble."

"No trouble," Shorty Shelbourne said, reaching under the bar to produce a big white mug. "It's already made."

Katie watched him pour. She went to the bar and gratefully accepted the cup.

"You want to saucer and blow it?" Shorty asked.

"No," she said, amused.

He shrugged. "Lots of folks don't think it tastes good any other way."

"Are you one of them?" Katie asked.

Shorty winked and inclined his head toward the top of the bar. There Katie saw a broad saucer filled with steaming black coffee.

"Want to try it?" Shorty asked.

"Another time," she said, but she softened her voice so he would be sure to know she was not rejecting the idea.

That softening was one of the things she had learned, she realized. A week or two ago she would have considered saucering coffee a real vulgarism, practically a social crime. Now she saw that it made no difference whatsoever and was a pleasant little idiosyncrasy that might even become endearing.

"Do a lot of people do that?" she asked.

"Quite a few."

"Does . . . Mike?"

"Lots of times."

She imagined Mike saucering his coffee, and smiled again. But it was a smile that held considerable sadness behind it. As she tasted the coffee, which was heavy and black and very strong, she thought of how she might have come here differently, more quietly, without all the fears making her act so—so overbearing and sure of herself.

She had been an awful fool, she thought.

What made her act that way? Had she always been cold, distant, hateful, ready to fight anyone and everyone who didn't live up to *her* exalted ideas of how people should be? Why had it taken her all these years to realize that people were not perfect, and never would be? How could she have existed so long in a vacuum of dusty preconceptions, set ideas, petty and narrow-minded concepts of how people should act in all circumstances? What miracle of fate had let her get this old before it was brought home to her with harsh clarity that she was *not* the arbiter of fashion, taste and morality for the entire world—that she had no *right* to try to force her ideas on others?

For that, she thought dismally, was what had been involved with Mike Kelly. He had not met her rigid specifications for a Cleveland gentleman, so she had hated him. His business had not measured up to her unyielding standards, so she had set out to take it from him.

178

And she had succeeded in large measure—but only as far as her wit and stubbornness could take her. Once the cafe and hotel had faced the *reality* of Salvation, Arizona, she had come face to face with disaster.

Then and only then, she thought, had she changed. And then she had found that she *liked* the change—heard her own personality whispering to her in ways that startled her . . . frightened her . . . made her wonder who she really was.

With a sigh, she finished her coffee.

"Want some more?" Shorty Shelbourne asked.

"Later, I think," Katie murmured. "Do you think they'll be getting up soon?"

The bartender shrugged. "They had a hell of a night. I expect Mike will be up shortly, but I wouldn't look for your kid brother to get up before noon."

Katie nodded and walked to the front window. She looked out at the street, where a few men walked around conducting business as usual. She thought about everything that had happened.

"Where are you going?" Shorty Shelbourne called after her.

She turned at the door. "Just down the street to my—to where the fire was. I'll be back soon."

She went out and walked slowly up the street to the corner. A few people along the way smiled and spoke to her. She answered softly. They all knew her now, she realized. She had been a part of the excitement that had had Salvation on its ear ever since her arrival.

Now, she thought, walking up the street toward the black ruin that had been her business, everything was different.

She did not have all of it put together by any means. But she knew several facts, and they were not happy ones.

Reaching the fire site, she stood on the remains of the plank sidewalk and looked at the rubble. She felt curiously calm, and yet strangely like crying.

Her only feeling, she told herself, should be relief. Heck was safe. Mike was safe. From what they had told her during that incredible hour after their return, a genuine Indian war had been narrowly averted. In addition, she had learned some things—about this new country she had just become a part of, and about herself.

The knowledge about Salvation and its people was not all clear yet, and perhaps it never would be. The knowledge about herself—and the way she had stupidly helped ruin things—was what she could not live with.

She was not the sweet, innocent, pure, perfect, clever person she had grown up thinking she might be. She was a meddler and a cheat, a virtual thief in the night, a dumb outsider, a bull in a china shop, a potential disaster for the entire town of Salvation, a pariah, and—*admit it,* she told herself—not even a very moral person.

The truth of the matter was, she admitted, that she had not simply danced for those men in the cafe because it was good business. It started as that sort of impulse. But once she had started, she had *loved* it.

And what did *that* make her?

What did it make her to know that last night she had not only liked Ruby and Dolores and the other girls—but in a tiny way had felt wonderment, curiosity—even a kind of *envy* of them?

She had lived her whole life deluding herself. It was no wonder Mike Kelly hated her. He acted nice, but he *had* to hate her. Who wouldn't? She had destroyed his business hatefully, stupidly, and she *wasn't even a very nice person.*

Standing before the ruin of the hotel and cafe, she felt like bawling. She fought the tears back. She told herself she had to be strong now, because of what she had to do.

Trying to postpone the anguish of really facing what she had to do, she forced herself to examine the wreckage.

There was very little left: where the cafe had been, a portion of the side wall, ragged and broken and black along the top, and the kitchen chimney standing solid, like a tombstone over the black ashes and water-soaked debris; where the hotel had been, simply a taller mound of broken plaster, charred lumber, unimaginably burned, unrecognizable trash.

She had brought it on, she thought again. She had had to play up to Ray Root, because she thought it made her more independent in Mike's eyes. She had had to dance and sing, to get more business. She had had to bring it all—all of it—upon herself.

If she could have done it over, she thought, how different it all might be!

But there was no going back, she reminded herself, trying to be cold. The past was dead. Her choice now was simple: stay here and try to rebuild, or leave and never come back.

Her heart told her to stay, to try again. She could try with *Mike,* too, she thought. Maybe somehow she could make him forget what a witch she had been. Maybe somehow—some day—she could even become the kind of woman he might—

Her mind recoiled bitterly from the conjecture. It was impossible! She had wrecked *everything,* not just these buildings.

And now, as much as she hated and dreaded it, there was only one course of action left.

A cheery voice called, startling her. "Hey, sis!"

She turned and saw Heck trotting up the street with Mike Kelly. Heck, bless his heart, looked as if nothing had ever happened, except his shirt was ten sizes too big—Mike's—and he looked pleased about that. As for Mike, he looked tired and drawn, but he was smiling, and Katie's heart flip-flopped and began to melt.

She tried to fight this feeling. It was mandatory—*vital.*

Mike and Heck walked up and joined her. She gave them a bright, bogus smile, and felt like a liar for doing it.

"We sure were surprised when we heard you'd already gone out!" Heck told her.

"I just needed some air," Katie said, watching Mike, who was watching her with puzzled quiet in his keen eyes. "Hello, Mike."

"Good morning," he said with sudden formality. "Are you okay?"

"Yes, I'm fine," she lied.

"We were thinking," Mike said, "about going down to Maw Jenkins's for some flapjacks. It can't touch the kind of cooking you do, but since you're out of business for a while, it's next best."

Katie smiled and nodded. "Fine. But I'm afraid I'm not just out of business for a while. I'm out permanently."

"Nuts," Mike grunted.

"No. It's true."

"You can get you a new loan. You can stick it out."

Katie shook her head, and her vision was bright with tears that embarrassed her. "I'm not going to do that, Mike."

"How come?" Mike asked, puzzled.

"Well, I—I don't know. I started it all just to fight *you*—I thought I had to be so—so *big,* and so—independent. And I just made a big mess of everything—"

181

"You don't spend your life looking backwards," Mike shot back. "Just get up and start again."

Katie shook her head. "No."

"Aw, sis!" Heck groaned.

"What *are* you going to do, then?" Mike demanded.

She looked at him and managed to get a smile through the blur. "We have just enough left for stage fare. I can find a nice job back in Cleveland and pay everything back—"

"Aw!" Heck cried again. "Mike—?"

Mike Kelly scowled at her. "You're talking crazy. You're just upset. It's natural. Give it a few days and—"

"No," Katie said firmly, although she was quaking. "I've made a mess of everything."

"So you're going to quit?" Mike exploded, shocking her with his sudden rage. "Just—*quit?*"

Katie got her chin up. "I know what's wise. I misjudged you, Mike. I misjudged a lot of things. The best for all of us is for me to sign whatever legal interest I have over to you, and—"

"Great!" Mike snapped bitterly. "That's just great! Suddenly you turn out to be a dadblamed quitter after all!"

Katie's temper tried to flare, but she wasn't up to any more fighting. There had been enough of that. She said softly, "You can call it that if you want to."

"Well, let me tell *you* something!" Mike shot back, grabbing her arm in a way that sent tingles all through her body. "I'm not *letting* you quit!"

"You have nothing to say about it," Katie said loftily.

"The hell I don't," Mike retorted, his face working. "The *hell* I don't, Miss K. Blanscombe! Now you listen to me! You came in here and fought me tooth and toenail! You got a business going. You pulled guys in off the street and you had it working. It wasn't your fault Ray Root got vicious. It wasn't your fault the place burned. None of it was your fault! And by golly, you're not going to quit now!"

"I ruined your buildings," Katie said, and the first genuine sob broke through her voice. "I ruined everything. Now I don't have any money and Heck almost got killed—*you* almost got killed—and you hate me, I know you do, and you *should*—"

"*Me?*" Mike Kelly gasped. "Hate *you?*"

"Of course you do!" Katie wailed. "And I don't blame you!"

Mike took hold of her other arm, so that he held her facing him. He seemed very big and very strong and gentle.

"Katie," he said softly.

She shook her head mutely and tried to get away. Heck was watching wide-eyed, and she hated for him to witness this—this degradation. He would never respect her again, no one would. She couldn't even respect herself.

"Katie," Mike repeated more firmly.

"Just let me alone," she sobbed. "My mind is made up."

"No it's not," Mike said.

"Don't try to tell me my own mind, *please!* I can't fight you any more!"

Mike laughed huskily. "I bet you can."

She looked up at him, not understanding the sound of his voice or the sudden new—closer, firmer, more controlling (and infinitely more exciting) way he was holding her.

"You," he told her, "are a lot too tough to give up, lady. I'm not going to let you give up. You're staying here. You're rebuilding. I'm going to help you. Then I'm going to move in next door. Then, between us, we're going to stand Salvation on its ear. The best of everything between us, you and me. *You and me,* Katie."

Katie stared into his eyes, and the weakness throughout her body was of a different kind now, frightening and beautiful in its intensity.

"No," she said feebly.

"Yes," Mike said firmly.

"No—we'd fight—I'm no good, and—"

"Sure, we'll fight!" Mike said triumphantly. "That's just it, you dummy! *Of course* we'll fight! We'll fight all the time! That's the beauty of it! Don't you see, Katie? Do I have to flat get down on my stupid knees in this stupid street and make a stupid idiot of myself? *You and me,* Katie! *That's* what I'm talking about!"

Katie felt fairly sure she was going to faint. "You mean—?"

Mike looked dazed. "I guess I *do.*"

"Hey!" Heck yelped. "Is this some kind of a dadgummed *proposal,* or something?"

Mike had never left Katie's eyes with his own. "I guess maybe it is, buddy," he said softly.

Katie stared at him, knowing it was all just ridiculous and impossible and silly and out of the question. She looked deep into him and saw and felt the strength there, the kind of strength she had longed for all her life, and she saw that she didn't have to have that strength *of her own,* because it was hers . . . with him.

"Well?" Mike whispered.

With a glad little sob, she let her head fall against his chest.

"Boy!" Heck yelled. "Wow! Hey! I just figured out what's going on! It *is* a proposal! Hey! Let's go celebrate, you guys! Let's go get us some of them flapjacks! Hey! You guys! *You guys—?*"

N